Sign up for our newsletter to hear
about new and upcoming releases.

www.ylva-publishing.com

Andi Marquette

the Bureau of Holiday Affairs

Acknowledgments

Publishing a book is, in some ways, like making a movie. There are lots of people working behind the scenes to make both happen, and usually, there are many different takes on many different scenes before they look and feel right. With that in mind, thank you to Ylva Publishing for welcoming another of my projects and setting in motion all the activity that went on behind the scenes in the making of *The Bureau of Holiday Affairs*. My lasting gratitude to my colleague-in-arms Jove Belle, who always puts me through my paces when she assesses and edits my work and this was no exception, and involved a lot of different takes on oh, so many different scenes. It is a much stronger story because of her time and effort (and coaxing and cajoling and well-placed one-liners). Thanks, also, to Glendon and the crew at Streetlight Graphics, who work hard on interior and exterior design, and help bring an author's vision to light through a book's cover. And thank you to everybody at Ylva—I know what you're doing is a labor of love, and I'm glad to be a small part of it.

And thank *you*, readers, for deciding to spend some time with me in another of my flights of fancy. Here's hoping you have as much fun as I did.

Chapter 1

Robin signed the paperwork and slid it aside. Maybe it was a dick move to fire people this close to Christmas— bleeding hearts would probably rag on her, but oh, well. The bottom line was the bottom line, and she didn't need to burden the company with extra weight into the new year. Even though sales were up a bit, Robin didn't want to take chances.

She answered a few emails and added a couple of figures to an upcoming presentation, which was sure to get her noticed as a CEO for a subsidiary, before she picked up the earlier paperwork. Robin walked the paperwork across the expanse of carpet in her office, past the sleek leather couch against the wall and the mini-fridge next to it, through the heavy mahogany doors to her assistant's desk, positioned behind short cubicle walls.

"I need these scanned and sent to HR before lunch," she said as she set the papers next to Laura's keyboard. She retreated to her office before Laura could give her one of her questioning looks. Laura was damn good at her job, Robin conceded, but sometimes she acted like Robin's conscience, like a little angel sitting on her shoulder. The last thing Robin needed or wanted was recrimination, silent or otherwise, on how she did her job.

Robin sat down and glanced at the clock on her laptop monitor. Not even ten yet. Her office door opened, and she looked up, irritated. Laura usually knocked.

"Good morning, Ms. Preston," the newcomer said in a clipped British accent as she shut the door behind her. She wore a burgundy pants suit and sleek black high heels that looked like something a woman might've worn in the forties. Come to think of it, Robin thought as she studied her, the visitor looked a bit retro, like a forties professional woman. She also carried a classic black briefcase.

"And who are you?" Robin asked.

The woman approached Robin's desk. "Your ten o'clock." She smiled, pleasant.

"I don't think—" Robin reached for her desk phone. How did Laura miss this? She picked up the phone. It was dead. She looked at her laptop. The screen was blank. She picked up her cell phone. Blank as well. She set it on her desk, wary.

The woman sat in one of the chairs in front of Robin's desk and placed her briefcase on her lap. "I'll just get right to it," she said. "I'm Elizabeth Tolson, senior agent at the Bureau of Holiday Affairs."

"Okay, you can stop right there. I don't have an appointment with you, I have no idea who you are, and—" She stopped, puzzled. "The Bureau of what?"

"Holiday Affairs." The latches on Tolson's briefcase clicked as she opened it.

"This is a joke, right?" Had to be Robin's brother. He was always trying to get her to loosen up, especially around Christmas.

"Absolutely not. The Bureau does not engage in such." Tolson removed a small case from the briefcase, opened it, and took out a pair of gold-framed eyeglasses that she put on. The earpieces looped around her ears. Very vintage. Next, she took a thick brown accordion file from the briefcase and set the briefcase on the floor by her feet.

"What is that?" Robin leaned forward, unnerved.

"Your dossier." Tolson undid the fastener—a string that looped around a small cardboard disk—on the accordion file. Robin hadn't seen one of those in years.

"My what? Who the hell are you?"

Tolson opened the file and took out a manila folder, which she opened with a practiced flip. "Preston, Robin Anne. Date of birth, June 15, 1978." She looked up from the file. "Seattle, Washington. Lovely city."

"Okay, this isn't funny. The joke is over." Robin pushed back from her desk. She would kill Frank, if he was responsible for this.

"Bachelor's degree at the University of Oregon. Business." Tolson regarded her over the top of her glasses. "But you started in art."

Robin was halfway to the door before Tolson spoke again.

"Master's in business, University of Pennsylvania."

Robin's fingers closed around the door knob, and she turned it. A strange sensation shot up her arm and into her chest, like a mild electrical shock. She pulled her hand back and started to reach for the knob again when she realized she was seated once again behind her desk. Her fingers trembled, and the small of her back was damp with nervous sweat.

"Somewhat of a business prodigy," Tolson said. "Rose quickly here at Frost Enterprises." She closed the file and let it lie flat in her lap. "The next logical step in your progression is CEO, most likely of an up-and-coming subsidiary." She took her glasses off, disengaging them carefully from her ears. She held them in one hand.

"How do you have all that information on me? That has to be illegal," Robin said, regaining some of her equilibrium amidst a flash of anger. "I assure you, Ms. Tolson, you will be hearing from my attorney."

"Gerald Moorhouse, of Moorhouse, Sanders, and Craig." Tolson sat back and regarded her with a gaze as readable as England's cliffs of Dover. "The Bureau has scheduled a meeting with him, as well. But that's neither here nor there." She smiled, the kind of indulgent but patronizing smile Robin remembered from some of her childhood teachers who were about to phone her mom.

"How do you know my lawyer?" She picked up her desk phone receiver again and held it to her ear. Still dead. She replaced it with extra emphasis.

"Ms. Preston, in all honesty, I argued against this meeting. At your annual case review—"

"My what? What are you talking about?"

"The Bureau analyzes hundreds of individual cases each year. At its discretion, it assigns certain cases to agents based on several factors. Those include whether the Bureau's Board of Advisors feels the individual is salvageable."

Salvageable? Robin's previous indignation dissolved into uncertainty. "What does that mean?"

"Redeemable, basically." Tolson tapped the file on her lap with her glasses. "Strong childhood, good deeds interspersed with the usual foibles and mistakes of children that carried over into high school. Overall, you displayed general acts of kindness along with the usual high school drama and angst, the latter of which was exacerbated most certainly by your struggles to keep your sexual orientation hidden until college." Tolson regarded her. "No doubt to cope with your father's indiscretions and continued absences."

Robin hadn't realized she was gripping the edge of her desk until her fingertips hurt. She forced herself to relax her hands. "That's personal. How the hell do you know that?" She would kill Frank. With her bare hands.

"We at the Bureau of Holiday Affairs know most everything about you, Ms. Preston. Within proper parameters, of course."

"What do you mean?"

"We know when you're sleeping. We know when you're awake. And we know when you've been bad or good." Tolson cocked her head. "Surely you're familiar with that adage."

Robin stared at her. She had to hand it to Frank. This was by far her brother's best practical joke since...well, it had been a while. She was unnerved enough that she didn't even remember sitting down after that weird shock at the door. And since it was clearly a joke—there was no other way anybody could know that much about her—she decided to relax and go along with it. Besides, who actually used that line from a goofy Christmas song?

"We noticed a change, however, your third year of college." Tolson tapped the manila file again, this time with one of her fingertips. Perfectly manicured, Robin noticed. Her nail polish matched her suit. Once this was over, and after she chewed Frank a new asshole, she might track Tolson down and ask her out.

"We attributed the change to Jill Chen's breakup with you, your mother's death, and in the following months, an overall existential crisis that left you bereft of previous foundations. And, unfortunately, drove you to engage in indiscretions in your personal life. No doubt modeled by your father."

"Really? An existential crisis? Care to elaborate?" She smirked, choosing to ignore the reference to her mother.

"I believe you would refer to it as, and I quote, 'an increase in general asshole-ness.'"

Robin's smirk shifted to a frown. That was a low blow on Frank's part.

"Not to correlate that with business school or business in general. There are thousands of individuals engaged in business pursuits all over the world who do not slide into asshole-ness." She added emphasis to the last word to indicate she was still quoting Robin. "In your case, however, it seems you used your new field as a way to mask older and better ways of approaching problems and to emphasize less desirable characteristics in their stead." Tolson paused and took another sheet of paper out of the file and put her glasses back on. "I'll cite one example here. Allison Wagner."

Robin clenched her teeth. "Her résumé wasn't as strong as mine."

"Nevertheless, deliberately misdirecting her with regard to the deadline date for the fellowship was simply not sporting. And Matthew Jacobs?"

Frank was toast. How did he even know about that?

"Mr. Jacobs developed the business plan that you submitted as your own to win the seminar competition your last year of classwork during your master's degree." Somehow, Tolson's accent made it sound even worse.

"To your credit," Tolson continued, "you did appear to experience some remorse about that. And about Wagner.

Unfortunately, it wasn't until after the fact." Tolson slipped the paper back into the folder and removed her glasses.

"It was just business."

Tolson raised her eyebrows. "There are standards regarding ethics in business as well, Ms. Preston."

Robin hunched her shoulders. "That was years ago."

"Lydia Evans," Tolson responded. "Joseph Spinelli."

Robin sat up straighter. "There is no way in hell you could know that. I just signed those papers this morning." Nervous sweat gathered at her collar. Had Laura tipped her?

"I told you, Ms. Preston," Tolson said. "It is the Bureau's job to know these things." She retrieved her briefcase from the floor, put the manila folder in it, and returned her glasses to their case before she put it inside as well. She latched the briefcase and returned it to the floor.

"Now. As I was saying, I argued against this visit because I don't think you're redeemable."

"Hold on. What does that mean?" Screw Frank. She'd drag more info out of Tolson.

"In more casual parlance, I believe you are a lost cause. Some people continue to engage in behaviors that are generally motivated by mean-spiritedness or a lack of empathy for their fellows. They learn these behaviors at some point during their lives and continue to use them as coping mechanisms. Some cases are, of course, genuinely unredeemable due to various psychological issues that the Bureau doesn't handle, but others might be, given the opportunity to change their ways." She tapped the arm of her chair a few times. "Many of these have what you might call an epiphany, and surprisingly, it does stick."

"So you're my epiphany?" Robin said, sarcastic.

Tolson smiled. "Of course not. I'm your current case manager. Not that I was pleased about that, since I have a one hundred percent rating at the Bureau for ensuring that my cases have their redeemable moment. Or moments. Some need a progression of smaller epiphanies to point them in the right direction." She straightened. "But I don't shy from a challenge, even though I am on record as strongly advising against this course of action where you're concerned."

Typical bureaucrat, Robin thought. Passing the buck.

"Regardless of your opinion regarding my place of employment and methodologies," Tolson said, as if she'd read Robin's mind, "I am here to do a job. With that in mind, you will have three more visitors between now and Christmas Day."

You have to be kidding. Robin fought an urge to roll her eyes.

Tolson stood and picked up her briefcase. "They will, of course, keep me informed on your case."

"Of course." Robin put extra snark in her tone.

"They don't necessarily share their tactics with me ahead of time, so I can't speak to those. But they all know they have two weeks before Christmas Day to schedule their visits in coordination with each other. And once this process has begun, the Bureau does not stop it for any reason." She paused, as if letting that sink in.

"What if I don't want your visitors?"

"Our cases never do. No one likes the mirrors we hold up to them." She smoothed the front of her jacket. "Good luck, Ms. Preston." She turned and moved effortlessly to the door, which she opened with no problem. It closed with a soft click behind her.

Robin let out a breath. "Frank, you dick," she muttered. She reached for her cell phone just as a knock sounded on the door. "Come in."

Laura entered. She held a stack of papers up and moved toward Robin's desk.

"Did Ms. Tolson leave a card?" Robin asked as Laura handed her the papers.

"Who?"

"Ms. Tolson. The woman who was just here."

Laura's brow creased in puzzlement. "Here? In your office?"

Robin studied her. "You didn't see her?"

"No. You were just at my desk with the other paperwork."

Robin glanced at her laptop screen, which was functional now. The clock on it read 9:59 A.M. "What the hell?" she muttered.

"Ma'am?"

"Never mind." Robin stood. She'd go for a coffee. A big, strong cup from the café at street level. That would cure anything. "I'll be right back." She left Laura in her office and headed for the elevators. She was just working too hard. She always got stressed this time of year. But she couldn't shake the chill wrapped around her spine.

The elevator doors opened onto the spacious lobby of the Frost building.

"Good morning, Ms. Preston." The guard at the info desk nodded at her. She could never remember his name.

"Did you see a woman come through here a few minutes ago? Burgundy suit, dark hair, briefcase?"

"No."

"You're sure? It would've been the last ten or fifteen minutes."

"No, ma'am. Hold on and I'll check the cameras." He appeared to be looking at something beneath the counter. "No. Nobody like that. Would you like to see?"

She shook her head and continued to the exit. She was definitely working too hard.

Chapter 2

"AM I AN ASSHOLE?" ROBIN asked from the bed.

Cynthia turned to look at her. She was putting her earrings back in. Her hair fell in tousled waves like golden silk around her shoulders, and her breasts filled her lacy bra just right. "In what sense?"

"In general."

Cynthia smiled and blew her a kiss. "Of course you are, darling."

"I'm serious."

Cynthia turned back to the mirror on Robin's closet door and finished with her other earring then put her necklace back on. "One needs to be less than savory sometimes, doesn't one?" She made a few adjustments to her skirt before she picked up her blouse and slipped it on. The color reminded Robin of the suit Elizabeth Tolson had been wearing two days ago.

"But am I an asshole more than sometimes?"

Cynthia seated herself on the bed next to her and ran her fingers along Robin's bare upper arm. It felt delicious but distant.

"You're fucking someone else's wife, darling. That qualifies as more than sometimes."

"You could have said no when I asked you to bed."

Cynthia laughed. "And you didn't have to ask. But you did." She stood and buttoned her blouse. "No one comes off clean in this, sweets," she said, but the endearment sounded sharper than it should have, and a weird little chill gripped Robin's chest.

"But given your reputation," Cynthia added, "I expected no less."

"What do you mean?"

"No less than uncommitted and enjoyable sex behind my husband's back." Cynthia finished with her blouse. "Surely you're not developing a conscience now." She gave Robin one of her sultry looks.

"That makes it sound like I don't have one."

Cynthia regarded her, expression decidedly cooler. "There are two types of people in this world, darling. Those who are doormats and those who are not. If you don't want to be a doormat, you ensure you get what you want. The ends justify the means." She adjusted her hair. "Call me next week. He's out of town again starting Tuesday."

Robin nodded and watched Cynthia leave the bedroom. She heard the door of her apartment open then close, and she lay back in bed and stared at the ceiling. Her phone rang from the bedside table, and she picked it up. Frank. About time.

"That was a dick move," she said when she answered.

"Hi, sis. Good to hear from you. How have you been?" he shot back.

"Don't act innocent."

He was silent for a few moments. "About what? What's going on?"

"That practical joke you pulled on me a couple days ago. Why the hell did you think it was okay to tell her those things about my past?"

"Whoa. Hold on there, speedy. What joke, what things, and who?"

Robin knew the nuances of Frank's voice. He was clearly confused. "Elizabeth Tolson."

"Who's that?"

"So you didn't send her to my office?"

"No."

"So this wasn't something you did?"

"No. The last time I did a Christmas joke on you was at least four years ago. And if I remember correctly, you did *not* appreciate it."

"A singing telegram dressed as a nutcracker sent to my place of employment doesn't go over too well."

"Maybe your whole company needs to lighten up. So what did this Tolson say?"

"Never mind. One of my other friends probably put her up to it."

"Put her up to what, exactly?"

"Just some be-good-for-Christmas crap."

"Well, even though I didn't send whoever it was, that's good advice for pretty much everybody. Speaking of which, what are you doing for Christmas?"

"I don't know."

"Why don't you come visit?"

Robin frowned. He sounded genuine.

"C'mon. Remember when we were kids? How much fun we'd have on Christmas Day?"

"You must've been at a different house. All I remember was Dad not being there and Mom trying to pretend everything was all right." And usually, her dad was off with some other woman, though he claimed he just had to work on the holidays.

"Look, I know that hit you hard. But we did still have some fun. You have to let go of Dad being a dick. Because hanging on to old crap can make you—well, you start becoming the crap. So come and visit this year."

She clenched her teeth. Every year he always asked her to come and hang out with him and his wife and every year she always turned him down. Wasn't that the definition of insanity? Doing the same thing over and over expecting different results? "I'll think about it," she said, another part of the annual ritual.

"At some point," he said, "you need to remember who you were. Catch you later." He hung up, and Robin tossed the phone to the other side of her bed. Remember who she was? What the hell did that even mean? Irritated, she got out of bed and padded to the shower, trying to figure out who might have sent Elizabeth Tolson to her office. The fact that she couldn't think of anyone else close enough to her to want to bother with a joke like that added to her irritation, but also fed a strange sense of loneliness.

Twenty minutes later, dressed in sweatpants and sweatshirt, she poured herself a Scotch over ice and made sure she locked the deadbolt on her front door, too. She turned her television on but didn't watch it. Instead, she stood staring out over the city through the sliding doors onto her balcony, which still bore the remains of the last snowstorm. In the distance, she could just see the outline of one of the myriad bridges over the Hudson. People practically killed for views like this in the city, even in a rather plain apartment like this one, with its off-white walls and beige carpeting. It might've been a hotel room, for all the personalization she'd done in here.

No real surprise, since she spent most of her time at work or traveling for work. She sipped her drink, but the usual velvet caress on her tongue of this brand of Scotch was missing. It tasted flat and a little rough, like her mood since Elizabeth Tolson's visit.

"Bureau of Holiday Affairs," she muttered against the lip of her glass. She had looked it up online, but the only thing that came close was, ironically, a 1949 Christmas movie titled "Holiday Affair." Christmas was for sentimental idiots who couldn't get ahead in life because they weren't willing to make hard choices. You had to keep moving, like a shark. Otherwise, you'd sink.

Her door buzzer sounded, and it startled her. What the hell time was it? Cynthia always called before she came over. Besides, she'd just been here and Cynthia never forgot anything. Robin picked her phone up from the coffee table. Almost eleven. Probably some drunk idiot hitting the wrong button downstairs. She took another sip and the buzzer sounded again.

She stared at it, positioned next to the front door of her apartment. This was an ultra-secure building, so she wasn't worried about people actually getting to this floor. Another buzz. She set her drink and phone on the coffee table, crossed the room, and pressed the button.

"Yes?"

"Hey," said a woman's voice. "Pizza."

"You've got the wrong address. I didn't order anything."

"You sure? I've got a large pepperoni pie here for Robin Anne Preston, born June 15, 1978. Extra cheese."

Robin's stomach clenched. "Who is this?" she said, but it didn't sound as forceful as she wanted.

"Pizza. Courtesy of the Bureau."

"Okay, you can stop now. This isn't funny anymore." Not that it ever was. "Get the hell away from my apartment building."

Silence. Robin exhaled in relief, shaky in the wake of her adrenaline surge.

"You want a big slice or a little one?"

Robin whirled as a surge of panic shot through her veins. A woman stood in the doorway of her kitchen, holding a pizza box.

"How the hell did you get in?" Robin clutched her phone like it was a weapon.

"Trade secret. So do you want a piece?"

Robin stared as the woman shrugged and set the box on the counter that separated the kitchen from the dining area. She wore blue surfer shorts, battered black flip-flops, and a pale-yellow T-shirt. A pair of sunglasses hung from the collar. Her hair—a cute jumble of spikes—was bleached blond.

"I'm Decker," she said. "And I'll be your tour guide this evening. Okay if I call you Preston? I'm not big on formality." She grinned, a flash of white beneath her tan, and opened the pizza box. She took out a slice.

"Tour guide?"

Decker took a bite and pointed at the letters across her chest, silk-screened in red in a seventies-style font. *Xmas Past*. They hadn't registered with Robin until Decker pointed at them. I'm dreaming, Robin thought. That's what this was. A weird dream, probably caused by stress.

"Seriously?" Robin asked.

"Mmm hmm," Decker said around the pizza.

"This is beyond ridiculous."

Decker shrugged.

"So you're going to take me on a trip into my past, and I'm supposed to get all emotional and change my ways."

"That's the general idea, yeah."

"That's completely stupid."

"That's what they all say." Decker took another bite. "You sure you don't want some of this? It's pretty good."

"No, I don't want any damn pizza. And I'm not going anywhere with you."

"They all say that, too."

Robin glared at her. "I could have you arrested for trespassing."

Decker finished chewing and swallowed. "You could try. Your phone's on the coffee table."

Robin moved and picked it up. "Fine. I'm calling the cops."

Decker shrugged again and took another bite.

Robin's phone was dead. Ice filled her chest. "What the hell is happening to me?" Was this it? Was she finally going crazy?

Decker finished the slice and brushed her hands on her shorts. "Think of it as an intervention."

"I don't need one."

Decker's expression might've been pity. "Let's go," she said, and she went to the front door and waited, her hand on the knob.

"I'm not going anywhere with you."

"Yep. You are."

"So you're kidnapping me?" Robin stayed by the coffee table, still gripping her phone.

Decker released the door knob and faced her. "Look. I've got a bag of tricks you would not believe, and full authority from the Bureau to enact this intervention. So put on your big-girl pants and take your medicine." She reached for the knob again.

"It's locked," Robin said, chastised, and wondered why she'd said that, as if she was searching for some sense of normalcy in the surreal. Even more, she wondered why she moved closer to the door.

Decker turned the knob and pulled it open, the locks clearly not an issue for her. She motioned at the hallway beyond, in which a mist gathered.

Mist. In the hallway to her elevator in a multistory apartment building. "I don't have shoes on," Robin said, as the mist swirled right up to her doorway but didn't enter. Oh, God. Was she going to crazytown?

"You won't need 'em." Decker stepped into the mist, and it curled and twisted around her limbs before it swallowed her.

"Hello?" Robin called, heart hammering. She approached the doorway and stared at the mist as she began to shiver. "Decker?"

"Come on," Decker responded from somewhere in the hallway. "Really. It's okay."

Without knowing why, without fully understanding the compulsion, Robin stepped into the mist. As a cool dampness engulfed her, she held her breath. She couldn't see anything beyond a few inches, and then she was falling, but softly. More like floating. Eventually, she felt floorboards beneath her feet, and the mist receded within seconds, revealing Decker, who was right next to her.

"Where are we?" Robin asked. It came out as a whisper.

"Go ahead and have a look around."

Robin took a tentative step, not sure her feet would carry her. They did. She heard a door slam and a kid yell, "Mom."

A dark-haired boy barreled down the hallway past her, followed by a slightly taller, equally dark-haired girl, all gangly arms and legs, apparent even in the jeans and jacket she wore.

"Oh, God," Robin whispered, recognizing herself at age eleven.

"When's dinner?" Frank shouted.

"Right now," came a woman's voice from the kitchen. A voice that shot right through Robin's chest. "Go get washed up."

"Mom," Robin said as her younger self followed Frank into the downstairs bathroom, and she heard the two of them laughing and splashing at the sink. They emerged, and Robin shrank back against the wall.

"They can't see or hear us," Decker said. "Go on."

Robin walked down the hall to the kitchen, remembering everything about this house she grew up in, a comfortable bungalow in one of Seattle's poorer neighborhoods. She knew the smell—a mixture of damp and meatloaf. It always smelled like meatloaf, though Robin's mom didn't make it too much. She remembered the dark wood of the banister as she passed the stairs to her right, and the time Frank fell from the landing and bit through his lower lip. To her left was the entranceway and the heavy front door that always made her feel safe when her mom locked it at night.

Her mom always decorated the house for Christmas, and Robin's chest tightened at the sight of the lights on the banister. The tree, she knew, would be in the living room behind her in the corner opposite the TV. Christmas music drifted in from the kitchen. Her mom kept a portable cassette deck in there, and loved playing it this time of year, even when her dad didn't show.

"Sweet potatoes," Frank said from the kitchen, his little boy delight spilling into the hall with the light.

"It wouldn't be Christmas without them," Robin's mom said just as Robin reached the doorway. Her mom put an extra spoonful of sweet potatoes on Frank's plate.

"Mom," she said again as tears gathered in her eyes. Mom. Wearing faded jeans and a baggy black sweatshirt, the clothes she always put on when she got off work. She'd seemed so vibrant when they were kids, always smiling and laughing, in spite of their dad's absences. As a kid, Robin hadn't noticed the exhaustion that marred her mother's face and slumped her shoulders.

"We should save some for Dad," Frank said as he dug in. Robin's younger self shot him a look, then transferred her gaze to her mother, worried.

"Sure, honey. If you want. He probably won't be home 'til late, though."

Robin recognized the lie for what it was. Her younger self did, too.

"Where was your dad?" Decker asked from just behind her.

"Probably screwing some woman. He did that a lot." An old pain slid between her ribs, its tip brushing her heart.

"It's okay, Frankie," Robin's younger self said. "We can play Monopoly and watch TV. It'll be a fun Christmas Eve."

Robin's mom looked at her younger self, relief in her eyes. "That's right. We'll all play."

"Did he miss a lot of Christmases?" Decker asked.

"Yeah. Hell, he missed a lot."

"And you looked out for your brother."

"Mostly." Robin watched the scene at the table, thinking that she sort of remembered this particular Christmas. Her mom was laughing at something Frankie said and her younger self smiled and got up and retrieved a pitcher of apple juice from the refrigerator, plastered with all her drawings. Frankie loved all kinds of juice then. Her younger self refilled his glass and checked her mom's.

"Thanks, honey," her mom said. She squeezed younger Robin's hand as she sat back down to dinner, and Robin swore she felt it, a warmth that traveled up her arm.

Mist gathered on the kitchen floor, twisting up the legs of the table.

"No, wait. Please?" Robin grabbed Decker's arm. "My mom. I just want to see her for a little longer." The mist thickened until Robin couldn't see into the kitchen. "Please. Mom," she called, a sob catching in her throat. And then the mist enveloped her, and she closed her eyes, falling, her arms wrapped around herself as if trying to hold onto her memories.

"You can open your eyes," Decker said.

Robin heard music in the background. She looked around. "Oh, my God," she said. "No way." She stood in the middle of her living room from her college days in Oregon. If this was a dream, the details were amazing, from the beat-up rugs that covered the scratched wooden floor to the peeling pale green paint above the TV that sat across from a sofa. Her roommate had put a tiny fake tree on the entertainment center. Cal had decorated it with little red and silver balls and lovingly hung tinsel all over it. Robin had laughed, but she admitted that when he did it that the tree reminded her of her mom, who had loved Christmas, and who had believed in it even when she was on her last one.

"Pretty nice for a college crib." Decker inspected the sofa. "Did you dumpster dive this?" she asked. "Good shape."

Robin shot her a glare and didn't respond.

"Who lived here who listened to The Clash?" Decker was reading the labels on the CD cases strewn across the floor. "And Joy Division. Nice."

"Me, thank you very much."

Decker raised her eyebrows, grudging approval in her expression. "There might be hope for you yet, Preston. Are these yours, too?" She pointed at the pen and ink framed sketches above the sofa. "Hard to do nudes. These are really good."

"Yes, they're mine. In another life." She stepped carefully over a couple of jewel cases past the mini stereo sitting on the worn shelves she and her roommate had rescued from an abandoned warehouse. She heard what sounded like crying in what had been her bedroom, just off the living room.

The door was barely open. She reached to push it open, but her hand went right through the wood.

"Jesus freaking Christ." She pulled her hand back and checked it. Still intact.

"You're here but you're not," Decker said, making her jump again.

"What the hell does that even mean?"

"Hard to explain. Just walk in." Decker motioned at the door.

"How?"

Decker shook her head in exasperation and walked right through the door, like a ghost might. Robin stared after her. This was so messed up. She held her breath and walked toward the door, flinching for what she just knew was going to be a smack in her face. Instead, she ended up in the bedroom next to Decker, who stood watching the forlorn figure who sat on the edge of the bed, staring at the floor.

Robin knew what day this was. She remembered it, and didn't want or need a reminder. "Dick move, Decker," she said through her teeth. The day the love of her life dumped her. Right around Christmas.

Decker shrugged. "Did you ever wonder why Jill broke it off?"

"I didn't have to. She told me." Robin fought an urge to sit on the bed with her younger self.

"Oh, yeah. The old 'I love you but I'm not in love with you' spiel. And you believed it?"

"What was I supposed to do? Tell her to change how she felt? Demand that she be in love with me?" She clenched her fists. "This is stupid. What the hell does reliving this bullshit have to do with anything?" She whirled on Decker, anger rising in her throat.

And then the room disappeared, and she was falling through mist. Her stomach lurched like she was on a rollercoaster. She didn't know how far down she had to go, and she instinctively braced for a crash, but it didn't come. She heard laughter, talking, and dishes clinking against each other. She stood in somebody's dining room. The big table in the center was piled with food, and Christmas decorations hung from the eighties-style chandelier above it. Lights twinkled above the picture window. The drapes were open, but with the lights on, Robin couldn't see outside. She was surrounded by people talking and eating, most of whom were Asian. They all ignored her, but she moved back against the wall anyway.

She glanced around. She hadn't seen furnishings like this since the nineties. And where the hell was Decker?

An older Asian woman emerged from what Robin guessed was the kitchen, and Robin froze. Chinese. She was Chinese, and she was Lin, Jill's mom. Robin had met her twice, and both times Jill had introduced Robin as a "good friend." Oh, God. She was in Jill's parents' house in Portland. Had to be.

"Have you seen Jill?" Lin asked a boy who looked to be about ten. He was reaching for another piece of fudge.

"No."

Lin's mouth tightened and she worked her way to a doorway opposite Robin.

"Might want to follow her," Decker said, and Robin jumped. She was sure Decker hadn't been there a moment earlier.

"Fine," she snapped, and she worked her way around the periphery of the dining room.

"You don't have to do that," Decker said.

Robin looked over as a man walked right through Decker.

"That is seriously—no. Just no." She continued hugging the wall and sighed in relief when she made it to the hallway, noting that though she could tell the carpet was thick, she couldn't feel it under her feet.

"Jill, it's time for this to stop," Lin was saying to a closed door at the other end of the hall. "It's rude."

"Give me a few minutes," came a response, and Robin closed her eyes as a voice she hadn't heard in fifteen years poked at an old wound.

"I'll talk to her." A young Chinese woman passed Robin. She looked about the age Robin had been when Jill dumped her. "Go back to the party, Mom. I'll take care of this."

Lin harrumphed and went back to the dining room. Robin squished herself against the wall of the hallway as Lin walked past her, barely two inches between them.

"Jill, it's Christie. Can I come in?"

Robin didn't catch the response, but Christie opened the door and went in. Decker motioned toward the door, and Robin approached it, took a deep breath as she shut her eyes, and walked through.

"Good job," Decker said when Robin opened her eyes.

Robin ignored her and stared instead at Jill, who was slumped in a chair next to a single bed. The room was probably Jill's before she went to college. Several awards for sports and academics hung on the wall next to Robin's head and they all had Jill's name on them. The walls had been painted pink, which might have explained why Jill hated that color so much.

Christie sat down on the bed opposite Jill, who had been crying. Robin's chest tightened. She hadn't seen Jill in years, hadn't wanted to after she'd gotten past the pain of the breakup, and she vowed that if she ever did see her, she'd make sure to remind her how awful it had been, getting dumped. But seeing her like this left Robin feeling a strange mixture of numb and raw.

She looked like Robin remembered, long straight hair pulled back in a ponytail, the elegant planes of her face still familiar, something that had always seemed incongruous with the mischievous spark in her eyes. Robin had caressed Jill's face many times, and Jill had always smiled when she did. But that was lifetimes and worlds away.

"You did what you had to do," Christie said.

"So how come it feels so fucking bad?" Jill dabbed at her eyes with a well-used tissue. Christie handed her a fresh one out of the box on the bed.

"You'll get over it."

"Really? I broke her heart. She thinks I'm the worst person ever." Jill blew her nose. "I am the worst person ever. I couldn't even tell her the truth."

Robin tried to swallow, but the lump in her throat prevented it.

"Do you think that would've made her feel any better? That you couldn't be with her because your family would disown you?"

Robin's teeth were clenched so hard that her jaw hurt.

"I'm a coward," Jill said through a fresh round of tears. "I'm not strong enough to fight for love."

"Come on," Christie said. "You know our family is extremely traditional. Did you really think you could be openly gay? What were you planning to do? Have some kind of commitment ceremony?"

"Maybe I was," Jill said, and tears stung Robin's eyes.

"I thought you weren't in love with me," Robin said, but Christie and Jill didn't react. "Why didn't you tell me?" Robin turned to Decker. "Why didn't she tell me?"

Decker looked at her, expression inscrutable. "There's usually another side to a story."

"God, I miss her," Jill said through her tears.

Christie reached over and squeezed her knee. "Look, breakups are hard. You'll get through it, and so will she."

"And then what? I can't express part of who I am. If I do, I lose my family. What kind of choice is that?" Jill got up and pulled another tissue out of the box.

"Well, you're not going to solve anything sitting in here. Go out and mingle for a little bit. You can tell people you're not feeling well after you do it and come back here."

Jill laughed, but it lacked humor. "Because it's so important to save face. It doesn't matter how bad somebody feels, or that my own family put me in this position. We must always keep up appearances." She wiped her eyes with the fresh tissue. "I'm going to the bathroom. I'll be out in a minute."

Christie nodded and gave her a quick hug. She left, but didn't close the door, and the sounds of the party floated down the hall.

Jill brushed past Robin, and Robin flinched though she didn't feel even a breeze from her passage. Instinctively, she reached out, but her hand passed through Jill's arm, and as bizarre as that was to see, it left her feeling even emptier.

"Can I go home now?" she asked. "Because this really sucks."

Decker shook her head as mist suddenly engulfed Jill's bed.

"Not again." Robin shut her eyes tight as the floor beneath her feet fell away. She landed a little harder this time, and stumbled forward to regain her footing. Where the hell was she now? She kept her hands out, waiting for the mist to clear. "Decker?"

"Right here," came the response to her right. She saw her form, solidifying as the mist receded.

"Here's to my big sis and her new job," Robin heard Frank say. She was standing next to the refrigerator in his kitchen, in the apartment he had shared with two other guys during his college years. At least they kept it reasonably clean, though the décor was frat boy meets jock. A football sat on the kitchen counter next to three pint glasses with different beer logos on them. A neon "bar" sign hung in the window above the sink. It hummed and threw pale blue splotches on the linoleum. Her younger self raised her glass and smiled.

Decker leaned against the door frame, arms crossed, watching with interest.

"Really glad you're here," Frank continued. "Merry Christmas." He gave her a one-arm hug, and Robin's younger self grinned.

She'd just finished her master's, Robin remembered, and gotten hired at a subsidiary of Frost.

"Merry Christmas," younger Robin said, and older Robin remembered how excited Frank had been for her.

"Mom would've been proud," he said and leaned back against the counter. Like their mom, he had a favorite pair of old jeans and a sweatshirt he always wore around the house. He looked a lot like her, too, Robin realized, as she studied his curly hair, the same shade of brown as their mom's, much lighter than her own. Both Robin and Frank had gotten their mom's eyes, a deep brown. She was grateful for that, because the less she shared with her father, the better.

"You think?" younger Robin asked as she sipped the beer.

"Duh." He smiled then lapsed into silence.

"Did you hear from Dad this year?"

He looked at her. "No. I stopped trying, though. No point in beating my head against that wall. You were right." He set his beer on the counter and sighed.

"Hey," younger Robin said. "It's okay. You've got me."

"I do. And I will always have your back, Rob. Always. No matter what happens. Don't ever doubt that."

His words dug into her chest as she thought about how she'd blown him off just a couple of days ago.

"I like your bro," Decker said from the doorway.

"Me, too," Robin responded, defensive.

"Got you something," Frank said to younger Robin. "Be right back." He left the kitchen, and Robin knew he was going into the living room where the beat-up little tree he and his roommates had "liberated" from the tree lot stood, decorated with cardboard bar coasters and Seahawks sports cards. She examined her younger self for a few moments. Seriously trippy, being on the outside of yourself. She looked stressed. Robin saw it in the way her younger self carried her shoulders and in the frown lines at the corners of her mouth. Grad school had worn her out. Hell, by that time, *life* had worn her out.

"Here you go." Frank returned and handed her a small, flat package. Her younger self put her beer on the counter and opened it. Robin already knew what it was, but watching herself see it for the first time made her smile. Her younger self took the framed photograph out of the wrapping paper.

"Oh, no way. I love this photo."

Robin knew it by heart. It currently sat on her dresser. Frank at age six, Robin at ten, and their mom, grinning as they stood on the porch of their house. Robin was dressed as a cowboy and Frank had his blue superhero cape on. Their dad had taken it. Robin considered it one of the rare good things he had done.

"Thanks," younger Robin said, smiling. She put it carefully on the counter and gave Frank a big hug. "No gag gift this year?"

He laughed. "Maybe next year. I was feeling all sentimental."

Robin watched, and a warmth she vaguely remembered spread through her limbs. She'd gotten Frank an autographed baseball and given it to him a few days before, signed by his favorite players from the Mariners. She knew that he had slept with it next to his bed for several months.

"So how about some Christmas pizza?" Frank asked as he opened his cell phone.

"Nice," Decker said, approving.

Younger Robin laughed. "Hell, yes. Extra pepperoni and cheese."

Frank grinned and pressed buttons on his keypad.

"Did you know where your dad was?" Decker asked.

"Not that year. Frank was in contact with him the year before, but then he stopped returning Frank's calls." Robin chewed her lip as she watched herself banter with Frank. They'd been tight, since they were kids. Until the last few years.

"How come you two don't hang out anymore?"

Robin didn't look at Decker. "I don't know. Life got in the way, I guess."

"Or it got in *your* way." Decker straightened and stepped into the kitchen.

"Whatever," Robin muttered.

"So next Christmas, should I find you a girlfriend?" Frank was asking her younger self.

"Oh, please. That's the last thing I need." She laughed and gave him a playful shove.

"I don't know. Maybe you could use a little bit of settling down," he teased. "Quit sowing so many oats and grow something instead."

"That's something Mom would've said."

"She probably did. I just assimilated it."

Younger Robin snickered. "How about we fire up the Playstation and shoot a bunch of bad guys?"

"No better way to celebrate Christmas." He followed younger Robin out of the kitchen. Older Robin remembered that night. They'd stayed up almost all night, playing video games and munching on pizza. When they were kids, their mom would stay up with them, watching old movies, playing games, and eating popcorn. And though their dad hadn't been around that much, those Christmases without him usually turned out all right. She heard Frank bellowing "Silent Night" in the other room and she smiled.

"Now that's a cool Christmas," Decker said.

"Yeah, it was." Robin moved into the living room, where Frank was getting the game console ready. Her younger self was on the couch, her stocking feet propped on the coffee table. It was a great Christmas, she realized, watching her younger self laugh at Frank's antics, and she wanted to stay, wanted to eat pizza and play video games and not care about anything but that moment.

But mist curled around her feet and moved up her legs like vines. "Just give me a few more minutes." That's all she wanted. Just a few more. Tears stung her eyelids, and the mist

33

wrapped around her arms and chest. She heard Frank singing again, but his voice was fainter, and then she couldn't see or hear anything and she was careening, weightless, through darkness. She wasn't sure if her eyes were open or closed, and she yelled all the way down—was she even pointed that way?—until she snapped awake.

Robin was lying on her couch, covered by a blanket. Morning light was trying to make its way past the closed vertical blinds on her patio doors, but it wasn't having much success. She heard the alarm going off in her bedroom, a series of insistent beeps. Thank God. A dream. She hadn't dreamed about her mom in a while, and usually it left her unsettled. Today, it left her sad and sort of lonely. And why the hell had she dreamed about Jill? Was it even true, what she dreamed?

She groaned and sat up, stiff. The blanket fell on the floor as she stood to go turn the alarm off in her bedroom. Thirty minutes later, Robin was showered and dressed and feeling much better about things, though she couldn't kick the sense of sadness she'd woken up with. She picked up her bag and slung it over her shoulder then went to her small, galley-style kitchen for a yogurt. She opened the fridge and automatically reached for the middle shelf. And then she stopped and slowly withdrew her hand. A pizza box sat on the bottom shelf, balanced on her cans of diet coke.

"No way," she said. The graphic on the box depicted a smiling Santa holding a piece of pizza. *Courtesy of the Bureau of Holiday Affairs*, the neat red script said underneath him. So was she still dreaming? Was this one of those weird dreams within a dream? She reached into her fridge to take the pizza box out but withdrew her hand before she actually touched it. Her cell phone dinged with a text, and she jumped as she closed the fridge. The message was from Laura, informing her that her nine o' clock meeting was delayed by fifteen minutes. That gave her time to get a cup of coffee on the way. A really big cup. Strongest coffee she could find. She left her apartment, unnerved and on edge.

Bureau of Holiday Affairs
Field Report: Preston, Robin Anne,
DOB June 15, 1978//Seattle, WA
Case Number 26901-15
Agent: Decker, T.M.
Date of Interaction:
December 14

Methodology Employed: Decker pizza delivery. Standard Christmas Past intervention: Childhood, early college/ Chen, sibling (Preston, Francis "Frank" Dean, DOB April 28, 1982), though I did include a visit to Chen after she dumped Preston for a dose of the other person's side.

Results: Preston may have a heart. Tried to be indignant at outset, then resigned. Really affected when she saw her mom and when she saw Chen in the aftermath of the breakup. Wanted to stay and watch a Christmas scene with brother when Preston was in grad school.

Observations/recommendations: Preston totally felt the scenes and engaged. Question is, will she recognize her own crap? I have a vibe that she will, but she'll need a good kick in the butt for that. Audio and video filed.

Personal Overview: Preston's breakup with Chen was a tough loss on top of her mom's death. If she can pull the asshole stick out of her butt and recognize it for what it is, there's a decent chance she could epiphany out of this rut. Her emotional responses to the scenes from her past were totally consistent with someone who has mad potential for an epiphany, but she might refuse this awesome opportunity out of pride and stubbornness. That's the biggest hurdle.

Chapter 3

IF SHE DIDN'T GET HER shit together, she could kiss her next promotion goodbye. Robin had been staring at the same image on her computer for a good hour. Just a mental block, that's all. Though she still couldn't shake the feeling that she might not be sane since that whole weird dream she'd had a few days ago. What kind of dream was so disturbingly accurate? That was part of what was freaking her out.

She clicked into email, answered a few, then clicked back to the presentation. Another few minutes crawled by. Frustrated, she stood and went to stare out the window, across the cityscape.

A long way from Seattle, in a lot of different ways. She and Frank used to spend summers mostly outside there, and even during the long, often gray winters it seemed she was outside more often than not. Here, however, she tended to stay inside. Too crowded to jog, too dirty and loud to spend much time outdoors, and parks were a pain in the ass to get to. When did her shift to the indoors happen, exactly? Because it wasn't when she moved here. College?

A helicopter swooped low over the river. She and Jill used to hike all the time. Jill was into landscape photography at the time. Even after Jill broke it off, Robin still spent time outside. Graduate school was when it changed, she decided as she watched tugboats and barges on the river. That's when she started living inside more than out. She had shifted to what she thought was urban and urbane, as if she'd been trying to leave her past behind, with its jeans and flannel and faded alt-rock T-shirts.

Her personal phone dinged with a text message, and she returned to her desk to check it. Christ. Cynthia. Robin hadn't called her yet this week, and Cynthia's husband had left town two days ago. Robin checked the text, just two words. "Call me."

She did, thinking that maybe if she got laid, it would help with her screwed-up mood.

"Darling," Cynthia said when she picked up. "You were supposed to call me this week."

Robin frowned. Cynthia was used to getting what she wanted and normally, Robin liked that she took control. It was nice, sometimes, to let someone else do that, since she spent so much time being a control freak on her own. But right now, it kind of pissed her off. She decided she wasn't in the mood to get laid. At least not by Cynthia. "Sorry. Busy."

"Well," Cynthia said with an extra layer of sensuous, "he's out of town until Saturday, and I'm all alone tonight. I'll be at the apartment at eight. Wear a tie. And don't be late." She hung up, which is what she always did when she gave an order like that. Robin knew that if she didn't show, Cynthia might not call her again, but she'd make life pretty uncomfortable at social gatherings.

It had seemed like a good idea at the time, seducing the wife of another Frost executive. Hot as Cynthia was, Robin figured she'd be able to get something out of it, like a good word to the guy, maybe some help up the corporate ladder. But Cynthia had no interest in putting in a good word for anybody but herself. And here Robin thought she'd been the savvy one, finagling Cynthia to bed to further her own career, while Cynthia was actually the one who held all the cards. It occurred to Robin at that moment that Cynthia could, at any time, get her royally fired.

You mess with a snake, her mom had told her on a hike once, you get bit.

Robin texted Cynthia a lie. *Dinner and drinks w/ clients tonight. Rain check?*

She sat back down at her desk and checked her calendar on her computer. Cynthia would make her wait a while for a response, in keeping with her dominatrix personality. "Damn," Robin said as she looked at the calendar. Meeting in twenty minutes. Good thing it didn't have much to do with her directly. She didn't need to prepare anything.

Her cell phone rang. She checked the ID. That was unusual. Cynthia, calling right back.

"Preston," Robin answered. She always kept it formal on the phone with Cynthia.

"Darling, I'm rather disappointed."

"Me, too," Robin lied.

"I can't tomorrow—let me check a few things. He's out of town again next week, but I'm not sure for how long." She tsk'ed. "I was so looking forward to fucking you senseless. Soon," she teased and hung up.

Relieved, Robin turned her ringer off, picked up her tablet, and went to the meeting.

<hr />

Robin finally left the office at eight, after she'd spent the last two hours working on her presentation. Or rather, trying to. She thought about calling Cynthia and saying that the "clients" had cancelled, but decided she'd rather not deal with her. Anybody else, and she might be into a night of sex and forgetting.

"Good night, Ms. Preston," said the guard in the lobby.

She gave him a perfunctory wave. She could never remember his name, either, and she worked this late several times a month. Robin exited through the revolving door into the cold, which carried the promise of snow in its wet, heavy greeting. Cab or walk? She debated the merits of both and opted for the cab. Just as she stepped to the curb, a sleek white limousine pulled up in front of her.

"Thanks, asshole, for blocking me." She turned to go around the back when the driver got out.

"Ms. Preston," he said.

She looked at him. Basic limo driver, she categorized. Stocky, pleasant face. Classy livery.

He came around the car and opened the back passenger door for her. "Your car, ma'am."

"I didn't order a limo—" Had Cynthia been spying on her? Was this one of her scenarios?

"Not consciously, no." He tipped his hat and motioned toward the car. "Lady Magnolia will see you now."

Robin stared. What the hell was this?

"Come on, sugar," said a voice from inside the limo. "Getting a cab in this city is impossible."

Robin stooped slightly to see who was in the car. An absolutely stunning woman smiled at her. She carried the kind of glamor Hollywood had fifty years ago, and she wore a form-fitting red evening dress with matching gloves that made her look as if she was about to host the Oscars. The white stole around her neck added a nice touch.

The driver smiled, encouraging. "We're here for Robin Anne Preston," he said. "Date of birth June 15, 1978."

Robin stared at him and her chest tightened. "Oh, no. Hell, no. This is the last thing I need tonight."

"Which is why you need to sit your cute, little, lesbian ass in this car," said Lady Magnolia. "Because Mama don't take no shit. And girl, you better hope I don't have to get out of this nice warm car to throw you in it."

Fuck, Robin thought as realization dawned. Of course her second visitor had to be a drag queen. Nobody could out-snark a good queen.

"What's it gonna be, sugar?" Magnolia asked.

The driver regarded Robin with polite interest.

Robin groaned, but she got in, and the driver closed the door behind her, leaving her in the company of a gorgeous RuPaul lookalike with a perfect Audrey Hepburn coif and a low Georgia drawl.

"That's better, sweetie. Have a tonic." She held up a silver flask and poured a bit into a shot glass, which she handed to Robin.

"So are you the good cop or the bad cop?" She sniffed the shot glass. Smelled like whisky. She sipped. Very smooth.

Magnolia screwed the top back on the flask and put it in a tasteful bejeweled clutch from which she now withdrew a compact. "Sweetie, I am either your worst fucking nightmare or the best bitch you've got." She inspected her makeup and gave Robin a sideways glance. "Whichever of those you get is on you."

"I'm already in a nightmare, so I'll go for the latter."

Magnolia tsked. "Sugar, this ain't no damn nightmare. This—" she made an expansive gesture, "is a chance, and not everybody gets one. Or my fabulous company. So I expect to hear some counting tonight."

"Of what?"

"Your lucky stars." Magnolia pursed her lips at the compact's mirror.

"So what's tonight's agenda?"

"Honey, all my agendas are gay. But in your case, I'll go lesbian." She made a soft kissing noise. "Now. Let me introduce myself. I am Lady Magnolia, your guide this evening." She handed Robin a card that said, in flowing formal script, *Christmas Present.*

"Seriously?" Robin held the card up.

"Honey, you have just been properly served. And a night with me is always a present." She flashed a wicked smile. "So you just settle your cute self and let's see where we end up." She tapped the glass between them and it slid open.

"Ma'am?" The driver asked.

"Ramón, do a lady a favor and give us some music."

"Yes, ma'am." The window slid closed and a club song Robin knew thumped softly from unseen speakers. She drained the rest of the shot glass and Magnolia took it from her.

"Much better, sugar. Because girl, bitch does not look good on you."

Robin started to retort but thought better of it and instead looked out her window, watching the mist that completely surrounded her. For all she knew, the car was flying, so completely were they enveloped. "Where are we going?" she asked, more to hide her growing anxiety than to get an answer.

"Where the night takes us. You just sit back and relax," she said with a little purr. "Magnolia's got you, and there is nothing you need to worry about. Except maybe the truth."

Robin closed her eyes, the beat of the song reminding her of her club days during college after Jill left. She'd ended up in a lot of different beds, then, but never for long.

"Time to get out," Magnolia said. The fog was already dissipating when Ramón opened the door.

Robin exited the car, knowing there was no point to trying to stay put. "Where are we?" She looked around at the buildings, shoved so close together that they probably held each other up. Many shared walls, while others were fortunate to have a walkway between them. Low income neighborhood, she automatically cataloged, in one of the boroughs, but she wasn't sure which. Signs on local businesses advertised services in a variety of languages. Trash bags piled on the curb for pickup. Cars lined the street, but Ramón had double parked, leaving room for drivers to go around the limo. Maybe he'd get a ticket. Robin wondered how the Bureau handled that.

"All in good time. Let's go, sugar." Magnolia adjusted her stole and walked regally in her six-inch heels to a beat-up metal door that Robin knew would take them to upstairs apartments. Magnolia went first up the stairs, walking as if she owned the place, stepping gracefully over an empty beer can and a crushed paper bag with *Deli* printed on the front.

The dim lights flickered overhead, and Robin smelled something cooking that might've been meat. Magnolia continued to the next floor.

"Okay, seriously," Robin said to Magnolia's back. "I've never been here. What does this have to do with me?"

Magnolia stopped and turned slowly to look down at her, a gesture that incorporated more drama than if she had done a hair flip. "Christmas Present isn't always about you." She raised an eyebrow imperiously then continued up the stairs to the landing. Here, Magnolia left the stairs and went down a corridor that had only one working light overhead, but she clearly knew which apartment she wanted because she stopped at a door on the right without checking any of the numbers.

She waited for Robin and pointed at the door. "After you," she said.

"Really?"

"Oh, girl. You do *not* want to go there with me." She smiled and ran a gloved finger down Robin's cheek. "Now get your sweet little ass in there."

Robin took a couple of deep breaths, shut her eyes, and moved toward the door, waiting for the feel of wood against her forehead. But like last time, she moved through the door and opened her eyes onto a cluttered apartment that smelled of hamburgers. This was the living room. Shelves made of boards and cinderblocks held a small flat-screen TV and a couch that had seen better days sat across from it. An overstuffed chair that might've been new twenty years ago hunkered next to the couch. She heard voices coming from what was probably the kitchen, right off this front room. Magnolia pushed her forward, and Robin peered in. A man she didn't know sat at a table, while a woman she also didn't know stood at a stove overseeing a frying pan. The window above the kitchen sink was open a bit.

"I have no idea why the hell I'm here," Robin said in a low voice, though she guessed the apartment's occupants couldn't hear or see them.

"That's Joseph Spinelli," Magnolia said. "Joe, as he prefers." She made a little growling sound. "I'd call him whatever he wants."

"Who?"

Magnolia placed her hand over her heart dramatically and gave her a withering look. "Girl, if he was a queen, his name would be Pink Slip. Courtesy of you."

Robin winced and looked back at him. She'd signed his termination papers a week ago.

"I'll see if I can get some more hours at the restaurant," the woman was saying. "We'll figure it out."

"How?" he asked. "We could barely afford her medicine before I got cut."

"I'll check to see if there's a program we can get on," the woman said, but Robin heard the strain in her voice.

The front door opened and a teenage boy entered. He took his coat and shoes off and left both by the door.

"In here, Mark," Joe called, and the boy went into the kitchen. He wore a shirt with a deli logo on it.

"Got paid," Mark said. He put a check on the table next to Joe, but Joe didn't look at it. The muscles in his jaw clenched. Mark squeezed his dad's shoulder. "Dad, it's okay. The college fund can wait."

The woman gave the boy a hug and a kiss. "Are you hungry?"

"Nah. Had a sandwich at work. You and Dad go ahead."

Another door in the apartment opened, and a girl about eight years old rushed down the hall. "Hi," she said as she gave Mark a hug.

45

"Hey, careful. Don't be running like that. It messes with your lungs," he said, and Robin noted how pale the girl was, though she smiled up at her brother.

"I took my medicine already."

"Okay, but don't get wild. There's only room for one of us to do that here."

She giggled and sat down at the table.

"Now just you look at that. Cute as a l'il ol' bug," Magnolia said, crouching to smile at the little girl though she couldn't be seen.

"What's wrong with her?" Robin asked.

Magnolia straightened to her full six feet and some. "Debilitating asthma. And girl, this place doesn't help." Magnolia moved to the sink and frowned as she looked at it. "Only so much you can do," she said, casting a critical gaze at the paint peeling on the ceiling.

"Look, sometimes people get laid off," Robin said, and it sounded petulant in her ears.

Magnolia turned back toward her, injecting the motion with extra flair. "Yes. They do. But honey, you'd better have a damn good reason when you make such decisions, and you'd better damn sure make room when those chickens come home to roost."

The girl started coughing, and both Joe and Mark scrutinized her. "I'll get her inhaler," Mark said as the girl wheezed. Joe moved over to her and Mark left the room. He went down the short hallway to what Robin guessed were the bedrooms.

"It's okay, honey," Joe said in a soothing voice. "Just relax, like the doctor showed you."

46

Mark reappeared with an asthma inhaler. He shook it up and handed it to the girl. She took it and managed a puff between wheezes.

"That's it. Sit still," Joe said. Mark caught his mom's eye and they exchanged a look. The girl's breathing improved and Joe stroked her cheek. "Why don't you go watch some TV?"

"Okay," she said, and Robin moved aside for her, though she knew it wasn't necessary.

"Mark, sit with me," she called as she got on the couch and turned on the TV.

He did and pulled her against him. "You all right?"

"Yeah. Are we going to be okay?" she said softly. Robin barely caught her question.

"Sure," he said, but he was lying, and Robin knew it. Her throat tightened, and she could feel Magnolia's eyes lasering the back of her head.

"Will Daddy get a job?"

"Oh, yeah. He'll find something soon," Mark said as he stroked her head. "Don't worry," he lied again.

"Why didn't his boss like him?"

Robin gritted her teeth.

"Sometimes companies are assholes, Annie, and sometimes bosses are, too."

She stared at him. "You said a bad word."

"I'm sorry." He smiled down at her. "Don't tell anyone."

"I won't."

"Here's Mr. Cuddles." He handed her a stuffed elephant, and she held it tight, snuggled against him.

"I'm tired of being sick," Annie said after a while.

"As soon as Dad gets a job, we can figure out how to make you feel better. Don't worry, okay?"

"I'm trying, but it's hard."

He gave her a little squeeze. "I know. But you've got me and Mom and Dad and we'll figure everything out." He smiled, male bravado and assurance in his voice, but Robin knew it was all for show. She clenched her teeth, realizing that it was a lot easier to lay people off when they were just names on a form. Here in Joe Spinelli's shabby apartment, watching Mark with Annie reminded Robin of her own childhood. Her mom had always scrambled to keep things together, to make sure she and Frank were taken care of, but at the end of the day, it seemed there wasn't much money to go around.

Mist started to gather in the room and this time, she was relieved and ready to go, ready to leave this indictment of who she was.

"This way, sugar," Magnolia said, and she grabbed Robin's wrist and they walked, but Robin didn't know where. All she could see was Magnolia's seemingly disembodied glove on her arm and then they were at the car. Ramón stood there, waiting with the passenger door open.

Magnolia got in first with a "thank you, sweetie" to him. Robin followed and settled back into the seat, glad to be out of that apartment and away from the evidence of how low she could go.

"Okay, sugar. Let's continue on our journey."

Robin decided she didn't want to ask. She should have taken Cynthia up on her offer after all. She pushed herself against the seat, as if she could disappear in it. There were lots of jobs in the city. She thought about the other person she'd laid off with Joe. Linda? No, that wasn't it. L-something. Lydia? That sounded right.

"Sometimes a company's bottom line means you have to make hard choices," Robin said, but she didn't look at Magnolia.

"Honey, where I come from, the bottom line is the lowest mark on your pitcher of margaritas, and the only choice you make is who's buying the next one."

The car glided to a stop, and Robin's door opened. She thought she saw some light through the mist, but she wasn't sure.

"Go on, sweetie. Shake a tail feather."

Robin stepped out of the car, and the mist settled around her like Magnolia's stole. She took a tentative step. And then another, on something that felt more like a floor underfoot than a street.

And then the mist parted, and she was standing in someone's living room. Oh, God. Frank's.

"Well, isn't this Middle America?" Magnolia said as she sashayed over to the photographs on the wall. "Look at you," she said. "A bouncing baby lesbian. Honey, you had the gay all over you from the get-go. Oh, and what's this?"

Robin joined her. A watercolor cityscape hung between the photos, a soft almost impressionistic depiction of Seattle and Puget Sound. She'd done that piece as a freshman in college.

"Girl, you have some skills." Magnolia gave her an appreciative look. "Put that to work, sugar, and use your powers for good."

Robin was about to say something when Frank walked into the room. She hadn't seen him in a year, and in the stress lines around his eyes, she saw echoes of their mom, who worked all the time to make sure they had the basics. Deb was right behind him, and her body language broadcast tension. Great. Magnolia had dropped her in the middle of a spat between her brother and his wife.

"I feel weird not telling her," Frank said. He was staring at the painting on the wall. "I mean, I'm going to be a dad. I want to share that with my sister."

Robin stared. Deb was pregnant?

"Oh, Lord," Magnolia said. "Drama." She fanned herself with one gloved hand.

"Baby, I get that," Deb said. "But she always blows you off. You barely see her anymore, and when you do, it's never because she wants to." Deb moved behind Frank and leaned her head against his back as she wrapped her arms around his waist. "Can you see where I'm coming from? I know what it does to you every time she blows you off. Do you honestly think she's going to be involved in the baby's life when she can't even be bothered to be in yours?"

"Oh, snap." Magnolia said, but Robin was too stunned to even glare at her.

"She's working through some things," Frank said, and the pain in his voice made Robin cringe.

"You've used that excuse the entire time we've been together." She released him and turned him to face her. "Look at me," she said. "Frank." She stroked the side of his face. "I know she's your sister, and I know that you used to be close. But that's not true anymore."

"She's just lost," he said, and Robin knew, again, what heartbreak felt like.

"And that's sad. But you can't help her. And she doesn't want your help, anyway." Deb brushed at the tear on Frank's cheek. He had always been a crier. Women loved it about him. And apparently queens did, too, because Magnolia dabbed at her eye.

"I'm not going to give up on her," he said.

Deb smiled and gave him a kiss. "I'm not asking you to. I'm just asking you to have a more realistic view of things, and to stop expecting anything from her. If you can get to that point, then it won't hurt so much when she doesn't come through."

He leaned his forehead against hers. "Should I tell her about the baby?"

"Generally, family members tell each other things like this. But she might not say what you want to hear."

"What do you mean?" He pulled back slightly.

"What I just said. You might be expecting her to be the sister you had years ago, and that things will go back to that. And if that doesn't happen—" Deb brushed his hair away from his eyes. "I don't like to see you hurt."

He sighed. "It makes me feel bad not to. I know she can be a total jerk, but she's my sister, and I want her in the loop for this."

"A jerk?" Robin's stomach felt as if she'd been punched.

"The reaction she gives might not be what you want," Deb said. "Be prepared for that."

"What the hell do you mean?" Robin demanded. "What reaction?"

"Sugar, quiet." Magnolia put her hands on her hips and stood, statuesque, listening.

"She'll be happy for us," Frank said, and it sounded defensive.

"I'm sure she'll be happy on some level." Deb put her hands on his shoulders. "But don't expect anything else from her."

"That's cold," he said.

"Yes, yes it is. Thank you, Frank." Robin shot Magnolia a look of triumph.

"No, it's realistic." Deb rubbed his shoulders. "In the five years we've been together, I've only been in your sister's company twice. And the first time was when I met her."

"Hey, I have a name," Robin said.

"Girl, is that true?" Magnolia raised her perfect eyebrows. "Twice? In five years?" She shook her head, a gesture that managed to convey both pity and patronization.

Frank smiled at Deb. "Okay, it's realistic," he said.

"Hey, wait a minute. Frank—" Dammit. He couldn't hear her. Robin clenched her fists. "What do you mean, it's realistic not to expect anything from me?" she asked anyway.

"But I think I'll still tell her, even if she decides not to be involved."

"Whatever decision you make about telling her is up to you. The baby will still have involved aunts and uncles," Deb said.

Frank nodded. "I just wish—"

"I know. Just keep in mind that your sister doesn't seem to want much to do with us."

"That is so not true." Robin was shaking, a mixture of anger, hurt, and pain. "Frank, that's not true. That is totally not true."

"When was the last time you had a face-to-face visit with him?" Magnolia asked.

"A year ago."

"Sugar, it was longer than that." This time, she almost sounded gentle.

"Frank, don't listen to her. I'm right here." Robin patted her chest emphatically. "Right here."

"Is she coming for Christmas?" Deb asked him.

He hesitated. "Probably not."

Deb hugged him, and he held her close. In his expression, Robin saw that Deb had made her point. The worst part was that Robin had given her all the ammo.

"It's not a war, sweets," Magnolia said. "It's just life. You make your choices, you own the consequences." She adjusted her stole.

Robin tried to swallow, but the lump in her throat prevented it. Frank was going to be a dad. And he hadn't told her. Maybe he had wanted to, the last time they talked, and she'd gone off on him about a practical joke that he said he didn't do. She gave him no room to talk about it. Robin hadn't felt this bad since Jill had left. No, this was worse. This was her brother, the little boy she'd tried to protect when they were kids, the man she'd somehow left behind. This was a red-hot poker to the heart. She gulped back a sob.

"My mama always said truth's a mean bitch." Magnolia took her arm and guided her through the mist to the car. Ramón closed the door behind her again, but Robin barely noticed. She touched her face. Tears. Her whole body ached with sadness. The car moved. Or maybe the mist did. Robin couldn't tell and she didn't care.

"Can I go home?" she asked after a while, glad that Magnolia hadn't said anything else.

"Soon."

"I hate this."

"Change don't always come with a hot meal and a highball."

The car stopped, and Robin's door opened again. "Please, I really just want to go home."

"Honey, we're still in the middle of our come-to-Jesus moment. Move your booty on out."

Robin stepped out of the car. Did Frank really have that conversation with Deb? Or was it all a setup? Her feet sank into carpet, and she smelled familiar cologne. Cynthia. This was the apartment she used with Robin if they didn't go to Robin's place.

She heard the unmistakable sounds of Cynthia and sex coming from the bedroom.

"This could be interesting." Magnolia model-walked to the open doorway. Her heels should have left indentations in the carpet, but they didn't. "Oh, no she didn't," she said, fanning herself.

Robin gritted her teeth and joined Magnolia at the doorway. "Seriously?" she muttered at the sight of Cynthia underneath a naked woman on the bed. Both were going at it hard.

"Mmm mmm," Magnolia scolded. "Careful where you dip your honeystick, sugar. Because Miss Thing here seems to attract a lot of flies." She gave Robin a sympathetic look, but it only seemed to make this whole trip worse.

Robin walked away, back to where she estimated they'd arrived, but she still heard the sounds emanating from the bedroom. Why was she surprised? Hell, Cynthia had screwed around with her, why wouldn't she screw around with someone else? She wondered how many more Cynthia had on her chain, and a wave of queasiness roiled her stomach. If she puked, would Cynthia see it the next morning? Or would it be invisible like Robin was? The thought amused her, and she fought a laugh, knowing that if she started, she'd probably cry, too.

"Hang on, sugar," Magnolia said softly near her ear. "And enjoy the ride."

At the sight of the mist gathering around her feet, she almost cried anyway, from relief. The mist seemed to swell, but Magnolia wasn't with her, and Robin was falling, like the last time she'd gotten a visit from the Bureau. She shut her eyes and braced for a crash. It came, but not as hard as she'd expected. Her feet hit ground, and she stumbled and went down, landing on cold concrete that bit into her palms and her knees. Hard enough to sting.

"Oh, my God, are you okay?" said a woman's voice. It sounded weirdly familiar.

"Yeah, for the most part."

"Here." The stranger took Robin's arm and helped her up.

"What happened?" Robin asked as she inspected her knees. Her slacks hadn't torn, fortunately.

"I don't know. You just seemed to fall. Are you sure you're okay—" the stranger stopped, and Robin looked at her. Her throat seemed to close, and she couldn't talk as they stared at each other.

"Uh," Robin managed after a few seconds.

"Oh, my God. Robin?"

Robin kept staring. "Jill?"

"It *is* you. Oh, my God."

"I—um." Robin stared again, at her amazing cheekbones and the still familiar sparkle in her dark eyes. "You cut your hair."

Jill laughed, and it broke the awkwardness of the moment.

"Oh, Jesus," Robin said. "I can't believe I said that. I mean, of course you cut your hair. It's been years. Why wouldn't you?" And it looked really cute, with the buzzcut on the sides and back and the punkish spikiness up top. She also had several piercings in one of her ears, each hole decorated with either a silver stud or a small jewel. And she wore a black leather motorcycle jacket, tight dark jeans, and combat boots. Jill had never dressed like that in college. She was always wound a little tight, but sometimes she'd show her rebel side with a punk rock T-shirt and a pair of black canvas sneakers that she'd decorated in art classes. But this—this was so not how she'd been in college.

"And you grew yours out," Jill said, still smiling. "Oh, my God. I cannot believe it's you." She started to move as though she was going to give her a hug but stopped, as if she remembered the circumstances that had created the length of time between them. "So—oh, my God, I have so many questions and it's so great to see you. But you're probably on your way somewhere—"

"No, actually, I'm not." Robin smiled down at her, wondering why it didn't hurt to see her, and wondering why it felt as though it hadn't been years between them.

"Oh. That's—that's great. I'm having an opening. Across the street." Jill motioned at a building ablaze with lights and people. And art. Lots of art. All over the walls, Robin saw through the front windows.

"Seriously?" Robin stared first at the building and then back at Jill.

"Seriously," she said with a little grin. "And you are now formally invited, if you don't think it's too fucked up to do that. Since we haven't seen each other in a while and you might still—"

"I'd love to."

"Okay. Come on."

And Robin followed her across the street, dodging traffic and smiling like she was in college again, going out to explore abandoned buildings looking for objects to use in their art pieces.

She entered the gallery behind Jill, who was greeted effusively by a guy who looked like a thinner, gayer version of Thor.

"You've sold five so far," he said, clearly pleased for her.

"That's great news. Samo, this is...an old friend from college. Robin."

"Charmed," he said with a nod, apparently not one to touch strangers since he didn't offer his hand.

"Nice to meet you." Robin returned his nod and several people converged from different directions on Jill, going on about her art.

"I'm going to wander," Robin said to her as she backed away.

"Thanks. I'll find you later. So please don't leave." Jill smiled.

"I won't." Robin half waved and left Jill to her fans. She took her coat off and carried it on one arm, the faint smell of paint that seemed to always linger in galleries taking her years back, to her days and nights in the studio when she was sure she was an artist, sure that was her path.

Something stirred within her as she stopped to admire one of the larger pieces Jill had chosen for this show. Mixed media, Robin automatically catalogued. Oils and found objects. Jill had painted a day scene of a city port that looked a lot like Seattle's, and she'd incorporated objects like antique fishing lures and hooks and a retro fishing rod. It seemed to be part of a port series she'd done, since this one was called "Port 9." She'd included hints of her Chinese background, in the characters she'd skillfully painted into spots on the canvas.

Bold, Robin thought, to use those kinds of objects, but Jill had placed them in such a way that they complemented the oils with their own bright colors and positions.

"I love this piece," said a woman next to her. "The colors are so vibrant and alive."

"Yeah," Robin agreed, automatically cataloguing the woman, too. Trust fund college student who liked art and the local scenes, she figured.

"Jill Chen is brilliant," said another woman who joined them. College student, probably not trust fund. Funky hipster goth-y, Robin decided. Nose ring and dreads.

"The way she places found objects in her paintings—I can't replicate it," funky hipster said.

"Maybe you shouldn't," Robin said, and both women looked at her as if she'd just slashed the painting. "I mean, maybe you should find your own way, and use media that best expresses *you*."

The women looked less appalled.

"After all, art is your personal creative journey, and how you travel is all you," Robin said.

Funky hipster nodded. "I feel you."

"What's your medium?" Robin asked.

"Mostly photography. But I work with others."

"What makes you feel the best?"

"Photography and collage, actually."

"Have you combined them?"

Trust fund leaned in, interested.

"Not really, no," funky hipster said.

Robin shrugged. "Maybe try it. See if you like how those two play together."

"Right on." Funky hipster nodded.

"Good luck," Robin said and she moved through the crowd toward some of Jill's other work. That had been a conversation like she used to have back in her art days. Sharing thoughts and offering suggestions. It felt good. Was it some kind of automatic response to art? To being in a place like this? Or was there something changing in her subconscious, brought on by Magnolia and Decker? A waiter in black tie slowed when he saw her.

"Wine?"

"Love some." Robin took a plastic flute from the tray and sipped. Some kind of chardonnay, she guessed. She moved to the back end of the gallery, which featured a few more of Jill's oils, all with found objects that echoed the painting themes or provided a juxtaposition that strengthened the relationships between internal elements. Jill leaned toward urban scenes, though she had a couple of landscapes of the Pacific Northwest that were gorgeous, and in each one, she'd included elements that related somehow to her Chinese background. Robin particularly liked how Jill had incorporated mahjong tiles in a few of her pieces. Jill's older female relatives loved to play that, and Jill's stories of particularly heated games had always make Robin laugh.

She sipped, seeing in these works a maturity and grace that the artist she'd met in college hadn't yet developed, though Robin definitely saw glimpses of her past, in some of her choices of found objects. Whimsical but maybe a little restrained in some instances. Playful and flirtatious in others. And weird, how Robin fell so easily into art vernacular, so easily into a scene like this. Weird, but somehow not.

Robin didn't know how long she'd been in the gallery, but she was nearly finished with her second flute of wine and she'd munched on a plate of cheese and fruit. Many of the pieces had sold already, which made her happy but somehow sad, because she'd lost that part of herself, and somehow, Jill had held on to the dream.

Maybe breaking up had been what Jill had to do in order to remain true to herself, Robin thought. After all, look what she herself had become. A corporate dick who burned her bridges and torched her memories. Another lump formed in her throat, and she tried to wash it down with the last of the wine. She managed to swallow it and then set the flute on a tray stand in a corner.

Robin went back to the painting of the city port, with the fishing lures and the hooks and the fishing rod. Someone had bought it, and Robin wondered if it was the trust fund student from earlier.

"Okay, I think I've pretty much talked to everyone who needs to be talked to," Jill said at Robin's elbow. "What do you think?" she asked, as if there were only a few days between now and the last time they'd seen each other.

"This one's my favorite," Robin said. "I really love what you did with the objects, and how you've got them positioned."

"Thanks. It might be one of my faves, too."

"So I'll guess you're in Seattle. Or Portland," Robin said.

"Not bad. Seattle. I moved there after college."

Robin nodded, and wondered at the sudden desire she had to pack up and fly across the country to the city of her birth.

"What about you?" Jill asked. She'd taken her motorcycle jacket off, and she wore a creamy white tailored blouse with the top buttons undone, exposing her neck and a bit of cleavage. She wore several silver chains, one with charms on it. When she moved her arm, Robin caught the flash of a blue jewel from her cufflink. Jill was much hotter now than she'd been in college, and she'd been gorgeous then.

"Nothing really to tell. I went business. Executive director of sales at a multinational here."

"Jill—" Samo said from nearby, and Robin was glad he'd interrupted because she didn't want to tell Jill any more about what she did. "When you get a minute?" he added.

"Be right there." Jill turned back to her. "Listen, I really would love to catch up with you." She handed Robin a business card. "I know there's some—well, some baggage between us, so if you don't want to, I understand. But it is great to see you, and I'm really glad I ran into you."

"Yeah. Sure." Robin took the card and smiled. "I'd like that."

"Great. I'm in town through New Year's. Call me."

Robin nodded and watched her walk away, and remembered her fifteen years ago, when she'd first seen her. They'd both been starting their second year of college, and Jill walked into art class that fall semester, conservatively dressed and maybe a little nerdy. But she had glitter on her sneakers and interesting glasses, so Robin introduced herself, and when Jill left class that first day, Robin had wanted to follow. She had that same feeling now.

She glanced around and realized she needed to figure out how to get home from here. Or not. Her chest tightened. Lady Magnolia was chatting up one of the servers not even ten feet away, a particularly handsome man—wait. He could see her? Did that mean Robin was still in some kind of Bureau mindfuck? She scanned the crowd for Jill, panic rising. There she was, still talking to Samo. Robin relaxed. Besides, this was Christmas Present, right? So it was, in fact, the present and this was happening right now. Then why was she able to interact with these people when she hadn't been able to earlier?

Magnolia caught Robin's eye and gave her a sly wink. She blew a kiss at the server and walked toward her, letting her stole hang suggestively on her shoulders. More than a few men tracked her with their gazes.

"I do love art," Magnolia said. "But come on, sugar. It's nearly bedtime, and I have to get you back before you turn into a pumpkin."

"Is this for real?" Robin asked as she followed Magnolia out of the gallery to the wet sidewalk beyond. Robin hadn't noticed that it had started snowing, but the limo was waiting and Ramón got out to open the door for her. "Am I really here?" she asked.

"Christmas Present can have many different meanings," Magnolia said as she got into the limo. Robin followed and settled herself against the leather seat again. She closed her eyes, tired and still emotionally raw.

"That's it, sugar. You just rest."

The music seemed to increase in volume, a rhythm and blues number, and Robin was so tired she couldn't open her eyes if she tried. Maybe Magnolia would let her stay here, on this really comfortable seat. Maybe she could stay here forever, and escape all the shit that swirled in her life. That would be nice, she thought as she drifted to sleep. So nice...

Bureau of Holiday Affairs
Field Report: Preston, Robin Anne, DOB June 15, 1978//Seattle, WA
Case Number 26901-15
Agent: your favorite queen
Date of Interaction:
December 19
Methodology Employed: Lady Magnolia special, with extra truth plus a dash of the past.

Results: Subject may have a soul.

Observations/recommendations: My mama always said that sometimes people just need a good size ten stiletto up the tush. Audio and video available.

Personal Overview: I have a soft spot for cute hard-luck lesbian cases. People create barriers to avoid dealing with pain, but they can become a weapon. I think there's a heart in there somewhere. The question is, can our little lost lesbian open it, not only to others, but herself? The Lady is cautiously hopeful, but she knows only too well the fallibility of humankind.

Chapter 4

ROBIN OPENED HER EYES TO the familiar sight of her apartment ceiling. Her clock radio was playing a song that sounded familiar. Some R&B number. She turned her head and looked at it. Time to get up and go to work, she knew, but she couldn't figure out why her alarm wasn't beeping. She never used the radio function.

She groaned and sat up, still fully dressed, though her shoes were off. The covers hadn't been pulled back, and she'd just slept on top of them wrapped in the blanket from the couch. Robin stripped and went to shower, though the hot water didn't settle her mood or her stomach, which was a little sour.

Had she really seen Jill? Or was that part of a dream? And was Deb really pregnant? She toweled off and dressed, another business power suit, and picked up her clothing from the night before. Something fell out of her pants pocket and she watched it fall to the floor. A business card. She picked it up and, when she saw the name, a mixture of emotions rushed through her chest. *Jill Chen, artist*. A pen and ink self portrait of Jill smiling and wearing sunglasses appeared in the lower right-hand corner of the card, and Robin remembered how Jill could create images of people like that in minutes or even seconds, the quick strokes of her brush or pen moving unerringly across the paper.

She slipped the card into her wallet and left the bedroom but returned seconds later. In her dresser, she kept a small wooden box. Robin opened it and stared at the contents, an assortment of rings and necklaces she hadn't worn in years. She closed it and started to put it away then opened it again and selected a couple of rings, both silver, one with a band shaped like the body of a snake, while the other's band was etched with tiny skulls. That one she slid onto her left pinkie, amazed it still fit. The snake ring slid easily onto the middle finger of her other hand.

She held her hands out and flexed her fingers. She'd put these rings away when she buried herself in business school, but here they were on her fingers as if they'd never left. Robin closed the box and put it back in her drawer. The thought of going to work made her stomach churn again, but she had several meetings, and she had to work on her presentation.

Robin grabbed her coat and shoulder bag and left without eating anything. She walked to work, hoping the air would help clear her head, and by the time she got to the office, she did feel a little better.

"Morning," she said to the guard at the information desk. He looked at her, clearly surprised.

"Good morning, Ms. Preston," he responded.

"Morning, Mike," said an older guy in a suit behind Robin as he passed.

"Mr. Watts," the guard said as Robin followed the guy onto the elevator. They'd lucked out. It was only the two of them.

"Floor?" he asked.

"Twenty."

He pushed the button for her. "How's it going?" he asked.

She looked at him. "Um, fine. You?"

"Excellent. Love this time of year. My kids will be home from college for Christmas."

"That sounds great." Robin nodded and sipped her coffee. Her stomach felt a little better.

"It is."

The elevator stopped at fifteen, and Mr. Watts stepped out as the doors opened. "Hope you have a great day and Merry Christmas," he said.

"Yeah. You, too," she said and meant it. The doors closed, and Robin leaned against the wall, though the elevator made it to her floor too fast for her to relax.

"Mr. Frost would like to speak to you," Laura said as Robin passed her desk on the way to her office.

"Okay. Did he call?"

"Yes. Ten minutes ago."

Great. She hadn't been at her desk. Frost hated it when people weren't at his beck and call.

"Thanks. I'll call him," she said with a smile.

Laura nodded, a puzzled expression on her face, and Robin noted that the dress she had on today brought out the darker tones of her skin. For the first time, Robin really looked at her. She knew Laura was married to a man and had a young child at home—a boy, Robin remembered. Her husband worked for the city, but she wasn't sure what department or what he did. Strange, the things that a person noticed or didn't.

Robin went into her office and tossed her coat and bag onto the sofa against the wall then she settled herself at her own desk and dialed Frost's extension. His personal assistant picked up.

"David Frost's office."

"Hi, Megan. It's Robin Preston, returning Mr. Frost's call."

"Oh, yes. He's on another line. I'll have him call you when he's done."

"Great. Thanks." Robin hung up and turned on her work laptop. Talking to Frost always made her nervous because she rarely had to deal with him except at meetings, so the fact that he was calling her directly made her stomach burn again. She retrieved her bag from the couch and took a folder out. A business card fell out onto her desk just as the phone rang.

"Preston," she answered.

"Good. I caught you," Mr. Frost said. He always sounded as if he'd had too many martinis and cigars the night before. "I got a call this morning from Bruce Schmidt. He was very impressed with the work you did on the Randall account."

"Oh. Well, thank you." That was a relief. Randall was notoriously stingy.

"And then Randall himself called to tell me what a hard-assed bitch you are."

Robin froze. "Sir?"

"In the best possible way. He's pretty sure you made up the figures, but he approved of your slash and burn approach and decided he wants to work with us. That's how you do business, Preston. Well done." He hung up.

Hard-assed bitch? Slash and burn? She thought back to the meeting she'd had last month with Randall, a man who bore a striking resemblance to the Monopoly game guy. He'd told her he had a problem with staffing, and he needed to lay some people off but didn't want to because he felt badly for them.

Robin winced and hung up. She'd told him to do a random draw to cut lower-level staff, so that he could claim chance. Her fingers brushed the business card that had fallen out of her file and she picked it up. *Christmas Present*. She dropped it as if it were hot. Was she going nuts? How much of last night was real? Gingerly, she picked the card up after a few moments and put it in her work satchel. Then she stared at her cell phone for a while before she finally speed-dialed Frank, who was probably at work, but sometimes he answered. Not this time, however.

"Hey, it's me," Robin said. "I was just, uh, thinking about you. Not sure about Christmas, but it doesn't look like I can leave. I have a presentation I have to do right after the holiday. I might be able to get away next month, so let me know what weekends work for a visit. Hope you're okay and hi to Deb." She hung up and picked up her tablet for her first meeting. It had been over a year since she'd seen him. Why was that?

Robin stared into the middle distance. Maybe Frank reminded her that she wasn't who she used to be, and maybe she was realizing that who she'd become wasn't someone she particularly liked, and who reminded her of her dad. So she avoided Frank, but in reality what she was doing was avoiding herself. From the scene she'd seen with Magnolia, Frank and Deb seemed to have a good relationship. Maybe that bothered her, too, because he'd found someone who made him happy, with whom he was going to be a parent, and Robin basically bed-surfed, never slowing down, always climbing the corporate ladder. No time for anything but work.

She wasn't sure she could get away next month, but for some reason, she didn't care. She'd make the time, as out of character as it seemed.

Or maybe it wasn't. Maybe all this business crap was what was out of character. She wasn't sure, anymore, and the last thing she wanted to do was sit through a meeting. How great would it be to just get on a plane for anywhere and start over? No more of this corporate bullshit or working long hours for the next promotion. How great would it be to fly out of here? Pretty great.

She took that thought with her.

Robin picked at the salad. Frank still hadn't called or texted, and she knew better than to try again. He was probably shocked that she'd offered to visit. But maybe if she did, then he'd tell her about the baby. And then maybe things could start getting better between them. She knew it was mostly her fault, that she'd let things get to this point. And worse, she realized it was something their dad had done to them as well.

She took Jill's card out of her wallet and picked up her phone. Why was she doing this? It wasn't as though she was looking for a date. Especially with a long-gone ex. That was the last thing on Robin's mind these days. Closure, maybe. She wasn't sure. She added Jill's cell phone number to her contacts then texted her.

> *Hi. It's Robin. Just touching base, seeing if you want to have lunch or something while you're in town.*

There. She'd reached out again. Twice in one day. That was a record for her because she was always too busy trying to climb the corporate ladder. Always trying to get ahead. She frowned. Maybe she just needed a vacation. It had been a while since she'd taken one of those. Robin stared at her salad for a while. She didn't feel like finishing, so she threw the rest away and went back to her office. This was deeper than a vacation. This felt like something was getting pulled up by the roots, and it left a huge hole that she had no idea how to fill.

Who the hell was she, exactly? The calendar on her laptop dinged, notifying her about her next damn meeting. Fortunately, this one was in the conference room just down the hall, and she probably wouldn't have to do or say anything. Normally she enjoyed verbally jousting with the old guard, but today, she didn't care. If she never did that again, she'd be fine with it. She picked up her tablet, and for reasons she couldn't explain, she also picked up a small notepad and a pen.

Robin took a chair at the end of the long conference table. Frost would be at the opposite end so he could intimidate whoever was giving a presentation today. Normally, she sat near there, too, but today she didn't feel like being near him. The table filled up, and unfortunately, Cynthia's husband Brady sat across from her, wearing one of his expensive suits. Maybe ten years older than Cynthia, he exuded money and privilege, and though he was in his late fifties, he kept himself up. Even with his receding hairline, he could pass for a guy twenty years younger. He smiled at her, but there was no warmth in it. That was the kind of man he was, Robin had figured out the year before. No wonder Cynthia had affairs. Then again, he probably did, too. He was gone enough to cover a few up.

It was kind of creepy, actually, sitting there across from him, and not only because she'd just screwed his wife last week. No, it was that his wife was screwing others, too, and she could relate to how he might feel if he knew, after what she saw last night. Not that she felt any emotional attachment to Cynthia. But seeing her last night made Robin feel sordid and dirty, and not in a good way.

She wasn't even sure anymore why she'd asked Cynthia to bed. Sure, she was attractive. Had Robin really believed that Cynthia would put a good word in for her with Brady, and that would travel up to Frost? That was messed up. She hadn't really considered Brady in her equation when she hooked up with his wife. He'd been unimportant to her. Her father behaved this way, and she hated that about him. The unflattering comparison between her and her dad left a bitter, metallic taste in her mouth.

Robin scrolled idly through her email. This thing with Cynthia was bad news, and she'd been in denial about it. The worst part about it was that she had pursued Cynthia even though Cynthia was married. She frowned, thinking about what she'd seen with Lady Magnolia. Robin had no one to blame but herself for this situation with Cynthia.

The lights dimmed and the slide presentation started. Sales were up, accounts were increasing, expansion opportunities looked good. Robin tuned out and idly started doodling on the notepad she'd brought. The lines slowly morphed into Oregon's iconic Haystack Rock. She sketched seabirds on its crest, remembering the roar and crash of waves against its slick surface and the screeches of gulls and kids running back and forth along Cannon Beach. It was as if she were in a trance as the pen seemed to move on its own, shading here, adding detail there, putting a dog in the foreground.

"—Preston?"

She looked up. Every pair of eyes was turned to her. The slide showed a bar graph with projected sales for the next quarter. "Sorry?"

Frost pursed his lips in what Robin knew was displeasure. He hated to repeat himself.

"Head cold coming on, sir," she fibbed. "Ears are stuffed."

"Can you add anything to the projections Hodges has?"

"Just that the Asia accounts are going full tilt and that should bump us to a record profit in the next quarter. I'd say maybe three percent more than what Hodges has up there." She hadn't given him the information. It wasn't the first time she'd withheld. Doing business at Frost meant you had to have a few cards up your sleeve, and make yourself useful to keep around.

Hodges shot her a glance that was both accusatory and pleading. Frost looked at him, and Robin actually felt a little bad for Hodges. Maybe she should say something. But he should've asked for the figures last week. Right? Suddenly, she wasn't so sure.

"Why don't you have the Asia figures?" Frost asked, and the air in the room seemed to cool several degrees.

"Um—" Hodges shuffled through a folder on the table next to him.

The door opened but no one else seemed to notice it. Frost was still glaring at Hodges, and everyone's attention was glued to him. Nobody was moving or making a sound.

"Hiya, Preston," Decker said as she entered. She wore jeans and a gray sweatshirt that said UCLA across the chest.

Robin stiffened. She glanced around, but still nobody moved. It was like being in a wax museum.

Decker went over to Hodges and looked down at his file, then back at Robin. "I know you've picked up certain ways of doing things in terms of business over the years, but really?"

"What are you talking about?"

"You know why Hodges doesn't have the Asia figures." Decker looked up at the image on the wall. "Don't you?" She turned back to Robin, like a teacher waiting for a student to answer.

"Okay, fine. I didn't give them to him. I haven't had a chance to get him up to speed."

Decker nodded. "So you'll just let him take whatever Frost dishes at him for that?"

It was actually on her, Robin realized. She glared at Decker. "I forgot."

Decker waited.

"Fine. It's a habit. But information can move you ahead here."

"Or knock you right off the ladder."

Robin knew Decker was right.

"Two words, Preston. Jenny French."

"How do you—"

"You did the right thing, then," Decker interrupted. "What are you going to do now? Because your boss doesn't look happy." The expression on Frost's face meant Hodges was probably about to get hung out to dry. Robin could prevent it.

"It's not his fault," Robin said.

Decker shrugged. "Do something about it," Decker said, and she disappeared as sound and movement returned. The door to the conference room remained closed.

"I—" Hodges said, and Robin saw, in the light from the image on the screen that he was sweating.

"Mr. Frost," Robin said, and everybody at the table looked at her. "It's not his fault. I haven't had a chance to brief him yet on Asia."

Frost's expression relaxed, and Hodges flashed her a relieved smile. The tension in the room dissipated though nobody spoke for a few moments.

"Take care of that," Frost said.

"Will do." Robin nodded for emphasis and waited a bit to make sure he didn't want any follow-up. He didn't. Somebody put the lights on and the meeting adjourned.

Robin gathered her things and moved to the door, not wanting to deal with either Frost or Cynthia's husband or the fact that she had just gotten a smackdown from someone who may not have existed.

"Thanks for that," Hodges said. "I should've checked in with you. Got too busy, I guess." He held the door open for her, and they stood out in the hall.

"Sure. I'll send you what I've got on Asia." She was about to move away when she thought about Jenny French. "Sorry I didn't sooner," Robin added, and meant it.

He gave her a puzzled look, similar to the one Laura displayed that morning. "You okay?" he asked.

"Yeah, fine. Just a bit of congestion," she fibbed.

"No, I meant—" He glanced at the notepad she was holding. "Wow. Is that Haystack Rock?"

Robin looked down at it, too, as if she was just seeing it for the first time. "Uh."

"It is. That's the best place. Can I see?" He reached for the pad, and Robin reluctantly handed it to him.

"This is really, really good. I didn't know you could draw."

"Hobby," she said as she took the pad back.

"I don't know much about art, but that could be more than a hobby for you."

"Thanks," she said, dismissive. "I'll go get those figures for you." She turned before he could say anything else and went back to her office where she did, in fact, email him the Asia figures and projections. Normally, she wouldn't give up information without some kind of deal, not even if she promised to. Never show your hand, Frost liked to say. But sending the figures to Hodges made her feel as if she was letting go of something that was weighing her down. She was trying to do the right thing, and she'd forgotten that it could feel good to do that, even if it might suck owning up to her part.

Robin leaned back in her chair. She hadn't thought about Jenny French in years. She remembered the night, junior year, she and Jenny had gone joy-riding in Jenny's dad's car without asking him. Jenny had let her drive, even though it was against Mr. French's rules, and Robin had put a long scrape and dent in the right front fender when she clipped one of those short concrete poles at gas stations near the pumps.

Jenny told her dad that she, not Robin, had done it, and got in a ton of trouble with her parents. It was expensive to fix, too, Robin remembered. Jenny had cried at school the following Monday, and Robin felt so bad that she went to Jenny's house that evening and told Jenny's parents that it wasn't Jenny who was driving, it was her.

They both got punished. Jenny was still grounded, though not as long, and she did have to pay about a quarter of the cost of the repair because, Mr. French said, she shouldn't have taken the car without asking and she definitely shouldn't have let Robin drive. Robin paid for the brunt of the cost by the end of the summer. She didn't have much money after that, but she did feel somehow as though she'd paid a fair debt, and she'd learned a very good lesson.

Robin checked her cell phone. Still no response from Frank, which made her anxious. Was he pissed? She hadn't been the nicest the last time he called. How bad would that suck if she finally tried to get her life on track with him and he wouldn't have anything to do with her? It would serve her right, she decided, and that thought made her feel even worse. Her phone dinged and she checked it, hopeful. Not Frank, but it made her smile anyway.

Jill's message was brief, too.

Sounds great. Do you have time for a longer lunch tomorrow?

That was Saturday, a day Robin usually worked. And she did have this presentation weighing on her. But the thought of coming to her office made her stomach hurt, while the thought of a couple hours with Jill made her feel good. A little worried, because she wasn't sure what Jill would have to say about their past, but good nonetheless.

Yes, she texted back. *You pick time and place. See you then.* She set her phone down and opened the slides for her presentation. Thirty minutes later, she was still bouncing idly between them, doing nothing beyond that. Her phone sounded with a text. Jill, again, with a time and place. Robin approved. It was near the piers. Jill had always loved being near water. She texted a confirmation and returned to staring at her presentation, wondering why Frank still hadn't responded.

She opened Google and typed "children" and "asthma" into the search bar. She played with her pinkie ring while she read the information on various sites. After a while of doing that, she called the HR department on her desk phone.

"Yes, Ms. Preston?"

"Hi—Mary?"

"Yes."

"Uh, I was wondering. What are the chances of hiring people back once they've been laid off?"

Pause. "What do you mean?"

"Just what I asked. If we—I—lay somebody off, can I hire them back?" She had laid plenty of people off in the past, no problem. There was no reason for it to bother her now. But it did. You couldn't make it in this business if you went soft. Could you?

Her personal cell started playing an R&B number that Robin remembered from Lady Magnolia's limo. She stared at it.

"Ms. Preston?"

Robin's cell went quiet, but the screen lit up. "Yes. Here."

"As I was saying, I don't really know. I don't recall that it's happened in the time I've been here. It would probably be highly unusual, since the parties might take exception to what could be seen as wrongful termination in the first place and that could result in some kind of legal action."

The R&B song started emanating from Robin's cell again. "Legal action?"

"But I'll find out for sure."

"Thanks." Robin hung up and reached slowly for her cell phone, which was still playing the song. Somebody was calling her, but she sure as hell didn't have that song on her phone as a ring tone. "Are you kidding me?" she said when she saw the caller ID. How was that even possible? "Hello?" she answered.

"Hi, sugar," Lady Magnolia purred. "Sounds like you need a little pep talk."

"For what?"

"For all the good things you're about to do."

Robin rubbed her forehead with her free hand. "I don't even know what those are."

"Oh, yes you do. But right now you're about as confused as a one-eyed dog in a house full of mirrors."

"How can I know what good things I'm going to do *and* be confused?" Was she really having this conversation? Maybe she only *thought* she was, because nobody in their right mind got phone calls like this.

"Sugar, you know what you have to do. And I know that some things you haven't done in a while might feel a bit strange when you try them out again. Sometimes you have to break a new pair of shoes in, a little at a time. But with a little patience, they're your most comfortable pair."

"I didn't get this far in this company without having to make hard choices." The words sounded flat, like a well-rehearsed speech she'd been reciting for years because she felt she had to, but as she sat there, she didn't have a solid reason for why.

"Honey, you've been singing that verse so long, it's lost its meaning," Magnolia drawled, low and sultry. "So go ahead and change the tune. You've got a little rebel streak in you, sugar. Or you wouldn't have put those rings on today."

Robin gripped the phone harder.

"As my mama says, we keep singing the same song because we know the words. Doesn't mean it's the right one. Bye, now."

The line went dead, and Robin set the phone carefully on her desk, as if it might blow up in her hand. She studied the ring on her left pinkie, the tiny skulls grinning up at her. She'd bought it at a flea market in northern California, the semester before she'd met Jill. Robin had worn clothing and jewelry then that looked kind of goth, kind of punk. She'd been listening to a lot of ska then, too. The skulls seemed to wink at her.

Rebel?

Maybe she was. Hiring people back after you fired them was definitely not part of the corporate world. Was it rebellion if she did it? Or getting back to herself? She wasn't sure, but it did feel good to think about Joe Spinelli being able to get medicine for Annie.

Robin brought up the company contact list on her laptop and dialed another number on her desk phone.

"Ramos," said a guy who sounded as though he should be calling an underground boxing match in the Bronx.

"Hi. This is Robin Presto—"

"Please tell me you're not cutting more of my staff."

"No, nothing like that. I was just wondering—how was Joseph Spinelli as an employee?"

"Is this a joke?"

"No. What was he like?"

"Christ, he was one of the best guys I had. Picked everything up really quick, had manager potential. And now that position's been closed, I don't know what I'm gonna do."

Robin frowned. She'd forgotten about that. When they closed a position, they then renamed it and brought somebody on at lower pay. "Okay, so if I get Spinelli back, would you work with me to bring him on at the same rate, maybe more?"

"Are you serious?"

"Yes."

"Currently, we'd have to hire him at the lower pay, because the new position calls for it."

"Have you posted with HR yet?"

"No. We were waiting until after the new year."

"So HR doesn't have the new job description?"

"No."

"Can you piggyback off that position and do a proposal that'll get Spinelli hired at his old rate of pay or a little better and send it up to me ASAP?"

"Jesus. You *are* serious. What about the higher-ups?"

"I *am* a higher-up. So get that to me as soon as you can so I can approve it for HR. The faster we get this done, the sooner we can notify him."

"Will do." He hung up and Robin dialed Lydia Evans's former department and made the same request of her supervisor, who was just as shocked as Ramos had been.

The phone rang just after she hung up.

"Hey, Mary," she answered.

"Well, Ms. Preston, I couldn't find anything with regard to your hypothetical situation because, like I said, it's just never been done. Legal seems to think it's a can of worms, but legally, it apparently is okay to do it, but the former employee could cause problems, depending on the circumstances of the layoff."

"But you're saying it could be done."

"It seems so. Between you and me, I doubt Mr. Frost would approve of such a thing."

No, probably not, Robin thought. Good thing he set the company up in such a way that he wouldn't have to approve every last hire and fire. "Well, I'm only interested in keeping the best talent on board, and I'm sure that's something Mr. Frost *would* approve of. Thanks for checking for me."

"Is this situation something more than hypothetical?"

"At the moment, no," she hedged. It was too soon to show her cards, and if Frost or his inner circle found out what she was up to, she'd pay in some way. It would probably cost her the promotion she'd been trying to get. Which didn't explain why she was doing this, other than it seemed as though she should. "But it occurred to me that letting people go to save money actually doesn't save money because we lose an investment, and we end up replacing those people with less experienced employees at smaller salaries, which guarantees they won't want to stick around. Sometimes I wonder if we miss the potential in human capital."

"I see," Mary said, but not in a way that convinced Robin that she got it. Hell, Robin wasn't even sure where she'd gotten that stuff she had just said, but it sort of felt as if it made sense. From some damn bleeding heart, Frost would probably say. "If I find anything else out, I'll let you know."

"Thanks." Robin hung up before Mary could dig any more. She wasn't sure what exactly she thought she was doing, but it felt better than the alternative, which was doing nothing. "Maybe I'm making amends," she muttered as she gathered her things to leave. Her cell dinged with a text. Frank, finally. She read it. He was out of town with Deb for the weekend and he'd call when they got back. *OK,* she texted back. *Hope you have a good time.* He texted a goofy grinning emoji back. She smiled. Maybe that was a little bit of progress between them. And how sad was that, finding hope in a damn emoji?

She slipped her phone into her coat pocket just as it signaled another text message, this one from Cynthia. Robin tried to be angry, but all she felt was empty. The message was brief. *I have tomorrow night free. Call me.*

She didn't want to talk to Cynthia. Not now, and maybe not ever again. She texted back. *Might have a cold. Will probably stay home.* She'd never refused Cynthia twice, but now she had to be careful, because Cynthia might decide to make her life miserable, and there were any number of ways she could do that. Robin put her phone in her pocket and left her office.

Laura looked up at her as Robin shut the door behind her. "Ms. Preston? Is everything okay?"

"Yeah. Why?"

"It's, um, early for you to be leaving. Do you have a dinner tonight?"

"I hope not. Because I'm not going to one." She waited, though, for Laura to check the calendar.

"I don't see one scheduled," Laura said after a few moments.

"Good. It's five-fifteen, on a Friday. Shouldn't you be leaving, too?"

Laura looked at her as if she'd grown an extra limb or something. "You have nothing for me to do?"

"No." And it hit Robin, then, that she loaded Laura up with work all the time, and often late in the afternoon, which meant Laura also stayed past five. "I don't," Robin said. "So go home. Or out to dinner. Whatever you need to do. Have a good weekend." Those were things she would never have said a week ago. She wasn't sure where they came from, but it wasn't as if she'd never said things like that in the past. Maybe her internal circuit boards were getting rewired. That would be a great thing to draw, Robin thought, and as she turned the corner to go to the elevator, she glanced back.

Laura was still staring at her, and it might've been funny, but it wasn't, because Laura was so used to Robin being an asshole boss that when it didn't happen that way, she didn't know what to do. So much shit, Robin thought as she got on the elevator. So much to unpack. The question she kept asking herself was why all of a sudden she felt the need to do it.

Chapter 5

IT WAS PRETTY ON THE pier, even with the cold and the gritty urban backdrop and the stray plastic bottles floating in the oily water. Robin's mom would've been horrified at the trash that bumped against the pilings. A group of stray clouds blocked the sun. Robin leaned against the railing and hunched further into her coat and scarf, glad she'd worn a winter hat. She inched her mouth above her scarf and sipped from the to-go cup of coffee she'd bought on the walk from the subway.

A patrol boat cruised past. Robin watched it. That would be an interesting job, probably. Hard, but sort of cool. Being out on the water would be neat, and there would be great opportunities for photos. She glanced at the clock on her phone. Time to go to the restaurant and meet Jill. Good thing it was only a couple of blocks away. She made it in about five minutes and stood outside the entrance, moving a little to stay warm. She could just see the river from here.

"Hi," Jill said behind her.

Robin turned. "Hi, back."

Jill wore baggy faded jeans, her combat boots from the gallery opening, and a thick tan cable sweater under her leather jacket. She'd wrapped a scarf around her neck and covered her spiky hair with a plain gray knit cap. She looked somehow adorable and sexy at the same time, but Robin buried that thought quickly.

"I was just—" Robin motioned toward the river with her coffee. "Admiring the view. No mountains, like Seattle, but sort of pretty. In a blighted urban landscape kind of way."

Jill laughed. "It has character. I enjoy it."

"You always did like being near the water. Glad that hasn't changed."

"Neither has your coffee habit," Jill said with a glance at Robin's cup.

"You can take the girl out of Seattle, but you can't take Seattle out of the girl," Robin said with a smile. "It's extra good on days like this."

"Nothing beats a good cup of coffee in those circumstances." She looked toward the river. "Thanks for doing this," she said without looking at Robin.

"Yeah. Of course. Did you want to eat? The blighted urban landscape will be here when we're done. If you still want to, we can go check out the pier."

"Sounds good. Lunch first. Pier second."

Robin held the door for her, and they were seated at a small table by a window, much to Robin's approval. Jill requested a small pot of tea, and when the server brought it, they ordered—Robin spring rolls and udon, Jill hot soba. The server took their menus and left. Jill poured herself a cup of tea.

Robin waited, a little nervous about where Jill would want to take the conversation.

"You look really good," Jill said.

"So do you. I like the—" Robin motioned at her hair. "Art girl is definitely a good look for you." Any look, actually, would have been amazing on her.

Jill smiled. "Thanks." She stared into her cup. "This is probably really weird for you."

"Maybe a little. But I've been through weirder." Like the past few days, which left her unmoored and unhinged.

"I've thought a lot about trying to contact you, but I wasn't sure you'd want to hear from me." She raised her gaze to Robin's, and Robin remembered how she'd always loved Jill's eyes, as much for what they didn't say as what they did. Now she saw in them the passage of time, and a sense of maturity and confidence that hadn't been there in college.

"Probably a safe bet," Robin said. "I was pretty fucked up after you left." Jill had always brought out the honesty in her. Apparently she still did, even after all these years.

Jill sipped her tea, still holding Robin's gaze with her own. "I wanted to contact you to apologize."

"Accepted. Except maybe I should've tried a little harder to make you stay."

Jill looked down into her cup again. "I don't know. The truth is—"

The server placed a small plate of spring rolls between them and set two more empty small plates next to it. He retreated quickly but Robin didn't move. She waited for Jill to finish her statement.

"The truth is," Jill said, "I hadn't fallen out of love with you when I left."

Robin didn't say anything, but it hurt a little, to hear that. Lost possibility? Regret? She wasn't sure what she should be feeling, so she just listened.

"I left because my family disapproved of our relationship and my parents threatened to withdraw my college funding and possibly worse."

Robin knew some of this. She'd seen and heard it a few nights ago, but hearing it from Jill now made it real, like a bucket of ice water to the face.

"I was a coward," Jill said. "And I spent a long time regretting it." Her eyes filled with tears.

"Thanks for telling me." Robin meant it, and she automatically wanted to make Jill feel better—a reaction from their past, mixed with burgeoning good intentions, perhaps. She started to reach over to squeeze Jill's hand then caught herself. That might make things even weirder. Instead, she handed Jill a tissue from the little packet she always carried in her coat pocket. "I wish I had been a little stronger myself and gone after you. But I didn't know what the hell I was doing. I had other stuff that I wasn't dealing with very well, and everything just kind of hurt. I carried that around for a while." A long time, she realized, staring across the table at her past. Her past stared back, and Robin felt a tug in her heart, and wondered how it was that she could still be drawn to Jill, after all these years and after all the things that had changed.

"I know. And I'm so sorry. If I could go back in time and make different decisions, I would." Jill wiped at her eyes.

Robin smiled. "Don't we all wish for that?" She took a spring roll and dipped it into the sauce. Jill did the same.

"These are pretty good," Jill said after her first bite.

"Yeah. Not as good as that place in Eugene we used to go, but it'll do."

"That was the best place," Jill said after she finished the roll and took another. She caught Robin's gaze again. "You don't seem as pissed at me as I thought you'd be."

"Oh, I was pissed at one time. I had all these scenarios about what I'd say and do if we ever met again. They all involved me making you feel really bad." Robin took the last spring roll.

"What changed?"

A really fucked up day, Robin wanted to say. The kind of day where you time travel or something like it and you don't know how the hell you're doing it and your guide is a butch surfer chick from the eighties, and she dumps you right in the middle of a epiphany-inspiring revelation. "I'm not sure yet," she said instead. "Maybe I stopped thinking about myself and tried to put myself in your shoes. I knew the pressures your family put on you. But I guess I didn't really get it."

The server removed the empty plates and left as unobtrusively as he'd come.

"I thought you'd probably want to say a few choice things to me." Jill picked up her cup. "So I was actually pretty shocked when I bumped into you the other night, and you came to my opening like, no big deal. It was really great, how that happened."

"Yeah. It was. Maybe I was too surprised to be mad." Robin smiled again. "And I guess I really wanted to see some good art." She wasn't sure why she'd gone, but she knew she had to, so she'd followed that instinct, though she still wondered why it had been so comfortable for her to do.

"Well, I'm glad you did."

The server returned with their main dishes and Jill dug in before he left.

"Look, we can hash out the past if you want, but..." Robin trailed off. Sort of like a business deal. Sometimes the other party had to say some things before moving to the next part of the negotiation.

"Okay. I'm not sure I'm in the space to go there, either."

Robin relaxed. "Maybe down the line. Right now, I'm glad to see you. So let's just go from there. Sound good?"

"Yes."

"So how are things with your family?"

Jill didn't answer right away, and Robin took a few bites of her own meal. Jill took a drink of water and took her phone out. "Things with the family are tense, but that's a normal state with them since I decided to divorce my husband and live my lesbian life."

The spoon stopped halfway to Robin's mouth. "Husband?"

Jill smiled. "You should see your expression. Yes, husband. I tried to be what my family expected, and I found a nice man. But I couldn't even do that right. He's not Chinese."

Robin chuckled. "You rebel, you."

"Maybe that was part of it." Jill swiped her fingertip over her phone's screen. "So we got married right out of college, and I got pregnant and here is Madison now." She handed the phone to Robin.

The photo showed a girl with long dark hair pulled back into a ponytail. She was about twelve in the picture, and she was holding a soccer ball, grinning. "Wow. She's beautiful. She has your eyes." Robin looked up at Jill. "Did you bring her with you?"

"No, she's with her dad and stepmom for the holidays. They live in Seattle, too. Drew and I have a very good relationship, and for that I will always be grateful."

"I'm glad that worked out." Robin handed the phone back, still a little shocked that Jill was a mom. "So do you have anybody sharing your lesbian life now?"

Jill laughed. "No. Madison spends half her time with me, so *if* I date, it had better be with someone I'm pretty interested in. I don't want people cycling in and out of her life. I find that the older I get, the less time I have for bullshit."

Robin smiled. "You didn't have much time for it back in the day, either."

Jill shrugged. "And you? Hitched? Shacked up? Kids?"

"Not at the moment, no. No kids. And yes, still gay." Robin had thought, before she entered business school, that she might want a child, but then things changed and there wasn't room for thoughts like that. She'd fallen into some kind of corporate ethos, where she thought the only thing that was important was working and getting ahead. She'd like to meet Madison some day, though. She wasn't sure why.

"Tell me about your work, then." Jill took another bite of her noodles, and Robin's stomach clenched at the thought of her job. For the first time, Robin didn't feel that internal thrill of being a shark of the corporate world. She was embarrassed by how gleefully she'd circled at the smell of blood in the past.

"Not much to tell," she said.

"Executive director of sales at a multinational sounds like a lot more than not much."

Robin laughed. "I forgot how you are about remembering things. But seriously. Not much to talk about."

"I'm getting the feeling that you're not entirely happy there." Jill continued eating, and her intonation left a lot of room for Robin to either follow up or not.

Robin shrugged. "I guess...I've had some weird stuff happen recently and I'm not sure what it means."

"Are you still doing art?"

Robin moved the bowl to the edge of the table. Suddenly, she didn't want the rest of her noodles. "Not like I used to."

"Are you okay with that?" Jill finished and put her bowl next to Robin's.

"Last week, I might've said yes. Now, I don't know." She smiled, but it felt forced. "You caught me at a strange time."

"There's nothing wrong with questioning things or changing careers." Jill poured the last of the tea into her cup.

"Did you continue on the art road right after we broke up?" It didn't hurt anymore to say those words, Robin realized. It was a statement of fact about the past, and the past had no power if she didn't give it any.

"No. My family was not supportive of that, so I worked in banking for about four years. But I kept doing art on the side, getting pieces in local cafés and places that liked to feature local artists. I started getting commissions here and there, and suddenly I realized I was doing okay as an artist. Drew and I were already divorced when I started doing art full-time and yes, it was hard at first, but it was good for me and expanded my career in different ways. It hasn't been easy, but it is who I am and it makes me feel alive. I spent too long trying to please everybody else not to do this." Jill took a breath and placed her napkin on the table. "And that was pretty deep for a lunch conversation."

Robin grinned. "I enjoyed it. Want to freeze your butt off on the waterfront?"

"Sure."

The server brought the check and they split the cost. Robin bundled up before she stepped outside, but Jill didn't zip up or put her hat on until they were already walking toward the river.

"So how's Frank?" Jill asked when they arrived at the railing.

"Married now. I think he and his wife are trying for a baby."

"That's great news. Do you see him a lot?"

Robin stared out at the water for a few moments. "Not as much as I should." She leaned over the railing a little more and looked down at the water's surface, choppy in the afternoon breeze. "The truth is I've been fucking up."

"What do you mean?"

"I've developed some not so great qualities." She looked at Jill. "And I've done some really shitty things."

"We all do."

"Yeah, well, I keep doing shitty things. And the worst part is I haven't seemed to care about the effects. At least not until recently." Robin thought then about jumping into the river. Maybe the icy water would knock the bad out of her...before the pollution in it made her grow another hand or something.

"Why not?"

"I don't know." Robin shifted her gaze back to the water. "Maybe it's armor."

"If that's true, then it's on backwards."

Robin looked at her again. "How do you figure?"

"Because the only purpose it's currently serving is to keep all the good things about you trapped inside."

"How very poetic of you," Robin said with a touch of sarcasm.

"You're talking to a woman who dumped the love of her life because she didn't have the guts to stand up for what she wanted, and to a woman who married a perfectly nice man who found out she was having an affair with another woman two years after their daughter was born." Jill turned her gaze to the river. "So, yes, I know a few things about armor."

"Sorry for sounding snippy just then," Robin said. "I've only just diagnosed my new asshole status. I'm not sure what the cure is. Or even if there is one." And then it occurred to her that Jill had just referred to her as the love of her life. And it made her feel even worse about who she'd become.

Jill smiled at her. "The cure is to forgive yourself and then find a way to like who you are, flaws and all. Everything else kind of falls into place after that."

"I'm going to try to believe that, because I'm actually a little worried that I got my dad's bad qualities and I'm doomed to be a dick."

Jill laughed.

"Hey, I'm serious."

"I know. But you reminded me so much of when we were in college. You said that then, too."

"I did?"

"Enough times that I used to think maybe you should track your dad down and just have it out with him so you'd stop thinking you were becoming him."

"Why didn't you ever tell me that?"

"I did, a couple of times. But your dad was a sensitive subject." She pulled her cap lower over her ears. Though it was sunny, the wind was cold and the tip of Jill's nose was red. It was totally cute, and Robin felt another little tug at her heartstrings.

"Maybe I should find him so I could thank him for having such a bad influence on me." Robin sounded less bitter than she expected.

"The only way that could have happened is if you let it. Because the woman I fell in love with in college had the soul of an artist, with all of its messy, beautiful, passionate elements. I think you're still that woman. You just took a few suspect turns." Jill adjusted her scarf. "And sometimes you have to backtrack before you can move forward on the road that's the better fit for you."

"Now you sound like we're back in college," Robin said with a smile, and she remembered how she and Jill would sometimes talk for hours into the night and then somehow still have time and energy to make love until dawn, both of them exhausted in class but loving all of it. The memory left her sad at what they'd lost but glad for this moment, reminiscing out here in the December cold.

"Some things don't change. But I try to work on the things that I should. And, no, before you ask, I haven't been successful with all of them. I'm a work in progress." Jill hunched her shoulders, as if she was trying to burrow deeper into her jacket.

"It's a bit brisk out here," Robin said. "Feel like going with me to have a look at the giant tree and Christmas decorations at the Center instead?"

"Sure."

"You can get some photos to send to Madison."

Jill smiled. "She'd totally love that."

"Then we'd better go. Plus I'm pretty sure there's coffee on the way." Robin started walking away from the water.

"Ah. The ulterior motive."

"It's a perfect day for another cup," Robin said as she waited for Jill to catch up.

"I'd have to agree."

"And I'm buying, since I'm trying to overcome my asshole streak."

Jill laughed again, and for the first time in over a week—hell, maybe longer than that—Robin felt at ease, flaws and all. As they went down to the subway, she hoped she could keep that feeling a little longer.

Chapter 6

"Do these people not have somewhere else to be?" Jill asked as she jockeyed for a position at the railing that overlooked the ice rink and the gold statue of Prometheus, who reclined opposite her, dwarfing the skaters.

"You're seriously asking that in this city four days before Christmas?" Robin maneuvered herself to the railing, reached back, and pulled Jill next to her. "Boom. Done. Awesome photo position for Madison."

Jill laughed. "I see you've lived here long enough to be able to deal with crowds in these circumstances." She snapped a few photos with her phone.

"Here. I'll take one of you." Robin held her hand out, and Jill gave her the phone and leaned back against the railing. Robin stepped back a few feet and took a couple more photos before people got in front of her, Jill in the foreground but the rink and Prometheus clearly in the background. She handed the phone back, and Jill grabbed her arm.

"Come on," Jill said. "Double selfie." She moved closer, and Robin automatically made a goofy face as Jill held the camera out and took a photo of both of them. "Serious, now. I don't want Madison to think you're totally insane."

"Too late." Robin did a genuine smile for the next couple of photos, and then they both did funny faces for the three after that. Robin laughed when Jill scrolled through them.

"Not bad," she said. "We almost look normal."

"Emphasis on almost." Jill looked over at the tree, a huge fir decorated from top to bottom with lights. "Think you can use your crowd management skills to get a photo of me by the tree?"

"Definitely." Robin took her phone again and secured her a spot that got almost the entirety of the tree behind her.

"Come on," Jill said. "More selfies."

Robin obliged and they mugged again.

"That should do it," Jill said. "Our insanity clearly documented." She scrolled through.

"Well, well," said a familiar voice behind Robin.

Oh, no. Of course she had to be in this part of the city at this time on this day. Robin braced herself and turned. "Hey, Cynthia," she said, trying to sound at least polite.

"I see you're feeling better." Cynthia shot a calculating glance at Jill, who looked up from her phone at Cynthia, then over at Robin, then back at Cynthia.

"Hi," Jill said, with a dazzling smile. "I'm Jill. A friend of Robin's from college."

"Oh?" That seemed to surprise her. Cynthia looked back at Robin, who nodded.

"Yeah. We haven't seen each other in years. Jill, this is Cynthia. I work with her husband," Robin said, pleased that she managed to sound smooth and professional. She held Cynthia's gaze, as if she was challenging her.

"Charmed," Cynthia said with one of her fake smiles.

"Doing some shopping?" Jill asked. She'd always been good at making conversation, no matter the circumstances, and Robin was glad she was there.

"In a manner of speaking." Cynthia looked pointedly at Robin, but then a woman who should have been leading an Amazon tribe into battle appeared out of the crowd, carrying two paper cups of coffee. Easily six feet tall, she was built like an athlete. Robin pictured her as either a soccer player or maybe basketball. She wasn't sure whether the newcomer was the woman who had been with Cynthia the other night and decided she didn't care.

"Hi," the Amazon said. "Greta."

"I'm Robin. This is Jill. I work with Cynthia's husband." Greta had to know Cynthia was married, since Cynthia didn't keep it secret and she always wore her wedding ring, even when she was having sex with people outside the marriage.

Greta nodded politely, but it was clear she didn't care. She handed a cup of coffee to Cynthia.

"Greta handles accounts for Diamant Mining out of Germany," Cynthia said.

"Sounds interesting." Jill put her phone in her pocket. "But I'm sure you'd like to get on with your afternoon. And it's a beautiful day to see the tree. Nice meeting you."

Greta seemed to appreciate Jill's out, because she took Cynthia's arm with her free hand and started to move away. Surprisingly, Cynthia let her, though she looked back at Robin. The expression on her face was cold and maybe a little predatory. Since Cynthia seemed taken with her latest toy, Robin opted not to care about any hidden message that might have been a part of Cynthia's gaze. As long as her attention was diverted, she'd probably forget all about her.

Robin did wonder, though, how long Cynthia had been screwing Greta. Probably as long as Robin had been in the picture. She wished there was a soap to wash away mistakes.

"Coffee." Jill said and Robin nodded, glad again that Jill was with her.

"Yes. Now. And before you ask, that was one of the things I'm not proud of."

"It's not my business," Jill said as she started through the crowd. "Unless you want to talk about it."

"No, I don't."

"Then let's focus on coffee, which I recall you said you were buying."

"That's right, I did. Part of my asshole penance."

"Stop with that."

"What?" Robin caught up with her.

"Calling yourself that. It's okay to own that you did some things that you're not proud of, and that you're still doing them, but now you need to quit dragging it around and do something about it."

"Yes, ma'am," Robin said with a half salute.

"I saw that. Now buy me some damn coffee."

"Right this way." She took the lead and, a few minutes later, stopped and gestured, triumphant.

Jill laughed. "Who knew there'd be a Seattle's Best here?"

"I figured you might be homesick." Robin pulled the door open and ushered her inside. As they stood in line, she thought about how she enjoyed that Jill called her out, because it was something she had done when they were together, and it was familiar and comforting. It meant Jill cared. Robin had felt it years ago, and in their exchanges over the course of the afternoon, she sensed that Jill was still

Jill, no matter the years that had divided them and whatever they'd both been through. Jill didn't waste time on a lot of words with people she didn't let into her inner circle, and Robin wanted to be in that circle again, and she liked this reconnection. Even though it was tentative because of their shared past, she liked that, so far, it involved no bullshit.

They found a place at the end of the counter that ran the length of the picture window. Jill took the empty stool, and Robin stood next to her, watching the people streaming past and thinking about the man she'd shared the elevator with who was so excited about Christmas. She used to get excited about it, even when her dad wasn't around. What had changed?

"So what are you doing for Christmas?" Jill asked.

"I actually don't know."

"What do you usually do?"

Robin stared at her coffee. "Work."

"Why?"

"Armor." Robin half smiled. "But I don't think I'll do that this year."

"I wish I'd known. I'm going to Vermont to visit some friends. I can call them and see—"

"Don't worry about it. Go have fun." Nice offer, but no matter how she and Jill seemed to be hitting it off right now, Robin wasn't sure she was ready to spend time with her and her friends. That might be a little too much for her to deal with right now.

"How about New Year's? I've got another showing scheduled for New Year's Eve. Weird art people. Wine and cheese. Any of that interest you?"

"Yeah." Robin grinned. "Nothing says Happy New Year like weird art people. Are you showing more of your mixed media?"

Jill stirred her coffee. "Yes, but also some watercolors and a few drawings."

"Sounds good. Text me the time and place."

"I will. It's a later gathering, so we can all celebrate midnight at the gallery. Is that okay?"

"Yes. Sounds fun, actually."

"Do you usually work New Year's, too?" Jill sipped her coffee.

"Yes. But clearly not this year."

"So do you have friends? A social life?"

"I manage." That was mostly true. "I told you," she added hastily, "I'm at an assessing point."

"Well, if you ever want to visit Seattle again, let me know. I've got a spare room."

"It's not Madison's, is it?"

Jill smiled. "No. She has her own. She's entering that age where it's important for her to get away from her uncool parents."

Robin nodded, empathizing. "I vaguely remember that age." Getting away from uncool parents was much easier, though, than getting away from yourself. "But I didn't really have the emotional room to do that."

"Because you felt responsible for Frank while your mom was working and your dad was out doing whatever he did. Maybe you need to let yourself re-do some of your early years."

"Maybe." She sipped her coffee and lapsed into silence for a while, but it was a comfortable, safe silence with Jill.

"You're not envisioning yourself living like Saint what's-his-name, are you? Might've been one of the Francises. Self-flagellating and hair shirt?" Jill said.

Robin laughed. "Busted."

"Okay, fine. If the hair shirt fits, wear it, I guess, since clearly, you're working some things out. Regardless, I'm really glad I ran into you."

"I am, too."

"I was really worried about what I'd say to you if you ever agreed to talk to me again and even more worried that you still wouldn't want anything to do with me, even after the fact."

"Honestly, I had several martyr scenarios about that." Some of them were funny, thinking about them.

"And now?"

"None. Guess I had a change in perspective."

Jill smiled. "I'm glad. And as weird as this should be—hanging out with you like this—it's actually not. It's... comfortable. That's the best word, I think, for how it feels."

Robin smiled back. "Yeah, it is."

"And sadly, I have to go. Art stuff and a Skype date with Madison."

"That's not sad. Tell her I'm not nearly as nuts as the photos suggest."

"But you are. And in a really good way." Jill slid off the stool, and Robin followed. They threw their cups away and emerged into late afternoon sunlight that sliced through the shadows that gathered between the buildings. Robin thought about how the light would affect her sketches—she caught herself. She hadn't thought in those terms in years, but there it was, automatic and unbidden.

She liked it.

"So I'll text you the time and place for New Year's Eve," Jill said as she zipped up her jacket and adjusted her hat over her ears. "I really hope you decide to come."

"I'll clear my schedule." She couldn't remember the last time she'd done that to attend an event that didn't have anything to do with work. She liked that, too.

Jill moved as if she wanted to hug her, but seemed to catch herself. "Great."

"It's okay," Robin said.

"What is?"

"A hug. I'm not that big an asshole yet."

Jill laughed. "Drop the 'yet.' That isn't something you want to strive for." She pulled Robin into an embrace before Robin had time to prepare. It was all too familiar but somehow new, and Robin automatically hugged her back, thinking that she hadn't really hugged anyone in a while, or felt as if the other person had genuine affection for her. Jill's cologne smelled sort of like teak or maybe sandalwood and carried none of the cloying sweetness that some women's scents did. Whatever it was, it smelled really good and triggered memories of incense and candles and the first time they'd slept together in Jill's studio apartment in Eugene on the futon in the corner of the room.

"See you later," Jill said as she pulled away and Robin nodded, trying to banish that image to the back of her mind.

"Yeah. Hope your Christmas is good."

"Yours, too."

Robin watched her walk away, and a few moments later, Jill looked back over her shoulder, smiled, and waved. Robin waved back, and the warmth from Jill's embrace seemed to linger. Somehow Jill had been able to retain the essence of who she was, even with the things she'd gone through. Robin was a little envious, actually, of that. When had things shifted so dramatically, that she herself had cut all ties to her past and tried to be someone so different? And why? Robin adjusted her scarf, which smelled a little like Jill, now. She started walking. Maybe she'd get dinner on the way home.

Chapter 7

"GOOD MORNING, MS. PRESTON. HAPPY Monday."

"Hi—Mike, right?"

The guard smiled and nodded.

"Hope things don't get too crazy for you between now and Christmas." Tomorrow was Christmas Eve, after all.

"Same to you. Hope it's a good one for you."

She got onto the elevator with several other people, some of whom chatted on their way up. Robin hadn't heard anything from the Bureau, which made her wonder if she'd been dreaming everything over the past ten days. Except Jill had texted her yesterday to thank her for a fun day and to send some of the selfies they'd taken. Was Jill real? She must be. Cynthia had met her. Or was that whole thing just part of some kind of delusion she was stuck in?

Robin really hoped Jill was real. She stepped off the elevator onto her floor and went to her office.

"Good morning, Ms. Preston."

"Hi, Laura." Robin paused at her door. When had she gotten so caught up in formality, that she wanted people to keep her at arm's length like that? She hadn't been that way before she came to Frost. She glanced at the rings on her fingers—three, now. Rebel streak, Lady Magnolia had said.

Maybe it was true. "It's Robin," she said, and it felt good saying it, but not so much rebellious as familiar, like finding some lost memento that she didn't realize she'd missed. "You've worked here long enough to call me that. Anything I need to know about today?"

Laura raised her eyebrows. "Just your usual Monday meetings."

"Thanks." Robin went into her office, leaving Laura to stare after her. Maybe all this good will she was trying to tap into meant the Bureau wouldn't have to send another visitor. Unless this whole thing was part of a giant hallucination, and she was going to wake up soon enough in a mental hospital somewhere. She tossed her coat onto the couch and dropped her bag on the floor by her desk before she turned her laptop on. Her office phone buzzed and the ID showed Laura's extension.

"Yes?"

"I sent all the Christmas gifts and cards out to the list of clients and colleagues last week. Everybody should have them this week. Was there anyone else you needed to add?"

"I totally forgot about that. But no, nobody else that I can think of." Fortunately, she'd already sent Frank's gift to him on Friday—a gift card to a local hardware store she knew he liked. Since he had mentioned, in what might or might not be a hallucination, that he needed to get a room ready, she figured he could use it.

"Then I'll be doing the severance paperwork for—"

"Severance paperwork? For who?"

"For the two people Mr. Olsen wants laid off. You signed the forms already."

She'd forgotten about those and winced. "Has HR signed off?"

Laura hesitated. "No. I was waiting until after the New Year."

"Good. Shred them."

"What?"

"Shred them. I'm not firing anybody else."

"But Mr. Olsen—"

"I'll deal with him right now."

"Yes, ma'am."

Ten minutes later, Robin hung up with Olsen, who was extremely relieved that he didn't have to lay anybody off after all. Speaking of layoffs, Robin checked her email. Ramos had sent her the job description she'd requested, and she approved it immediately and sent it on to HR with instructions to re-hire Joseph Spinelli. She did the same with the job description she'd gotten from Lydia Evans's former supervisor.

By lunch time, she'd dealt with three meetings, several phone calls, and gotten some praise from Frost's second-in-command about a client's satisfaction. She was about to go get something to eat when her desk phone rang. Mary from HR. Robin answered.

"Hi, Mary."

"All right, Ms. Preston—"

"It's Robin. You've known me a while." She liked this going against the grain stuff. It made her feel more human, more like she'd felt years ago.

Pause. "I've streamlined this procedure to bring Mr. Spinelli and Ms. Evans back on January second, at their same rate of pay. We hadn't posted the other positions yet, so there aren't any hitches."

"That's great news. Can they get reinstated without having to start all over on everything?"

"I suppose we could do that. I tend not to cut people off too quickly at a holiday layoff," she added, with a bit of condemnation in her tone.

"Could you please notify both of them and give them the offers?"

"If they don't accept?"

Robin considered. There was a chance they'd gotten jobs in the interim. Or they'd be too pissed to come back, though she doubted it. "Then we'll post the positions after the New Year."

"What do I tell them if they do accept and want to know why they were initially let go?"

Robin frowned. "Tell them to call me. Make sure they have my work line and my work cell." She'd made the mess. She'd clean it up as best as she could. Jenny French came to mind again.

"I must admit, I'm a bit surprised, Ms. Preston."

"Robin."

Mary didn't acknowledge the correction. "I've never approved of layoffs as a general principle. That's off the record, by the way."

"Noted."

"I'll let you know what Mr. Spinelli and Ms. Evans say."

"Thanks."

"And Merry Christmas, Ms. Preston."

"Robin—" but Mary had already hung up. She was old-fashioned in a lot of ways, and might never call her by her first name.

Robin sat on the edge of her desk for a while, staring out the window at the river and neighboring skyscrapers. She thought about how easy it had been for her during her master's degree to close herself off and put on the smooth business persona. How easy it had been to ignore her better self, and to bury her pain under narcissism. She studied her rings again. And underneath her button-down shirt she wore an old black tee with the name of a nineties riot grrl band from Portland. Why she still had it, she wasn't sure, but it and two other tees from her past had been in a box in her storage closet. So had some of her art supplies.

Those she'd taken out yesterday and, tentatively, sketched a few things on an old pad she still had. She tried charcoal and pastel, too, and by the end of the day, she had a few studies of the river and its bridges. It had felt good, doing it, and it was as if she was filling something within that had been empty too long. Something was stirring, coming to life again, and she hoped she could keep that going for a while. Especially if the past week really was an epic slide out of sanity. Robin decided to enjoy the feelings for as long as she could, before she woke up in a psych ward. Which might not be so bad if Jill could visit. They could plan an escape and then—

And then what? Robin frowned. Jill made her feel safe, made her feel as if…She pondered. Like herself. Jill made her feel like who she'd been, when she was comfortable in her skin and spent hours immersed in either art or Jill.

Her personal cell phone rang. She looked at the ID. Cynthia.

"Preston," she answered, a little bit of anxiety percolating in her stomach. She wasn't as comfortable with personal confrontations as she was with business. Cynthia rarely called her, so this was clearly important.

"Hello, darling," Cynthia purred into the phone. "I'm getting the distinct impression that you're not too interested in continuing our liaisons."

Robin considered her response, actually appreciating that Cynthia had come right out with it. "It might be for the best."

"Your new toy from Saturday?"

"She's an old friend from college." Robin somehow kept anger out of her tone at Cynthia's sarcasm. "And it seems you have plenty of toys of your own. I doubt you'll miss one less."

"Oh, darling, that wasn't kind."

"Sometimes the truth isn't." An image of Cynthia screwing whoever that was (Greta?) filled her brain.

"Be careful, darling." Cynthia still managed to sound sexy, but Robin knew the warning was real. "I don't like being made to look a fool."

"I'm not making one of you. I'm stating a fact. You're busy, and I'm not a good fit for your schedule."

Cynthia didn't respond right away, but Robin heard her breathing. Cynthia was rarely at a loss for words. Maybe she'd never had someone break it off with her. Although this was hardly what Robin would call a relationship.

"Then I suppose this is goodbye," Cynthia said. She didn't sound sad.

"It is. Take care," Robin said, but Cynthia had already hung up. Take care? Did she really mean that? She thought about Cynthia's husband, and about Cynthia stepping out on him every chance she got. Yes, she did mean it. People like Cynthia needed something, but they didn't know how to get it. Robin hoped she could figure things out, because she really didn't want to turn into a Cynthia.

Her office door opened. "Ms. Preston?"

"Robin." She looked at Laura as she set her phone on her desk. "What's up?"

"I found some discrepancies in the European figures."

"Oh?"

Laura placed a spreadsheet on Robin's desk. "It looks like Mr. Hodges transposed these two figures here, which throws off the percentages quite a bit. The good news is, correcting them actually boosts the final sales figures."

Robin looked over her shoulder. "Huh. You're right. So do you do this with all the figures that come through my office?"

"Yes. In case you're traveling and you or the other executives need information, I make sure I have it and can provide it."

Robin studied the spreadsheet a while longer. "When you say information, are you just referring to sales figures?"

"No. I pay attention, Ms. Prest—Robin. There's a lot that goes on in a business, no matter what size it is, that higher-ups ignore or don't notice."

"And I'll bet those little things are a lot more important than people think." Robin straightened. She liked not being "Ms. Preston." She'd been using formality as a barrier, and though she felt a little exposed without it, she felt more human.

"In my experience, yes."

Robin nodded. Laura was good at her job. Better, probably, than Robin thought. Eighteen months she'd been working here, and Robin had given her more than enough to do, and usually without much thanks, she realized.

"So tell her that, Preston," Decker said. She was standing behind Laura, wearing jeans and a different sweatshirt than the last time Robin had seen her.

Robin stared past Laura's shoulder. How was she going to explain Decker to Laura? And then it occurred to her that Laura hadn't turned around at Decker's voice.

"Well?" Decker raised her eyebrows. "You know you want to."

"Ms.—Robin? Are you okay?" Laura looked over her shoulder then back at Robin, expression puzzled.

"Yeah. Fine." Robin shot a last glare at Decker. "Um, listen. I've been thinking and I guess I'll just say it. I haven't been the best supervisor." She kept her eyes on Laura, but she could just see Decker out of her peripheral vision.

Laura didn't respond, but her expression agreed.

"I'm not sure how to fix that, but I hope you bear with me as I try to turn this damn ship around."

"Ship?"

"Mine. I don't think I've been sailing the right direction—never mind. Anyway, thanks for this. And please keep paying attention." She handed the spreadsheet back to Laura, noting that the blue blouse she had on picked up her eyes.

Laura stared at her for a few seconds then walked toward the door, moving right past Decker, though Laura didn't react.

"Nice," Decker said when Laura shut the door.

"Seriously? You're like a damn ankle bracelet for somebody on probation."

A smile flickered at the corners of Decker's mouth. "I missed you, too, Preston. But it felt good, didn't it?"

"What?"

"Doing the right thing." She gave Robin a thumbs-up and disappeared. Robin stared at the spot where she'd been standing. Decker was right. It did feel good. Even if it was part of losing her mind. Robin grabbed her coat. She wanted lunch and another large coffee.

"Morning, Laura," Robin said the next day when she arrived. "Anything not quite right pop up?" Besides me, she finished silently.

"Morning, and no. You do have a meeting at eleven and another one at two."

"And then?"

"That's it for the day."

"How does your day look?"

Laura had apparently decided to accept this strange new persona Robin had adopted, and she replied, "Nothing pressing. I took care of all the packets for the executive staff for the meeting on the twenty-seventh and sent the turkeys and hams out to the administrative staff."

"Then why don't you leave at lunch?"

"Ma'am?"

"Consider it holiday time. You probably have things to do for the holiday, right?"

"Yes, I do. Thank you."

"Oh, I was wondering—would you mind having a look at this presentation I'm putting together for the meeting on the twenty-seventh? It's about the state of the company, and

I'm pretty sure I'm missing things that the higher-ups tend not to notice."

"Certainly."

"I appreciate that. I'll email it to you and don't worry if you don't get to it today." Robin went into her office before Laura could respond. Ten days ago, the thought of giving something like that to Laura to look at would have made her laugh and say something sarcastic and probably demeaning. Now, however, it was liberating. Losing some of her control freak was nice. A little scary, but nice.

She spent the morning responding to emails and doing web searches on art and art supplies. At one point, she went to Jill's website for probably the hundredth time since the night she'd gone to Jill's opening. It soothed her, clicking through Jill's online gallery, as if Jill's art helped connect Robin to a part of herself she'd forgotten. Or hidden. Her calendar dinged with notice of her eleven o' clock meeting. Robin stared at the screen, and it dawned on her that she'd just been looking at rental property in Seattle.

Had to be crazy. That's what this was. She was slowly losing her mind, and it was too bad, because she was enjoying some of it, and she was enjoying not caring about this meeting or even about the company. All she'd been thinking about for the past two days was art and how it made her smile to see ink, charcoal, and pastel on her hands again. She rubbed at a spot of charcoal on her fingertip that hadn't come off in the shower. With a sigh, she dragged herself away from her desk.

An hour later, she was back at her office door. Laura was getting ready to leave.

"See you after Christmas," Robin said.

"Yes. Thank you again for the extra time."

Robin smiled and waved and opened her office door.

"Merry Christmas," Laura said.

"Same to you." She closed her door and spent the next two hours getting the things done that came up in her last meeting so she could take those results to her next damn meeting. Robin hadn't eaten anything except some coffee cake while listening to a droning voice share useless corporate facts, so she rushed to the food court and got a sandwich. Finally, the last meeting came and went, and she sat in her office to make sure she was caught up with everything, since she'd decided to take Christmas Day off—the first time in a long time.

When five o'clock rolled around, she shut down her laptop with relief. Going crazy was making her irritable toward her job.

"Good evening, Ms. Preston," said a man's voice in a clipped German accent.

Robin looked up. She hadn't heard her door open. A man dressed in a gray suit cut in a modern, slim form stood between her desk and the door. His white shirt sported a banded collar, so he wore no tie. His hair, however, was slicked down in a way that made Robin think of men in the twenties. She was good at gauging people's ages, but this guy—he could've been anywhere between thirty and fifty.

"Can I help you?" She wished Laura were still in to screen traffic. People showing up in her office unannounced made her cranky, but something about this guy made her really nervous. The kind of nervous people get when they're walking down an unlit street at night.

"I believe it is I who should be saying that to you," he said.

A chill shot down her back. Whoever this was, Robin wanted as little to do with him as possible. If she moved right now, she could probably dial security before he tried to stop her.

"I'm afraid your telephone will not work, Ms. Preston."

And then it dawned on her, and her stomach clenched with anxiety. "The Bureau, right?"

"Indeed." He approached her desk and handed her a card. If the Bureau had hired him, then he probably couldn't kill her. *That* was a lovely thought. Could people die in their own delusions? *K Rampus*, the card read in raised engraver's block letters. Beneath that, *Christmas Future*.

"So this is where you show me my funeral, and there's nobody there because I didn't change my ways and I have no friends or family and I'm supposed to regret squandering my life."

He clasped his hands behind his back. "Normally, Ms. Preston, that might be something that would help with your epiphany, but I'm pleased to see that you have already started to address some of the things in your life that concerned the Bureau."

"Does that mean you can go and we're done?" She really didn't like this guy's vibe. She preferred stoic Decker to this. Or even Lady Magnolia's little barbs.

"I'm afraid not. Once the Bureau begins an intervention, we must see it through to the end. And though it does appear that you have started to deal with a few things, the Bureau is not convinced your intentions are genuine."

Robin frowned. "What do you mean?"

"You may simply be changing your ways out of self-serving intent." He held his hand up to keep her from interrupting. "We understand that, yes, there is a bit of that in someone's shift of worldview. After all, a subject wants to ensure that she is redeemed, and to do that, one must act in certain ways. But the question remains whether the subject is truly interested in connecting with the larger world through a changed worldview or simply in keeping a tally of good works, in order to make some kind of claim on redemption. In other words, Ms. Preston, the Bureau is not yet convinced that you—how do you Americans say—have bought into changing your ways for the right reasons."

"Don't you have an intention machine or something you can hook me up to?"

"My dear, that would defeat the purpose of Christmas Future."

Robin stifled a groan and looked at the card he'd given her again. The name looked familiar. K Rampus. Something about Christmas lore. Krampus. Santa's allegedly evil twin, a demon who beat the bad out of kids this time of year. She looked at the gentleman standing in front of her desk, who carried himself formally, like a butler at a state event. If he was a demon, that might explain why he made her skin crawl. She caught herself. Demons? Really?

"Krampus," she said, and she held the card up.

"Well done. Not many here have heard of me."

"Is it true you beat children for being bad during the year?"

"Only if warranted. Usually when they see me, the problem is solved."

"I'm not really clear on how a man in a suit would do that."

He gave her a tight smile and suddenly, a pale red mist encircled his legs and torso. His body stretched until his head brushed the ceiling, a good ten feet above. His skin darkened to a deep brown, like old damp wood, marred with bristly hair across the carved musculature of his arms, chest, and legs. Claws extended from his hands and toes and, holy shit was that a forked tail?

Robin stared, horrified, and two horns emerged from his skull as it elongated into a shape like a grotesque goat's head. He opened his mouth, and a long, sinuous tongue snaked out, moving with his grin.

She tried to speak but couldn't, tried to move, but her muscles refused to respond.

And then the demon was gone, and the dapper man with the slicked-back hair stood in its place. Robin's heart continued to pound. How could this be happening?

"Perhaps you understand, now, how the bad behavior of children can be corrected with a simple visit. And do be careful in your use of names. Sometimes one conjures things one really shouldn't."

She nodded, still stunned. This had to be it. Her one-way ticket to la-la land. Because things like this did *not* exist. *Should* not.

"Ah, but we do, Ms. Preston," he said, and she realized she'd voiced her thoughts aloud. "There is quite a lot that exists that humans insist on denying. Unfortunately, it is a bit more difficult with adults, even if I reveal myself. My actual appearance may ensure good behavior for a short while, but not always beyond that." He clasped his hands behind his back again. "Adults need to understand the consequences of their choices." He smiled, and this time it was almost genuine. "So, Ms. Preston, let us explore this idea of consequences."

Robin suddenly fell through cold darkness before she had a chance to answer, but she was sure she was yelling as her speed whistled past her ears. Please let there be a big air bag to meet her when this was over—she stopped moving and the darkness faded to reveal a large room, painted white. Artworks hung on the walls. A gallery of some sort.

A woman stood at the opposite end, studying a painting. She was dressed in black trousers and a white blouse. Her dark hair was gathered into a bun. Compelled, Robin took a tentative step. The gallery's wooden floor was solid beneath her feet, and she continued walking. The woman didn't turn around at Robin's approach and she completely ignored her when Robin stood next to her.

"She cannot see or hear you," Krampus said from behind her.

"I kind of figured that out," Robin half muttered as she, too, studied the painting. At first glance, the painting seemed like a typical landscape, but the artist had cut squares in the canvas in a few places, giving the appearance of windows. Within those squares the artist had created completely different scenes. A child reaching toward the viewer in one, a car parked on a pier in another. A pile of smartphones in another. Something resonated within her, and she moved closer to see the signature in the bottom left-hand corner.

"R. Preston," she read aloud. "What the hell? This is *mine*? I did this?"

Krampus merely inclined his head.

Another woman approached, dressed in a sleek red dress that accentuated her dark skin.

"What do you think?" dress woman asked.

"I love it," black pants responded, and Robin started. Jill. She moved so that she could better see Jill's face.

"Oh, wow," Robin said. Jill had aged. She was easily in her sixties, though her hair didn't have much gray in it.

"It is one of the artist's more recent works. Do you know her?"

"I used to."

Used to? Robin waited for more details.

"Do you collect her work?"

"I have a few pieces." A shadow of sadness appeared in Jill's expression, and Robin's stomach clenched. "And I will add this to my collection."

"Excellent. Allow me to prepare the forms." Dress woman moved away, and the door to the gallery opened and another woman entered, this one younger—maybe in her forties, also wearing black pants. Her tunic-style shirt was a deep green. She looked a lot like Jill.

"Mom," the newcomer said, and Jill turned.

"Madison?" Robin stared.

Jill waited until Madison had joined her at the painting. "What do you think?" Jill asked.

Madison glanced at it. "You're buying another one of hers?"

"I like it."

"Okay, so like her art. Stop buying it. Stop supporting her with your money."

"Honey, she's a fellow artist. Personal issues should have nothing to do with whether I support someone's journey or not."

Madison shook her head, barely hiding her disgust. "After what she did to you?"

"What?" Robin asked, a hard, cold knot in her stomach. "Jesus, what the hell did I do now?"

Jill didn't respond to Madison.

"I can't believe you still care about her." Madison stared hard at the painting, as if willing laser beams to come out of her eyes and burn it.

"Robin has her own burdens. I just happened to be part of the fallout."

"She broke off the engagement."

Robin's jaw dropped. "Engagement? We were engaged?" She looked at Krampus. "Is that what she's talking about?"

He remained implacable. "It does appear thus."

"You are the most unhelpful Christmas visitor I've had," Robin snapped.

"This is a future that may or may not come to pass, based on decisions you make now," he said, patient. "Listen."

Engaged. How the hell did that even happen between them?

"She's not the first and she won't be the last woman to do that," Jill said. "I don't carry grudges."

"Stop making excuses for her. She led you on for weeks. Months. Broke off the engagement then used your good graces to build her audience for her own art. Never once thanked you. Slept with your agent and then poached her—"

Robin clenched her teeth.

"Which I think says quite a bit about my agent," Jill said, anger in her tone.

"Why the hell do you insist on holding on to this woman?" Madison asked, a little less strident. "She has done nothing for you. She wasn't who you thought she was in college, and she sure as hell wasn't who you hoped she was when you ran into her in New York all those years ago."

Jill crossed her arms and glared at Madison.

"She played you, Mom. You made the right call when you broke up with her in college, and you should have stuck by that decision."

Madison's words were like a physical punch to Robin's chest.

"She allowed her past to define her," Jill said, keeping her tone low. "I won't judge her for that."

"Do you honestly think she gives a damn about you or about the little forgiveness thing you have going on?"

Dress woman approached with an incredibly thin device the size of her palm. Madison's smile was forced.

"Hi," Madison said to her. "I'm sorry we troubled you, but she won't be taking the painting after all."

"Oh—" dress woman looked at Jill, who shook her head once. "Well, if you change your mind, just call. I'll keep you on file for a bit." She moved her fingertip above the device's surface before she retreated quickly, clearly ascertaining the mood.

"I'm not going to let you throw your money away on her," Madison said to Jill. "And please, for the love of God, let go. Some people are unredeemable."

Jill's expression tore at Robin's heart. "You're right," Jill said. "But sometimes, I hope."

"I know. For whatever reasons, she got under your skin, and she's stayed there ever since." Madison put her arm around Jill's shoulders. "Like some kind of fungus."

Jill managed to laugh. "Maybe I should think about it that way."

"Maybe. Let's go." Madison led Jill outside, and Robin stared after them with a painful tightness in her chest.

123

"This isn't the actual future, right?" Robin said to Krampus. "It's one *possible* future, but it's not set in stone."

"Indeed."

"How the hell did we end up engaged, anyway? I mean, that's—we broke up in college, years ago. We're on two completely different trajectories, now."

"It's one possible future. The decisions you make now can help determine whether this one comes to pass or not."

"Well, that one sucks. I somehow became the world's biggest dick, and I somehow hurt Jill. How the hell does anybody do that? She's this amazing woman and apparently she kept giving me chances. Why did she do that? Because from seeing this future, it was a total waste of her time."

"Was it?"

Robin stared at the painting. "For this future, yes."

"Ms. Preston, I'll reiterate that this is only one possible future. There are myriad ways a future can express itself."

"Well, it seems that the reason Jill's not happy in this one is because of me."

"That may not be entirely fair to say. Ms. Chen could have decided not to—what's the saying—carry a torch for you."

Robin glared at him. "But it looks like she did. So in order to prevent her from ever having to make that choice, she shouldn't get involved with me." She caught herself. Why was this even an issue? She didn't want to get involved with Jill again. Right?

Krampus might have been a statue, he was so immobile. "Or you could examine your own motivations for doing so, should it come to pass." He cocked his head. "If your intentions are good, and you are moved by genuine care toward Ms. Chen, then that will influence whatever future comes to pass."

"Didn't you learn in demon school that the road to hell is paved with good intentions?"

"Hell has no roads. It is only what you make it, my dear."

Robin looked back at the painting. "So if Jill doesn't get involved with me again, she'll be safest from this future." She turned back to Krampus.

"Possibly. There's no guarantee that she won't have a similar future, no matter who enters her life."

"But this one, where she's stuck on me, won't come to pass if we don't end up together." Robin gestured at the painting. "If somebody else, say, got involved with her, it would also prevent this."

"Ms. Preston, this future may not come to pass even if you *do* get involved with Ms. Chen," he said, patient. Surprising, that a demon could sound that way. "If you enter a relationship now with Ms. Chen, and you do so with integrity, then you will already have altered this future."

"Suppose, though, that Jill found somebody else before that happened. Like, maybe if I introduced her to someone, and she was a much better match for that person than for me. She'd be safe from this, right?" Robin again gestured at the painting.

"Ms. Preston, if you work on changing your present, this future will not materialize. I hardly think attempting to find a date for Ms. Chen will change a trajectory of which you are a crucial part."

Robin decided she hated this painting and what it represented. "It'll save her from me." She looked back at Krampus.

"Perhaps you should instead save yourself from you." He clasped his hands in front, and Robin noticed a ring on his left pinkie with a single red stone in the band. "If you change something about the source, you change the outcome. Perspective, my dear." He turned toward the door. "Shall we?"

"Like I have a choice." And the darkness descended like a heavy drape and wrapped her in cold, but she wasn't moving. She was floating, somewhere. Or nowhere, so complete was the silence and blackness that enfolded her, only to abruptly recede. Robin opened her eyes to blazing sunlight. She stood on the sidewalk in front of somebody's house, but she didn't recognize it, a low-slung brick ranch style. It needed work on the roof, and the gutter in front sagged in a few spots, and the chintzy metal roof over the porch was pulling away from the wrought iron supports near the door.

What should have been a lawn was instead smooth, round stones the size of golf balls, their expanse broken by a few tired yucca plants that looked as if their best days were decades behind them. A couple of burly guys carried furniture from a moving truck onto the cement slab that served as a porch. Another man stood on the front porch, directing. Frank. A few years older and a few pounds heavier.

"Hey, Dad," a teenaged boy said from the driveway. "The car's not open." He wore baggy blue shorts, sneakers, and a black T-shirt. His hair was a mop of unruly dark curls.

"Oh. Here." Frank dug into his pocket and pointed it at the car. "Where's your sister?"

Frank had two kids?

"With Mom. They're on their way."

Frank nodded and said something to one of the movers as he emerged from the house. The mover nodded and wiped his forehead with a bandana. Where were they? Southern California? Arizona?

The teenaged boy opened the back of the car and took out what might have been a framed painting, from its shape, maybe two feet square. Whatever it was, it was wrapped in a blanket. He almost dropped it.

"Hey, careful with that." Frank hopped off the porch and took the object from the boy, whose expression was classic teen irritation.

"It's not like it's worth anything."

"Maybe not in terms of money. But it does have sentimental meaning."

"Too bad that doesn't pay the bills."

"Travis," Frank said, and his tone carried a warning. "This is special to me. At least have some respect for my feelings about it."

"Yeah, okay. Fine." He reached into the trunk again and took a box out. "What's so special about it, anyway?"

"It was one of her first paintings. She quit doing art, but when she was an artist, she was pretty cool."

Robin watched as Travis carried the box to the house. He looked like Frank had when Frank was a teenager. "Well, sorry, Dad, but she's not like that anymore."

"She's still your aunt," Frank called then followed him into the house.

Robin groaned, and Krampus suddenly appeared at her elbow.

"This isn't set in stone, right?" Robin looked at him.

"It is another possible future."

"How many are there?"

"Infinite, my dear. A future is a response to choices you make in the present, and your motivations behind those choices. Let's go in, shall we?"

She started walking, but before she'd taken two steps, she was in the house, standing in a hallway. The paneling hadn't been updated since the eighties, and the floors underfoot, though hardwood, were scuffed and faded from years of neglect. At some point in the past, the paint had probably been a crisp, fresh white. Now it was a dingy light gray, and the outdated light fixtures only worsened that effect.

"Maybe if she gave a damn about you, she would've helped after you got canned," Travis said as he put the box down in what clearly was going to be a bedroom. Mattresses leaned against the wall.

Robin's heart sank. She'd let Frank down like that? What kind of sister did that? One like her, clearly. There was no way she could correct this unless she herself changed. And she wasn't even sure how to do that. But she had to. She wanted to be redeemable. That much she knew.

"Language," Frank scolded. "Running a corporation is a lot of work." He took the painting into one of the other rooms then reappeared without it. Oh, God. Robin had made CEO, or something comparable. A couple of weeks ago, she would've reveled in that knowledge. Now it just made the hole within her deeper.

"You're family." Travis stood in the doorway of the bedroom he'd put the box in. He was almost Frank's height, and once he filled out, he'd probably have Frank's athletic build. "Family is supposed to help each other."

"Ideally, yes. But sometimes things get in the way."

"Like what?" Travis crossed his arms, challenging.

"Like whatever demons from your past you can't shake."

"That's bullshit."

Frank gave him a parental look.

"I'm sorry, but it is. You grew up in the same house with her, with the same parents, and you turned out okay. You don't write people off like she does. You're there for them, and you try to help. She's making boatloads of money. The least she could've done was offered you a loan until you got another job."

Robin glared at Krampus. "I'm tired of finding out how big a screw-up I am in the family department."

He shrugged. "There are many different possibilities for the future. The smallest actions can cause large ripples. Whatever future this represents, the choices you made played a role in it. But so, too, do the choices of others. No one ever operates in a vacuum, but thinking you do and behaving that way can lead to futures like this." He shook his head slowly and appeared genuinely sad, for a demon.

She might be able to introduce someone to Jill to prevent Jill's future, but how the hell did you find somebody to step into a family and be a sister? This was on her, she realized. And, if she was being honest with herself, so was whatever happened with Jill.

"Travis, there's a lot of baggage in my family where Robin's concerned," Frank said. "I can't pretend she hasn't let me down or that I'm fine with whatever she's doing now. But I have a past with her that you don't. I remember her as a big sister who was there for me throughout our childhoods when our dad wasn't, and when our mom was working several jobs to keep us fed. That's the sister I try to hold on to, and that's why that painting means so much to me. Because it was done by *that* Robin. Not whoever this other Robin is."

Travis stared at the floor.

"I don't think you'll get to meet the Robin I still care about. And that really bums me out. But you know what? It's her loss. Because she doesn't know you. Or Mallory. Or Deb. You guys are *my* family. And that's what counts." Frank put Travis in a playful headlock and ruffled his hair until Travis laughed. Robin's chest ached. It *was* her loss, and that made everything hurt even more.

"Okay, Dad. Relax with the hair."

Frank laughed, too, and released him. "C'mon. Your mom will kill us if we don't get the car unloaded." He passed within inches of Robin.

Mallory. Robin loved that name. How the hell could she have stayed out of Frank's life this long? What the hell was wrong with her? She headed outside, needing to see more of Frank and Travis and wanting desperately to find out more about her niece. But before she even reached the front door, she was once again cloaked in darkness so complete it was almost viscous, like oil. Cold, slimy oil. It was like being immersed. Or maybe buried alive. Robin fought a rising panic and when light finally penetrated, she was so relieved she wanted to cry.

This was somebody's office, Robin surmised, looking around. Somebody with a lot of money and power who enjoyed a panoramic view of the city from at least thirty stories up. The desk looked heavy and expensive and the conference table did, too. Both were fashioned out of some kind of hardwood and polished to a sheen that reflected the paintings on the walls, which were mostly cubist and abstract in primary colors. The room was beautiful in a museum kind of way. But there was no soul here. No sense of the person who worked here.

Krampus turned away from the floor-to-ceiling windows. "A most excellent vantage point," he said, hands clasped behind his back. When he wasn't in full-blown demon mode, he could have passed as a professor.

"Whose office is this?"

He pointed at the door to the office, which stood half open.

Robin moved closer to the door. "Oh, hell, no." She stared at the one-inch-high gold letters fastened to the door. R.A. Preston.

"Your hard work was rewarded," Krampus said, tone mild. She shot him a look, trying to ascertain if he was being sarcastic, but she saw nothing in the smooth planes of his face or the black depths of his eyes. He motioned for her to step out of the office, so she did, half dreading what she'd find. Two nondescript white men in suits stood chatting in a sitting area outside the door. The furnishings were urban minimalist, and Robin wondered if she'd been responsible for the design, and when she'd come to like that sort of thing.

"Are you going to the service?" Grey suit asked brown suit.

"Probably not. I didn't know her."

Robin's chest tightened. Service. Somebody was dead, and she had a very bad feeling that it was probably her.

Grey suit shrugged. "I didn't either, but it's a good way to suck up to the board."

"Seriously, is anybody actually going besides them? I heard she didn't have any family."

"Of course she didn't. Nobody could stand her," grey suit said.

"She had a brother," a prim woman with close-cropped red hair said as she approached carrying a vase of flowers. She wore a black skirt suit with a cream blouse. Grey suit coughed, embarrassed.

"Suck it," Robin muttered at him.

"And I believe he will be attending the memorial." Red hair brushed past the suits and went into the office. Robin followed her and watched as she placed the vase on the conference table. She leaned a white card against the vase then left.

"Okay, so I'm guessing the memorial is for me," Robin said to Krampus, but he didn't respond because the room faded. The darkness lasted only a few seconds this time, and when it dissipated, she stood in another room, white marble underfoot and on the walls, as if she were in an updated Grecian temple. A casket was positioned in the center of the room on a wheeled stand, its wooden surface reflecting the dim light from the wall fixtures.

Robin stared at it, a weight she couldn't name crushing her inside, holding her in this spot. A man entered from behind, wearing a dark suit that might have been a little too big for his frame. He had the complexion of someone from South Asia, and he carried a device in his palm that looked like the world's smallest tablet.

"Sam? You ready?" said another man who entered, and this one looked as though he might have played football for a Midwestern college team. His suit, also dark, looked a little too small.

"Just clearing the paperwork." Sam's fingertip brushed the device. He held it next to the corner of the casket then looked at it. "Preston, Robin Anne. DOB June 15, 1978."

Her name seemed to burn in her ears. She looked around for Krampus but he wasn't here.

The bigger man went through the same procedure with his own device. "Check. Scheduled for cremation." He put his device into one of his jacket's inside pockets. "Heard she was a CEO of some big company."

Sam put his device in his own pocket. "That is correct."

"Weren't too many at the memorial. Maybe six or seven."

That's it? Only six or seven came to her memorial? Robin bit her lip so hard it hurt.

"That is also correct." Sam took a position at one end of the casket.

"Kinda sad," the other man said. "She wasn't that old." He went to the other end of the casket and released the wheel brake with his foot. Sam did the same on his end, and they started rolling the casket out of the room.

Not that old? What did that mean? How old was she in this future when this happened? And how had it happened?

"I hope people come to my service," the bigger man said, checking to make sure his feet weren't getting in the way of the wheels.

"Live well, and they will."

"You're like one of those—what do you call 'em—gurus."

Sam chuckled as they got the casket through the doorway, and Robin lurched after them. "Wait," she said, and she tried to grasp the side of the cart but stopped when she realized she could see the casket through her hand. "Oh, God." But she tried anyway to stop them from wheeling the casket any farther. She might as well have been trying to stop an ocean liner with a canoe.

Where was Krampus? Was this it? He was going to leave her here?

She was plunged into darkness again. But this was different, because she heard Sam and the other man talking, voices muffled as if they were wrapped in cloth. Or—Robin tried to move and her shoulders bumped something solid on either side of her. Her fingers brushed fabric, and she tried to raise her arms above her head, but her hands hit another surface.

Oh, God. She was *in* the casket. "No," she said, disbelieving. "Hey," she shouted. "I'm in here. Guys. Let me out!" Robin sobbed and flailed, kicking as best she could and pounding against the sides with her fists. "Please," she yelled. "Krampus! Please help me!" Her fists and feet ached from her efforts but she continued. Why didn't anyone hear her? "Please!"

Was that heat? Was it getting warmer? "No," she shouted. "Please get me out of here!"

And then she was falling, but she landed quickly on something soft. Carpeting. She thrashed, trying to free herself from the blanket—blanket? Robin stopped moving and assessed her new location. Home. She was home. This was her apartment, and she was lying on the floor next to the couch in her living room. Her television was on and the vertical blinds were open to morning light. She never opened those, but right now, she welcomed the light, and would hug it if she could.

Robin sat up, shaky, and examined her hands for bruising, but they were fine. "I'm okay," she said, trying to convince herself that it was true. The blanket was wrapped around her legs, and she kicked it off and moved her feet around. They were fine, too. "I'm okay," she repeated, not sure she believed it. Her phone sat on her coffee table, and she grabbed it and checked the time. Eight in the morning, Christmas Day. "I'm more than okay," she announced. "I'm fucking alive." She speed-dialed Frank, smiling so much it almost hurt.

"Hey," he answered on the second ring. "What's up?"

"Merry Christmas, Frankie."

"Robin?"

She heard confusion in his tone. "Did I wake you up?" she asked. "I'm sorry."

"No, no. It's just—wow. Kind of a surprise. Been a while since you did that."

"I know. And I'm really sorry. Anyway, I just wanted to make sure I called—"

"Rob, is everything okay?"

"It's fine." She moved her fingers around, still trying to convince herself that she was all right, that her rings hadn't somehow gotten dented or bruised her fingers. No marks. Nothing. "Actually, it's more than fine." So much better than fine.

"Seriously. Are you okay? Did something happen?"

She laughed. *You have no idea.* "Kind of. Listen, I would take you and Deb out to dinner in the next few days if I could, but since I'm a thousand miles away, I'm going to PayPal you some money, and you have to promise that you'll take Deb and go somewhere nice, okay?"

"Uh—"

"Promise me, Frankie."

"Okay, okay." He laughed. "I promise. I know better than to turn down a dinner. Oh, thanks for the gift card. Deb and I were just talking about re-doing one of the bedrooms."

"Great. Send me before, during, and after photos."

"Jesus, Rob, what the hell's gotten into you?"

"I'm not sure. But I like it. So work with me, here." She opened all the other blinds and flooded her apartment with more light, and it seemed to burn away the residue the night before had left. Maybe it was burning a whole lot of residue away.

"I—damn," Frank said. "You sound like your old self. Your old, back-in-the-day self. I really missed you."

To her surprise, Robin's eyes filled with fresh tears. "I'm trying to get some shit together. No guarantees, but I'm working on it." She cleared her throat and wiped at her eyes. "So can I visit next month? Or February?"

"I would love that. It'll have to be February, though. School's cranking up and I've got a ton of stuff to get ready for. How about the third weekend?"

"Great. Let me know, and I'll get a flight—wait. Run it by Deb, first, and let me know if it's okay with her."

"I'll check right now. Hold on."

Robin waited. She could hear Frank saying something and then Deb responded. They talked for a few more moments and then Frank addressed Robin.

"All clear for the third weekend in February." He sounded excited.

"I'll come in on Friday afternoon and be out of your hair Sunday evening. Don't worry. I'll rent a car and get a hotel." The scene she'd witnessed between Frank and Deb was still fresh in her mind, and Robin didn't want to put Deb in a position where she had to deal with Frank's prodigal sister.

"What are you talking about? You can stay with us."

"Don't worry about it. I don't want to impose."

Frank didn't respond for a few moments, and Robin heard him talking to Deb again. "Deb wants you to stay with us," he said.

"We'll figure it out closer to the time." Robin watched watercraft on the river in the distance. She hadn't cleared her schedule at work for this trip, but she didn't care. She'd take a sick day if she had to. "Okay, I'll let you go. It's Christmas, after all. Figure out where you want to go to dinner with Deb."

"Wait. We have some news."

Robin smiled, hoping it was what she thought it might be. "What?"

"Well, um, you know how you told me once that you thought it would be weird for either of us to be parents?"

Her smile widened. "Yeah. But we were young. And it would've been weird then."

He laughed, a mixture of nervous and giddy. "That's true. But neither of us is that young anymore."

"Are you saying what I think you're saying?" Robin played along, trying to coax it out of him.

"I might be. If you think I'm trying to tell you that Deb and I are going to be parents, then yes."

And even though Robin already knew, hearing him tell her made her heart swell. "Oh, my God. That's the best news ever! When is—" she caught herself because she almost said "he"—"the baby due?"

"Mid-June."

"Hell, yes. My birthday. That's a smart baby."

Frank laughed again. "We've been sort of holding off telling everybody until we're sure things are on the right track."

Robin accepted the fib for what it was—an attempt to connect. "How's Deb holding up?"

"Pretty well. Some morning sickness, but so far, she feels good."

Deb shouted something in the background.

"She says as soon as she starts feeling really sick, she's going to give me a lot of hell for it."

"I'll back her up on that." Robin closed her eyes and enjoyed the way the sunlight felt on her chest and face. "You're going to be a dad," she said. "Wow."

"I know. I'm freaking out a little."

"You'll be the best dad ever."

He didn't say anything for a while.

"Frank?"

"Yeah. I'm here. I guess I'm a little worried, since we didn't have good fathering in our lives. I don't want to screw up, you know?"

"Parents always screw up."

"You know what I mean."

Robin turned around so the sun could warm her back. "Yeah. I do. But you know what not to do, now. You'll see. You'll be great at it."

"Thanks for the vote of confidence. And you're going to be an aunt."

"Yeah." She thought about that, and about Travis as a teenager. No way was she going to miss the years before that. "I'm actually really excited about it. Do you know if the baby's a girl or boy?"

"No. We want to be surprised."

"Cool. So have you thought about names?"

"Sort of. Nothing for sure, yet. Every day is a step closer, and I want to get the baby's room ready. It's really cool that the gift card you sent was for a hardware store."

Robin grinned. "Sometimes I get stuff right."

"Yeah. Sometimes." He laughed. "Okay, I have to go. Deb's making breakfast."

"Dude, you need to help a pregnant woman out. I'll talk to you later."

"Definitely. I'm so glad you called. Talk to you soon."

"Yep. Bye." Robin hung up and turned to stare out the window again. A tear rolled down her cheek, and she wiped at it, surprised. Was this what insanity felt like? Or sanity? A mixture of raw and unformed, as if she herself had just emerged into the world, wide-eyed and new, uncallused and unscarred. Or maybe she was an explorer in her own life, preparing to blaze a new trail.

But before she did that, she needed coffee. Robin padded into the kitchen and put water on for her French press. As she took her jar of coffee beans out of the cabinet, something caught her eye on the counter next to the refrigerator. A business card, and in elegant raised engraver's block letters, it read *K Rampus, Christmas Future*.

She didn't touch it. Instead, as she waited for the water to heat, she sent money to Frank then texted Christmas greetings to Jill and several other people who no doubt would think she had lost her mind when they read her message. After the water was hot, she poured it into her press and texted a few more people while the coffee brewed. Cup in hand, she returned to the living room and stood in the sunlight pooling across the floor. She was alive. And this was a good day to draw, she decided, liking the way the morning light hit the distant bridges. A very good day to draw.

"My report, Agent Tolson." He set the manila folder on her desk and stood back a step, clasping his hands in front. He preferred to create a hardcopy. Tolson allowed it, and he appreciated that. He also liked her office, which might have come out of a 1940s American movie set.

She looked at him over the frames of her eyeglasses. "Mr. Rampus," she said by way of acknowledgement. She knew better than to use his true name too much, and he appreciated that, too. "I understand you unveiled."

He nodded once.

"Not a usual procedure with an adult."

"Most don't know who I am, so there's no need. Ms. Preston, however, did."

Tolson rested one of her hands on the folder. She wore pale pink nail polish that matched her blouse. She always presented well. Understated yet classic. A look he himself favored in his own wardrobe when he affected a human persona. "How did she take it?" she asked.

"Fairly well. After the initial shock." He offered a smile.

Tolson smiled back. "I've already watched the video. Nice choice of scenarios."

"They seemed appropriate."

"Entirely. Your assessment?"

"I understand why you wished to engage this case, madam." He had little time for the foibles of humans, but he had been working with Tolson long enough to know that she had a soft spot, as Americans said, for cases like Robin Anne Preston. Curiously, he rather liked her, too. She had spirit.

Tolson took her glasses off and set them on her desk next to the file. "Is that your assessment?"

He inclined his head. "I concur with my colleagues with regard to this case."

"Recommendations?"

"I included them in the file. You do realize that Ms. Preston may not accept the choices the Bureau would like her to make." He had no investment in whether she did or not. He merely offered the statement as a possibility.

"According to all our calculations and projections, they are the ones that will provide her and others the greatest fulfillment and thus create the best kind of change."

"I have no argument with that. But humans are quite maddening. I presume that this, too, has been taken into account."

Tolson smiled. "We are indeed quite maddening. And sometimes, a nudge provides all the incentive necessary for a first step down a new path. Thank you, Mr. Rampus. I greatly appreciate your assistance in this matter. I know you had other duties, given the time of the year."

"I am a superb multitasker, as you know. Until next time, Agent Tolson." He half bowed and turned in a clean, precise motion and was across the room without taking a step. He shut the door quietly behind him.

Chapter 8

ROBIN GOT HOME AROUND TEN. She almost didn't believe she'd accepted a last-minute dinner invitation from a few acquaintances and ended up having a good time. Maybe she was rediscovering this social life stuff. Her phone rang as she poured herself a glass of cold water. Jill's name showed up in the ID. That was a nice end to what had turned out to be a great day.

"Hey," Robin answered. "Off the slopes finally?"

"Hey back. For a while. I had some time and wanted to properly wish you a Merry Christmas Day."

"Thanks. Merry Christmas to you. How's Madison?"

"She is having a fabulous time with her dad, but she did make it a point to say that she missed me."

"She hasn't hit full-blown teen yet, I see."

Jill laughed, and Robin remembered how much she loved Jill's laugh. Rich and fun-filled, always genuine. It was one of the many things she'd missed when Jill left. She took a drink, trying not to think about the possibility that they might be together once again. She'd have to figure out what to do about that.

"Did you do anything fun today?" Jill asked.

If she told Jill what she'd been through, Jill would no doubt commit her to some sort of mental health facility. "A bit of drawing. Had some dinner with a few friends. Low-key but, yes, fun."

"Drawing? Did I hear you right?"

"You did." She looked at her fingertips. Once again, she thought she'd gotten all the charcoal off but maybe she hadn't, since the light from the nearby lamp indicated otherwise.

"I'm really glad to hear that."

"Pretty sure none of it is ready for a showing."

"It doesn't matter. Just the fact that you're doing it means something's shifting."

"I hope it's in a good way," Robin joked. She knew, though, that Jill was right. Something within was coming alive, and it sort of scared her because it had been so long since she'd felt anything like it, but she welcomed it, too. It fed something that had gone hungry too long.

"Definitely."

"I do feel a little different."

"You sound different."

Robin laughed. "Well, it has been several years since we last talked." She ran her finger down the side of her glass.

"No, it's been three days or so."

"And I sound different now than I did then?"

"Yes. Lighter. A little freer, maybe. I hope it continues. It's a good vibe."

Lighter. Maybe that was the descriptor Robin was looking for. "Oh, I talked to Frank this morning, and I was right. He's going to be a dad." She was still excited about it, and it must have carried through the phone because Jill offered a little whoop.

"Do they know the sex?"

"No. They're going to try not to."

"I didn't want to know, and I'm glad I didn't. Madison surprised me."

"Did you already have names picked out?" Robin turned the light off in her kitchen and carried her glass into the living room where she turned those lights off, too, before she sank onto her couch.

"No. For some reason, her name came to me about an hour after she was born. Guess she let me know."

Robin heard the smile in Jill's voice, and she remembered when she'd asked her out for the first time over the phone, how nervous she'd been, and how Jill had said yes. The undercurrent of Jill's smile in her voice then had both turned Robin on and made her feel grounded. She had that feeling now, but she had nowhere to put it, so she pushed it gently to the back of her mind.

"It's a great name," Robin said. "Kind of badass."

Jill laughed again. "Badass?"

"Yeah. I have a feeling that Madison—as awesome as she is now—is going to blow that out of the water when she hits adulthood." And she was going to be a solid foundation for Jill, but Robin didn't say that because she wasn't sure how much of the past two weeks was dreams or hallucinations. For all she knew, this was a dream, and she'd wake up with the hole in her deep down that she would never be able to fill. Thinking that the time she was currently spending with Jill might be some kind of delusion was painful. Pretty awful, actually. And Robin hoped this wasn't a dream, because she had to make sure that Jill found someone who was worthy of her. No way was Robin going to allow *that* future to come to pass.

"She is pretty amazing," Jill said with parental pride. "And you'll get to experience some of that in your super aunt role."

"I hope so. I want to be the cool lesbian aunt."

"As opposed to the uncool one?"

Robin grinned. "Yeah. As opposed to that one. I'm working on not being that."

Her blinds were still open, and she stared out at the neighboring buildings, their dark facades broken by interior lighting that emanated from myriad windows. Beyond those, the river was a smooth black, darker than night, beneath the spiderweb cables of the closest bridge. She'd never really noticed the lights on the bridges, never really appreciated how a nightscape was its own kind of life under the cover of darkness.

"I think you're going to be an excellent aunt," Jill said.

"I'll probably need tips, so can I keep you on speed dial?"

Jill didn't answer right away, and it dawned on Robin that maybe Jill thought she was flirting.

"Absolutely," Jill said. "When's the baby due?"

Robin relaxed. Jill's tone hadn't changed. "June. Right around my birthday."

"That's almost too perfect."

"Smart kid."

"Must run in the family."

"Probably Deb's side—Frank's wife." A red light approached the closest bridge. A helicopter, Robin figured, and she wondered how she'd managed to miss all the little things that happened outside her windows.

"Maybe that's it," Jill said, and Robin could tell she was teasing.

"So when are you done playing in Vermont?"

"A couple of days. I have to be back no later than the twenty-ninth so I can get things ready for the show on New Year's Eve."

"Don't forget to text me the location and time and all that." Robin toyed with the idea of asking her if she wanted to grab lunch again, but decided not to. She'd see her in a few days, after all, and she still had to figure out how to change the future's trajectory. How, basically, to save Jill from Robin.

"Don't worry. Thanks for talking. I'll see you later."

"Yeah. Bye." Robin hung up and thought about her friends and acquaintances. Did she know anybody who would be a good match for Jill? The lights on one of the distant bridges blinked, and she watched it for a while. Three of her single friends came to mind who might be possibilities. Robin decided to text them and find out if they wanted to come with her to the art opening. If they all came, that was three opportunities for Jill to click with one of them.

Robin stretched out on the couch with a blanket, deciding she wanted to fall asleep with her blinds open to the night, and to whatever possibilities might be in it. Tomorrow, she'd text her friends about the art gallery.

"Hey, Mike," Robin said to the security guard. He looked at her, surprised. "Didn't get a chance to give this to you Christmas Eve." She placed a Starbucks gift card on the information counter.

He picked it up, still staring at her. "Did you have a good Christmas?"

"Yes. You?"

"Lots of family. Hectic, but nice." The phone at his station rang. "Thanks, Ms. Preston." He held the card up and answered with his free hand.

Robin nodded and waved and caught the elevator to her floor. She had not wanted to come to work, and it should have bothered her, how little she cared about Frost Enterprises and its bottom lines. It was like the movie *The Matrix,* she thought as the elevator ascended. Everything she'd thought was real and important and defining in her life wasn't, and she wanted something real, something simple, something that fed whatever it was that stirred inside. Maybe she should watch more movies. She'd gotten out of the habit when she started working at Frost, only taking time once in a while these days to stream something.

"Hi, Laura." She put a gift card for a nearby restaurant on Laura's desk. Her outfit today was a tasteful but conservative navy suit with a light-blue blouse. "Forgot to give this to you before you left Tuesday."

Laura looked at the card, then at Robin. "Thank you. How was your Christmas?"

Robin smiled. "Revealing. Yours?"

"Fun with my family." She said it with an expression that conveyed how important that was to her.

"Glad to hear it. Sorry we're back in the fray today. I'm pretty sure I have at least one meeting, and I'll be working on my presentation for tomorrow, so I'll be around if you need anything." Robin went into her office. She started to shut the door, thought better of it, and left it partially open. For the first time since she'd been working here, a closed door made her feel claustrophobic.

Fortunately, her current office wasn't the one from Christmas Future, and for that she was glad. Still, it looked and felt corporate, like how someone who thought she was important would set up an office. Heavy desk—both expansive and expensive—leather chairs and couch, track lighting, and art she hadn't chosen herself. Most of it was generic photographs of parts of the city that probably came from a visitors' guide. Jill's "Port 9" would look really good in the light from the windows—she caught herself. None of Jill's art belonged in this fake, sterile, and cutthroat environment.

Robin threw her coat onto the couch and set her satchel on the floor next to her desk but then changed her mind and took it over to her couch, where she set up her laptop so she could put her feet up on the coffee table. No punk T-shirt under her blouse today, but she wore three rings and tiny skulls-and-crossbones earrings. She'd left her hair down. It made her feel freer, somehow, not to have it pulled back all the time.

She checked her calendar. Meeting in an hour. Then to her email, one marked urgent from Mary in HR. Fortunately, Lydia Evans and Joseph Spinelli had agreed to return and could she please sign the paperwork? Damn right she could, and she printed it out and did just that.

"Ms. Pres—Robin." Laura poked her head in.

"Just a sec." She checked to make sure she'd initialed everything. "Could you make sure Mary in HR gets this ASAP?" Robin handed it to Laura.

"Yes. I just wanted to let you know that I have some ideas about your presentation, if you have some time this afternoon."

"I think you'd know whether that was the case. If I do, put yourself in that slot, and we'll go from there."

"Yes, ma'am." Laura retreated, but Robin thought she saw her smile.

Time to get ready for this damn meeting. She'd much rather be drawing, she thought as she plopped down on the couch again to work. Twenty minutes later her personal phone dinged with a text message. She checked it and smiled. Jill, sending her the time and place for the art opening. Robin knew of this gallery, though she'd never been inside. If she recalled correctly, it had been a shipping warehouse in the early twentieth century. She vaguely remembered a lot of brick and two huge windows in the front.

With this information, Robin texted her friends, hoping all three could come. That would be ideal. She was about to put her phone down when instead she looked at the selfies she'd done with Jill. She stared at them for a long time, thinking about the few weeks before the breakup.

Jill had been distancing herself, Robin realized, but not because she wasn't in love with her. Robin hadn't fully recognized it and instead figured something was going on with Jill's family, which was usually the case when Jill withdrew. She knew now that was correct, but when Robin finally tried to get Jill to tell her what was going on, Jill withdrew permanently. But here she was now, making goofy faces with Robin, like they used to do in cheap photo booths in Oregon. Robin scrolled to a photo she took of Jill alone, and she studied Jill's face, seeing the woman she'd loved long ago, but also someone else who'd gone through her own difficult times but still managed to bring her old self along and fuse it to the new.

Robin set her phone aside. Dangerous, looking at those photos, because she had a future to prevent and looking only seemed to make her poke through ashes in hopes of finding an ember. Which was just as off-the-wall as what had been happening for the past two weeks.

Her calendar dinged its fifteen-minute pre-meeting warning and Robin set her laptop aside and retrieved her tablet from her bag, not looking forward to spending the next hour with a bunch of men, some of whom might resent her for her title. Her *Matrix* comparison sprang to mind as she walked down the hall, and she wondered if the Bureau handed out red pills, in addition to its "scared straight" program. Those thoughts amused her, and she took a seat toward the end of the big conference table, opposite where Frost usually sat.

Cynthia's husband came in and sat across from her. She greeted him, but he ignored her. Whatever. Frost's executive guys weren't always the friendliest bunch and a lot of them had issues with women. Hopefully, Cynthia moved on to her latest toy, and she'd forget all about Robin. That would be one less mess to deal with.

The meeting started, and Robin dutifully recorded updates from the departments who'd shown up, but she didn't care. She surreptitiously looked at rental properties in Seattle again, as if that provided her a lifeline, though she wasn't sure she had the gumption to grab it. Baby steps.

Finally, the meeting wound to a close, and she got up, dutifully chatting to others as they left. She and Brady were the last two in the room, and he shut the door before she exited, sealing them in, and proceeded to get right up in her face.

"Listen up, Preston."

"What—"

"Shut up."

"Excuse me?" Adrenaline surged through her, and she checked the door, debating her chances of making it out before a scene erupted in here.

"I'm going to say this once," he said in a low, dangerous tone. "You stay the hell away from my wife."

Stunned, she could only stare. So this was how Cynthia was going to get back at her. She should have figured as much.

"Goddamn dyke, coming on to every woman you see."

Robin regained her voice, and she kept it level despite her rising anger. "That's way out of line."

"I'll tell you what's out of line," he snarled. "Sexually harassing my wife."

"Harassment? What the hell are you talking about?"

Her tone may have conveyed adequate outrage, because he stepped back. "Don't play fucking stupid."

"And don't make bullshit accusations."

He glared at her. "Do you deny trying to seduce my wife?"

"I don't have to answer any of your goddamn questions. Maybe you should ask your wife what she does in her spare time instead of throwing crap like this around."

His face flushed red, and he clenched his fists. Robin was reminded of a documentary she'd seen on volcanoes. "This isn't over," he said.

"It damn well is. I don't want anything to do with you or your wife. Stay the hell away from me." Nobody was going to push her around. Especially not like this.

"Watch yourself, Preston," he said, raising his index finger in her face to emphasize his point.

"Fuck off," she snapped back as he stormed out of the room, leaving her to stare after him. Maybe she shouldn't have said that last thing. Not very professional of her. But then again, neither was accusing her of sexually harassing his wife. *Fuck you, too, Cynthia.* Good thing she'd saved all her texts, though there was nothing overtly sexual in them. But they did prove that Cynthia sure wasn't uncomfortable with Robin contacting her.

Once the adrenaline from the encounter wore off, her stomach churned with anxiety. What exactly had Cynthia told Brady? More importantly, what would he do with her lies? She clenched her teeth and went back to her office, but she couldn't calm down. Should she contact Cynthia and have it out with her? No. Bad idea. It would only add more fuel to her sick revenge fantasy.

She glared out the window. What options did she have? She couldn't go to Frost, because that might bring down an investigation. Even though her relationship with Cynthia had been consensual, a whole lot of dirty laundry would get aired, and they'd find a way to get rid of her. Going to Cynthia was out of the question, because she was setting Robin up to take a fall. Cynthia would probably demand sex to make the story go away, and there was no way in hell Robin would allow Cynthia to blackmail her. That thought made her stomach twist even more.

What about Brady? Maybe if he saw the texts to Robin from Cynthia, he'd back off. Or he'd push for Robin's resignation or firing, whichever came first, to make it go away. Plus, he wouldn't want to be made to look like a fool if he knew his wife was playing him, too. Still, that was an angle Robin could exploit. Join forces with Brady, and isolate Cynthia.

The idea faded quickly. Cynthia was the quintessential trophy wife, from an equally monied and powerful family. She could no doubt make all kinds of trouble for Brady, too. For all Robin knew, she had dirt on her own husband and she probably used it. She forced herself to take several deep breaths. Robin didn't have to approach Cynthia in the first place and talk her into bed. Some of this was her own fault. She grimaced. Now that Brady had put her on notice, maybe the issue was over.

But she doubted it. Brady had lackeys who would love to see Robin take a fall. She groaned. This was revenge on Cynthia's part, but it was also politics. And nothing got uglier than a mixture of those two toxic ingredients.

She'd also bet money that no matter what she did or said at tomorrow's meeting, there was no way in hell she'd get promoted or even recognized. Especially if Brady went to Frost and planted ideas with him She half laughed. All this time, she'd been playing politics so hard, working the system in ways both moral and not, and ultimately, it probably didn't mean dick. If she hadn't gotten mixed up with Cynthia, something else might have knocked her off the corporate ladder.

And what did it matter, ultimately? She'd either gone nuts in the past few days or had an epiphany and neither of those was conducive to her current corporate culture. What to do about it was a whole other matter, and not one she was ready to deal with.

Robin went to get some lunch, though she wasn't hungry. But she'd be damned if she let Brady or any of his people see her sweat about this.

Chapter 9

"Ms.—Robin."

Robin looked up from her couch, which was proving infinitely more comfortable than her desk, though this area of her office was starting to look like her brother's college bachelor pad. Her to-go containers from lunch were stacked on the coffee table next to a couple coffee cups, and she'd tossed her shoes on the floor next to it. Laura stood in her office doorway holding a stack of papers and a tablet. Her gaze swept the coffee table and her expression went from confused to amused in a matter of seconds.

"Oh, yeah. Time to talk about the presentation. Where do you want to sit?"

"The table is probably easiest. I have some things to spread out, and it'll be easier for you to see them over here."

"Sure." Robin got up with her laptop and padded over to the table in her stocking feet. She loaded the presentation and positioned the laptop so both she and Laura could easily see it. Laura spread some documents out on the other end of the table and placed her tablet next to the laptop, also with a slideshow loaded. The two of them sat down.

"I've done two different versions," Laura said. "One falls more in line with what Frost has been doing for years. The other—" She stopped. "Well, that's my wishful thinking presentation, based on trends I've been seeing in business and corporate policy.

"Let's see the one that's in line with Frost."

Laura obliged, and Robin noted that it had incorporated most of Robin's slides in a slightly different order, and with better accompanying figures in some cases. Laura was good, and Robin wished she'd tapped her expertise earlier.

"Okay, let's see the other one."

Laura switched to it and halfway through, Robin stopped her. "This is brilliant."

"You haven't seen all of it."

"Fine. Let's go through the rest, but I'm pretty sure my opinion is not going to change." Laura had brought in about a third of Robin's slides, but she'd contextualized them in terms of progressive corporate policies that emphasized investing in human capital over bottom line, citing several examples from many successful businesses of varying sizes, up to a multinational. It was everything Robin wasn't until recently, and everything Frost's culture stood against.

"I love this." Robin started it from the beginning. It was refreshing, and rebellious, two things she was enjoying more of these days. "How long did it take you to do it?"

"Not very. These are all things I've been following for months, and they're issues that I dealt with in college. I'm one of those bleeding heart social sciences majors. I studied sociology with an emphasis on business culture."

Robin vaguely remembered that from Laura's résumé. She turned from the tablet and looked hard at Laura. "Can I use this tomorrow? And I'd like you to come as well, and team with me in presenting it. I can do a quick background read on most of this, since I'm familiar with it, too, but I'd like to have you there as the expert."

From Laura's expression, she probably would have been less surprised had Robin asked her on a date.

"Don't worry," Robin assured her. "If they hate it, I'll deal with it. They'll think I forced you into doing it, as an assistant, and you're in the clear. Or, if they like it, then I'll give you all the credit."

Laura glanced nervously at the door, as if checking to make sure it was closed. "I told you that I pay attention to a lot that goes on around here."

"Yeah. And?"

"I know this meeting tomorrow has huge ramifications and can determine whether people advance or not."

"That's the rumor."

"So why are you willing to go so far out on a limb? Mr. Frost wants new ideas within the party line."

"But I don't. Maybe we should be thinking outside the box." Red pill, she wanted to say to Laura, but she was pretty sure Laura thought she had lost her mind, and that analogy wouldn't help with her opinion. "And if you didn't want me to consider it, you wouldn't have created this presentation." She gestured at the tablet.

Laura appeared to be considering her next words. "I took a chance doing that, especially since you seem more approachable over the past few days. But I didn't expect that you'd buy the whole thing."

"Why not? They're great ideas. Businesses need to think about all kinds of approaches, not just the usual. That's what keeps them competitive. So will you help me?"

"Yes."

"Great. Let's sketch out how this'll work." Robin got up to retrieve a scratch pad and pen off her desk.

"Can I say something?"

"Sure."

"They're probably not going to promote you." She looked at Robin, expression troubled.

Though Robin had suspected that, hearing it aloud rubbed a little salt in the wound. "Let me guess. You've heard things."

She nodded.

"Is it a woman thing or the gay thing? Or both?"

If Laura was surprised at Robin's coming out to her so directly, she didn't show it. "Woman, mostly. But the other probably doesn't help, though I haven't heard anything bad about that. Just questions."

"Trying to figure out if I am?"

"Yes."

"Guess I shouldn't be surprised. Not like corporate culture is a bastion of girl power."

"No. It isn't."

Robin sat down and tapped her pen on the scratch pad. She could approach the impending meeting in a variety of ways. She could present Laura's information and see where the chips fell, or she could engage some of the tactics she'd learned over the years. She still had a few things up her sleeve where some of her peers were concerned, and she'd made it a point to cultivate relationships with a few of the board members who weren't always drinking Frost's Kool-Aid.

She could set Frost and a couple of board members against each other, and that would keep her position secure for a while longer. She also had some good dirt on a couple of Brady's lackeys. There were ways to get that across in meetings like this, and ways to plant information with the right people to run a little discrediting campaign.

Her personal cell rang, an R&B tune. She didn't need to look at it to know who it was.

"Go ahead and take that," Laura said. "I'll be at my desk."

"You can hear that?"

Laura looked at her, puzzled. "Yes. Why wouldn't I?"

"No reason." She waited until Laura had left before she answered.

"Hello," Robin said.

"Sugar," came Lady Magnolia's drawl, "my mama always said that a house is only as good as the man that built it. Or, in your case, the cute little lesbian."

Robin frowned. "I'm not sure—"

"Honey, you reap what you sow. Plant corn, you've got something worth sharing. Plant ragweed, and Lord have mercy, you're miserable for weeks. Build a good house, and you have a place for dinner soirees and family gatherings. Build something raggedy, and sugar, nobody's gonna want to live there."

"Are you saying what goes around comes around?"

Magnolia laughed. "Bingo, sugar. So think long and hard about what exactly you want next in your life, and how you want to live those days. Whatever you put in motion, you better be sure you know how to ride it. Bye, now."

Magnolia hung up, and it dawned on Robin that this was after Christmas. Why was the Bureau still contacting her? She put her phone on the table. Was this a last-ditch effort to save her because she'd failed some kind of Bureau test?

She slumped back in her chair. What exactly did she want out of Frost? If she did the standard presentation, she wouldn't advance. But chances were, that wasn't going to happen, anyway, given what Laura had said. If Robin did Laura's presentation, the board might notice and she might advance in spite of Frost. But then, he'd spend a lot of time making sure she had a hard time getting things done. Or Brady would. There were no guarantees she was going to move ahead. The only thing that she could count on at the moment was staying in her position. So no matter what she did at the meeting, her chances of advancing weren't very high, even if she employed behind-the-scenes warfare.

How would that make her feel, engaging in the kind of cutthroat take-no-prisoners approach she'd employed in the past? And how badly did she want to advance in this company? Did she even want to stay? Robin picked up her phone and looked at the call log. There was no evidence of Magnolia. No number, no "unknown caller," nothing.

"Robin?" Laura reappeared. "Do you want to keep working on this or wait a bit?"

"No, we can keep working on it."

Laura rejoined her at the table. "I didn't mean to upset you."

"What do you mean?" Robin put her phone down.

"About advancement. I just don't think it's a good idea to get your hopes up about it."

Robin smiled. "The truth hurts."

"It's not about you personally. It's about the culture here."

"I know. It doesn't matter what I do or don't do at this meeting. So my attitude is, why not just put your presentation out there? Nobody is expecting it." Robin's rebel streak sent a little jolt of energy through her. "At this point, I've got nothing to lose."

"Maybe you do. Brady Herrington went to see Mr. Frost after your meeting this morning." Laura held Robin's gaze. "Your name came up, but Megan wasn't sure what the context was. She could tell by the tone, however, that Brady wasn't happy."

Megan. Mr. Frost's assistant. She'd given Laura a heads-up and Laura had passed it on to her. Maybe Laura was warming up to her a little. Regardless, Robin shook her head in irritation. In addition to her sour stomach she had a headache coming on, too. "Bad, probably. Brady and I don't mix well." She grinned. "Not that I wouldn't gladly take him on."

Laura smiled back. "He has it in for you for some reason. Those are the rumors."

Rumors already? Had he gone to Frost with Cynthia's accusations? Sneaky bastards, both of them. She rubbed her forehead. She'd known that about them. After all, she'd watched them do the same thing with others. Why she thought it couldn't happen to her, she wasn't sure. Thinking about both Brady and Frost made her queasy. Why would she want to stick around in a company with those two on the ladder above her, able to pee down it? As long as that was the case, she was screwed. And honestly, did she even want to stay? She was leaning no, but if she had to leave, it would be on her terms.

"Robin? Is everything okay?"

"Yes. I wish I had tapped into your information pipeline a long time ago, but like I said, turning this damn ship is a little difficult."

"Do you still want to do this presentation?" Concern showed in Laura's eyes, and it made Robin feel a little better. Nobody worried about assholes, after all.

"Definitely. She picked up her pen. "So let's plan how this is going to work."

Laura smiled, encouraging, and re-started the presentation.

⎯⎯⎯◄◊►⎯⎯⎯

The next day dawned cold and overcast, with a threat of either icy rain or snow or both. Two of Robin's friends couldn't make the art opening because of prior commitments, but they appreciated the offer. The other said she'd check her schedule, and Robin really hoped she could come. Of the three, this one seemed the best match for Jill. She was into art and music.

Which felt weird, thinking that way. Trying to set up her ex from years ago with someone had to be a new level of strange in her life, though given what she'd been through—if that wasn't some kind of delusion or fever dream—it was tame.

Robin was already halfway through her extra-large coffee by the time she got to her office. A day of reckoning, she thought as she hung her coat on one of the hooks near the door. She hadn't felt so untethered since she'd switched her major to business.

Thinking back on it, doing that was probably a reaction to her mom's death and Jill leaving. Art was too painful for both those reasons, and she thought business would be a better route to a job to support her and maybe Frank, since their dad wasn't in the picture, either. Turned out, she was pretty good at business, but like Agent Tolson had said, she'd done some things that she hadn't needed to, things that ended up hurting others. Did she use her prickly, unapproachable self to protect her regular self from further pain? Had she been that caught up in her grief that she hadn't learned to balance strength and vulnerability?

Change wasn't easy. What was it Lady Magnolia had said? It doesn't always come with a hot meal and highball. Robin smiled in spite of her mood. She checked her personal phone, and for the thousandth time in the past few days, she went to the photos of Jill. She had been beautiful in college, but the years since had added all kinds of layers that enhanced not only her physical appearance, but her spirit. Jill was definitely one of those women who became even sexier as she aged.

"Ready?" Laura asked from the doorway, and Robin clicked out of the photos. She assessed Laura's outfit, an olive power suit that brought out her eyes. Good choice, Robin thought. She'd opted for a black suit with a cream blouse, and she'd put her rings on this morning, but switched the skulls and crossbones earrings for small diamond studs.

"Let's do this." Robin gathered her tablet and file of materials as well as her laser pointer. "Nervous?" she asked. She hoped Laura believed her, that Robin would take the hit if the presentation didn't go well. Robin would follow through because, she was really enjoying doing the right thing. "A little."

"You'll be great. Good suit, by the way. Very chic, very professional. Frost will appreciate that."

Laura murmured something in response. She carried her own tablet and file and was silent the rest of the way to the large conference room three floors up. Frost used it for his showcase meetings, and the table was big enough for the nine primary board members. Who, Robin noted, were all in attendance.

"We'll be the last presentation," she said to Laura as they took their seats about halfway down the length of the table. Which could be either good or bad, since the last presentation was usually the one people took with them after the meeting, especially if it stuck out for any particular reason.

Six of the board members present Robin knew and had spoken with at length over the past few years. She acknowledged all with a nod and a smile. There'd be no chance to draw during this meeting, and she put herself in full-attention mode so she could address anything that came up in the presentations before hers.

Brady sat across the table from her, slightly to her left. He avoided looking at her even when she pointedly stared at him. Score for her, she decided. Soon after, Frost issued the opening remarks, paid respects to the board, and then ordered the lights dimmed.

Each of the five presenters was allotted fifteen minutes, but Robin knew at least two would go over, and substantially. She was right. Frost called for a break after the third and Robin went to the bathroom. On her way back to the meeting room, one of the board members waved her over.

"Mr. Pruitt," she said by way of acknowledgement. "Thanks for coming. How are things with your wife?"

"She's much better, thank you." He was pushing seventy, and wore a more traditional, classic cut men's suit and matched his pocket square with his tie. The ruby in his tie clip picked up the accent color in both. "I do hope that you have something new to add to this meeting."

"I just might." She smiled. "And I promise we won't go over fifteen minutes."

He smiled back, and she went back to her seat. A few minutes later, the meeting resumed, and the second-to-last presentation dragged on for thirty minutes, going on about successes over the last couple of quarters and how that was probably due to better marketing. Sure, Robin thought. But marketing can get you only so far if you don't follow through with personal service.

She scanned the faces around the room. Most seemed to be bored. Brady was looking at something on his tablet, and Robin guessed it had nothing to do with what the presenter was droning on about. She felt a little sorry for the presenter, actually. Phillips hated doing presentations, and he always sounded nervous.

Finally, he finished, and Robin took her laser pointer out of her pocket. "Here we go," she said in a low voice to Laura. She stood, and Phillips gratefully handed her the remote that controlled the computer and the slides.

"Thank you," she said. "I'm joined today by my assistant, Laura Navarro, who will keep me on track and help with explanations as necessary."

That got the attention of four board members, since it wasn't standard operating procedure. Frost's brow creased, and he leaned back in his seat, fingers steepled.

Robin glanced over at Laura, who gave her an encouraging nod, so she launched into what they'd dubbed "out of the box." Robin had added some music and video clips and brought Laura in several times to provide figures and some background. Midway through, Frost was scowling, Brady was smiling smugly, but almost all the board members were scribbling notes, as were a few of the people from other departments.

By the end, the board members were nodding and whispering to each other. They applauded when the lights went on, and Frost stopped scowling, but from his hard expression, he wasn't pleased. Robin had basically taken Frost to task for ineffective internal practices. She remained standing, because she knew Frost would end the gathering.

"Thank you, all," Frost said by way of dismissal. "We appreciate your time."

"Nice work." Robin gave Laura's shoulder a squeeze. "Stick around. See if you notice anything." She moved away before Laura could respond.

"Well done," Pruitt said to her. "It's about time somebody brought this place into the twenty-first century."

Frost overheard, and his eyes narrowed, assessing Robin the way a predator assesses a threat. Well, she was pretty scrappy herself. She met his gaze squarely, and he shifted his to Pruitt, who addressed him directly as another board member moved in to talk to her.

Now came the post-meeting power play. All the board members made it a point to talk to her directly, which didn't sit well with either Frost or Brady, from their expressions. Screw both of you, Robin thought.

"How long have you been looking at these issues?" Pruitt asked as they moved slowly to the door. "Because it's high time."

"Not long enough, sir. My assistant was instrumental in educating me about this, and she created the slide show. In this case, I'm the messenger. It's all Ms. Navarro other than that."

"Well, that was a damn good hire, Preston. I see you walk your talk."

"Sometimes I just get very lucky."

"Regardless, we could use more people like you. Finding the right people for the job is half the battle, I've always thought, to saving money. Give people a reason to be loyal. Used to be, they were, and we all took care of each other. I'd like to see more of that in this day and age. And I'd like to have a personal assistant like Ms. Navarro. If you find me one, let me know. I'm currently in need." He gave her an avuncular smile.

Two other board members echoed him.

Robin smiled. "Yes sir," she said, and the image of a chessboard crossed her mind, because that's what corporate maneuvering was like. Pruitt had liked her presentation. So had a few other board members. Which put Frost in a vulnerable position, along with Brady. She could press this advantage, and most likely derail Brady for a while—she caught herself. Jesus, she'd been conditioned well in this kind of backroom thinking. Why should she engage when she wasn't even sure she wanted to stick around?

"Keep in touch, Preston," Pruitt said. "I want to hear more from you. Pity you can't join us for lunch. But do give me a call, and we'll set something up separately."

Score. Robin smiled and nodded. "Yes, sir. My best to your wife." She headed for the elevators, Laura right behind her.

"Thanks for that," Laura said when the doors slid shut. They were the only two passengers.

"For what?"

"The credit."

"The board appears to have liked your work," Robin said as she pressed the floor number. "If they didn't, I would have taken the hit." She grinned.

"I guess I was a little worried."

"About what?"

"That you might let me take the blame. Or that you'd take all the credit."

Robin started to retort but remembered Decker's last visit. "I get that. But like I said, I'm trying to turn my ship around."

"I appreciate that. For the record, Mr. Frost isn't a fan."

Robin shrugged. "We knew he probably wouldn't be. Did you catch anything else?"

"A couple of people thought you were, and I quote, a 'libtard'."

Robin made a disgusted noise in her throat. "I have a pretty good idea who they are."

"A few others were cautious, but thought your organization was great. And they liked the music."

Robin laughed as they got off the elevator. "Well, that's something."

"The entire board is pleased."

"That is also something. Want to grab lunch?"

Laura looked at her, surprised.

"The board is eating with Frost and friends."

"You got an invitation."

"I called Pruitt's temporary assistant directly a couple days ago and made my excuses. Client issue, and we want to present Frost in the best possible light, of course." She smirked. The truth is, she didn't feel like sucking up, and she didn't feel like bringing her little rebel out and stabbing Brady with a fork. After yesterday's conversations with both Laura and then Magnolia—if she hadn't imagined that—she was glad she'd made the decision.

"Why wouldn't you want to go to that?"

"I'd rather have lunch with someone who at least gives me the benefit of the doubt than a bunch of guys who really don't give a shit who I am or what I do. Although after today's presentation, it would've been fun to see Frost trying to say nice things about me to the board members that liked it."

Laura raised her eyebrows at Robin's assessment and smiled. "You could probably still go."

"Lost my taste for that kind of meal. How about you? Lunch?" Robin asked again.

"Yes."

"Great. Let me get my stuff." She went into her office for her coat and turned her personal phone back on. Caroline had texted to say she could come to the opening, but Robin wasn't as sure as she had been about that. Krampus had said the future she'd seen with Jill and Madison could change based on changing the present. Wouldn't one option for changing the present be making sure she doesn't hook up with Jill? And wouldn't it be that much easier to avoid if somebody came into Jill's life who she hit it off with? Because Robin wasn't sure she trusted herself to make the right decision where Jill was concerned. She put her coat on and left her office.

Chapter 10

ROBIN WAITED FOR HER COFFEE to achieve its required strength. Krampus's business card was still on the counter but she refused to touch it, afraid it might conjure him or the Bureau. She'd ignored checking her work phone yesterday evening and instead made plane reservations to visit Frank and then contacted her accountant and checked a few financial things. Frost was a dick, she realized, and would probably throw her under the bus sooner rather than later. She wanted to get her ducks in a row and prepare for the hatchet. He had the weekend to plan something, after all.

Funny, how she didn't care. She'd spent all the years since college making sure she was smart with her money, and her business degrees had taught her a thing or two about investing. She'd built a decent portfolio. She'd be all right. All kinds of things were in motion in her life, and though she wasn't sure where everything would settle, she'd decided to go with her feelings, and see what opportunities came up. Not her usual approach, but it was one she'd used years ago. Until her mom died and things went south with Jill, it had served her pretty well.

Where would she be if she hadn't worked so hard to stay unattached and uninvolved?

Happier, probably. She poured herself a cup of coffee and left it next to Krampus's card as she retrieved cream from the fridge. Her personal cell dinged from the living room with a text message, but she finished doctoring her coffee first. When she did check and saw Jill's name, she smiled. She'd sent a photo. Robin opened it and kept smiling. Jill was skiing again, and she'd taken a selfie at the top of the run, grinning beneath her racing goggles and bright red hat. *Bet you'd enjoy yourself up here*, the message said, and Robin read it a few times, knowing she shouldn't like the way it set something to glowing within. But she didn't try to stop the feeling, either, because it was deep and safe—two things she hadn't experienced in a while.

The memory of Krampus's visit knocked that sentiment right out. Clearly, in that alternative reality, hooking up again did Jill no favors, though Robin had caught herself thinking about it, and what it would be like to kiss her— and more—again. The clouds parted, and sunlight streamed into her living room. She opened her sliding glass doors and stepped out onto her balcony into the juxtaposition of winter cold and teasing warmth from the sun.

Bet you're right, she texted back to Jill. *Hope you're having a great day*. She sipped her coffee, and after a few more minutes admiring the view, the cold sent her back inside. She'd accepted a dinner invitation with a friend and a few acquaintances, but she had the whole day to kill, and she wondered at herself, taking her second Saturday in a row off. But it felt really good, so she poured herself another cup of coffee and opened her sketchpad.

———◄◯◯►———

"Girl, don't make me put this size ten stiletto up your behind."

Robin jerked awake and lay still in bed, listening. She'd already had her three visits from the Bureau, plus some bonus hallucinations for good measure. What was Lady Magnolia doing in her apartment? After what might've been a minute, Robin relaxed. Damn dream. Her clock read a little past three in the morning. She'd only gotten into bed a couple of hours ago, spending time drawing after dinner. Good thing it was Sunday. Hearing nothing but the competent whir of her refrigerator from the kitchen, she closed her eyes again.

"Didn't you hear anything Mr. Rampus said, child?" Lady Magnolia's drawl sounded, both close and far away.

"What are you talking about?" Robin mumbled, half asleep but deciding that she'd play along with the dream. It took less energy than waking up.

"Change your perspective, and you change the outcome," Lady Magnolia said.

"What the hell does that mean?" And who had said that first? Oh, yeah. Krampus. Her limbs were heavy and warm, like she was lying in oatmeal. She giggled, but she was so relaxed that it sounded more like a soft little bark and a snort.

"Oh, Lord, sugar. My mama always told me that when opportunity knocks, you don't leave her waiting on the porch."

"Thanks for the advice. Can I sleep now?" Robin was really tired, and there was nothing she could do about whatever Lady Magnolia was talking about. Besides, there was nobody at her door. This was a secure building. She'd just sleep for a while. Robin sank into darkness, and when she woke up, daylight flooded her bedroom.

She didn't remember opening the blinds in here, but it wouldn't surprise her if she had, since she'd developed the habit of doing it in the other room. Almost ten. She never slept this late on the weekends, but she realized that, for the first time in a long time, she enjoyed sleeping in. How long had it been since she'd done that? Too long. Much too long.

Her phone rang from somewhere else. She listened to it for a couple of seconds before she remembered it was in the living room, and then it dawned on her that the ringtone was one she'd programmed for Jill. She didn't normally do that, give people their own ringtones. She wasn't sure why she'd done it for Jill's number, but maybe their shared past gave Jill extra weight in Robin's life. It was too late by the time she got to the phone, dragging one of her blankets behind her. One foot had gotten wrapped up in it.

Robin speed-dialed Jill.

"Good morning," Jill answered.

"Hey."

"Oh, hell. Did I wake you up?"

"Um. Not really."

"You sure? You have your just-woke-up voice on."

"No, I was up. I haven't had my coffee yet, though."

Jill laughed. "You want to call back after you take care of that?"

"No, it's okay. But I will start making it while you talk." It occurred to Robin that Jill remembered what she sounded like in the mornings, after all these years. She smiled as she kicked the blanket off and went into the kitchen.

"Okay, so I'm done with all that skiing in Vermont, and I got back into the city last night. I'm wondering if you wanted to have lunch again," Jill said.

Robin finished pouring coffee beans into the grinder. God, she wanted to…"Yes," she said and then wondered why she'd voiced that aloud. Was this even a good idea? "But hold on a sec. Grinding." She pressed the button on the grinder down but could still hear Jill's laughter over the phone. A few seconds later, Jill spoke.

"All done?"

"With that part, yes. Go ahead and tell me your plan for lunch." Robin prepared the French press, filled her electric kettle, and turned it on.

"Feel like meeting me somewhere near the gallery?"

"Sure. Just tell me where and when."

"How much time do you need for your coffee?"

Robin grinned. "It'll be ready in about ten minutes."

"And then there'll be about twenty minutes for that first cup, another twenty for the second…unless you're feeling mellow. How about a later lunch? Meet me at one-thirty?"

"Done."

"Great. I'll text you the restaurant."

"Need-to-know basis. How James Bond of you." Robin poured the boiling water into the press.

Jill chuckled. "You know, for someone who insists she's an asshole, you sound pretty relaxed. And a lot like the woman I met in college."

"You say that now, but seriously, a month ago, there is no way in hell you'd be asking me to lunch."

"What changed?"

Robin hesitated. "Epiphanies, maybe." Sure, Jill would have lunch with her now, but if she knew about Decker and Lady Magnolia and Krampus, she'd back slowly out the door. Then again, maybe she should tell Jill. That would ensure Jill's future would be secure because she'd think Robin wasn't quite right. She pressed the plunger on the press with a slow, practiced motion.

"I know a few things about those," Jill said, and she sounded thoughtful but also empathetic.

Robin poured herself a cup and sipped it black. "I'm betting you do. Some can be a real kick in the butt." An image of Lady Magnolia's stilettos came to mind, and she stared at Krampus's card, still on her counter, and wondered if she'd dreamed last night's conversation. God, she hoped so. But still. What the hell was that about opportunity? Something tickled her brain about how Magnolia had phrased it, but Robin couldn't put her finger on it.

"Agreed. I'll let you drink your coffee in peace. Let me figure out what restaurant needs us to grace it with our presence. See you in a bit."

"Yep. Later." Robin hung up and put her phone on the counter then leaned back against it. She sipped her coffee and remembered how Jill had made her coffee in a battered espresso maker on a hot plate after their first night together. Jill had been wearing a baggy flannel shirt and nothing else, And when she'd rejoined Robin in bed with two cups, her lips tasted of coffee. How young they'd been, even with their respective baggage. Jill used to joke that the trick was making sure your luggage complemented your partner's. It didn't have to exactly match, because that would be boring. And then Jill would kiss her, sometimes soft and searching, other times hard and needy. A pleasurable chill sent tingles up her spine, and Robin took another drink from her cup to try to tamp it down.

This was not part of her plan, these feelings. They were dangerous. Getting mixed up with Jill would only fuck up Jill's future and, after all the shit Robin had seen over the past two weeks, being responsible for that made her feel sick. Hopefully, Jill would hit it off with Caroline, and then she could get on with whatever came next. Whatever it was, Robin was pretty sure it wouldn't involve Frost Enterprises.

What should she do about that, she wondered as she sipped again and stared out at the city. There wasn't much she could do, she realized. No matter her own title, she was just some outsider lesbian who had sealed her fate with that presentation on Friday. But wasn't that one of the five things that would ensure victory, according to Sun Tzu? "He will win who knows when to fight and when not to fight." She'd read *The Art of War* her second year of business school. This was a fight she knew she couldn't win, because even if she managed to curtail Brady and bypass Frost, she wasn't sure she could live with the results of it.

The worst-case scenario was that Frost would fire her. Or rather, "let her go," in corporate parlance. If not that, he could demote her and send her to one of the company's other departments, maybe in the far reaches of the building. No more corner office with the great view. And then she'd have to put up with the pitying looks from some and the supercilious sneers from the younger men striving to be in the good old boys club. The second scenario would force her to put up with it or resign.

175

Robin topped off her coffee, a little surprised that she didn't seem to care what Frost decided to do. And if it came to resigning—she took another swallow of coffee and ran that thought through her mind for a while. How did *that* feel, to actually contemplate resigning?

Fine, she realized. Maybe even liberating. Had she been that stifled, and she didn't even realize how much? The view out her balcony doors beckoned, and she left the kitchen with her coffee cup.

The sun glinted off the river, and a couple of barges moved slowly, almost regally, under the closest bridge. Robin imagined them as giant turtles, one swimming with the current, the other against, and that made her think about the way Northwest Coast Indians portrayed turtles, geometric stylized shapes in bold, primary colors.

Should she wait for Frost to show his hand? Or should she resign because it was the right decision for her, to hell with what Frost decides? Frost would be careful, because she could play the gay card and claim she was discriminated against because of it. That would get ugly, because she'd demonstrate that Cynthia didn't seem to have a problem texting her or calling her, so how the hell could Robin have possibly sexually harassed her?

Or she could pull the woman card, and Laura might be able to help her with some kind of documentation regarding that, because women only made it so far at Frost but no further. God, that would be a long battle.

And as Robin stared down at the water and thought about Seattle, she knew it wasn't one she wanted to fight.

So Frost would probably go for demotion. Or rather, transfer. Some unknown department, where she'd keep her title and salary, but get loaded down with crap work and not have anything more to do with building accounts and attracting clients. She'd be effectively silenced unless she resigned. Frost's hands would be clean. He could claim that her talents were needed elsewhere.

That's how people disappeared in corporate America. Robin finished her coffee, pissed that Frost could basically get away with whatever he wanted, but she'd built up a nice financial cushion, and she had a hell of a network. Resigning wouldn't hit her in the pocketbook. Not really. It was preferable to being fired, but Frost probably wouldn't do that, especially since he knew a few of the board members liked her.

She still had a card or two up her sleeve where Frost was concerned. Robin would engage in self-preservation if she had to. She'd been doing it for years and she was damn good at it. Her phone dinged with a text message, and she returned to the kitchen to check it. Jill, telling her to meet her outside the gallery where her New Year's Eve showing was scheduled. Robin texted an affirmative back, left her cup on the counter, and went to shower, thoughts of Jill supplanting Frost, and they were far more pleasant.

Chapter 11

THIS GALLERY WASN'T TOO FAR from the one Jill had taken her to a little over a week ago. It felt as though it had been much longer since the last opening. This building looked more upscale, but that might have been because of its nearly full-glass front. The door was also glass, the handle a sleek steel vertical bar.

Robin peered inside at the honey-colored wooden floor and the white walls, mostly empty because Jill and gallery staff hadn't put Jill's works out yet. Track and recessed lighting. Nice for bringing out various aspects of whatever art was being shown. The colors and forms in Jill's pieces would look really good here, Robin knew.

And there was Jill, approaching from inside, her hair not spiked today, but rather falling to the side in a way that made her look Asian boyish. She wore faded jeans that fit her just right, a pair of battered black Converse sneakers, and a baggy blue flannel shirt with the sleeves rolled up, exposing the long white sleeves of the T-shirt beneath. In a moment of déjà vu, Robin saw Jill walking into that classroom the first time she ever saw her, except this Jill—the one who was using a key to open the gallery door from the inside— carried herself with the confidence acquired through a life truly lived and surviving hard choices. Beneath the warmth and humor in Jill's eyes, Robin saw that Jill knew both of those—hard choices and a life lived.

"Hi, there," Jill said with the kind of smile that meant she really was glad to see Robin. "C'mon in."

Robin did, immediately comforted by the faint odors of paint, canvas, and wood—the universal smell of artists' studios and galleries everywhere. She took her gloves off and shoved them into one of her coat pockets while Jill closed the door behind her and relocked it.

"I had a cool thought," Jill said, and Robin was disappointed that the statement didn't come with a hug.

"And that is…"

"Let's eat in."

Robin waited for her to elaborate.

"This place has a studio apartment upstairs where they house visiting artists—that would be me—and it's furnished."

"Um. So we're cooking?" Robin looked past Jill toward the back of the gallery, dubious.

"That is an option, but I'm not feeling it. So I ordered Thai."

Robin relaxed, because cooking with Jill signaled the kind of intimacy she craved but didn't want to engage in. Not now. "I'm down with that."

"I thought you might be. Come on. I'll show you my temporary abode."

Robin followed her toward the back, disappointed again because Jill was wearing the flannel shirt untucked, and it covered her ass. She wrenched her gaze away, thoughts of Christmas Future knocking those ideas right out of her head.

"So here's where all my art stuff is," Jill said as they entered the back storage area. To the left was a metal industrial-looking staircase. "I'll be putting some pieces up this evening with some help. They'll be in around four or so."

Robin glanced around at the paintings, encased in layers of bubble wrap and leaning against the opposite wall. "How many pieces are you displaying?"

"Fifteen large, fifteen mid-size, and a few smaller ones that I haven't decided on yet. The gallery staff will have a say in that, too." Jill started up the stairs, and Robin followed, careful to keep her gaze off Jill's ass, which was slightly visible from this angle. She gripped the railing, more to keep herself concentrating on something else, and waited a couple steps below the landing as Jill pushed open the door to the apartment.

"It's pretty nice," Jill said as she entered. "There're hooks by the door where you can hang your coat and stuff."

Robin stepped inside, unbuttoned her pea coat, and hung it dutifully on the hooks as Jill suggested. She put her scarf and hat on an adjoining hook then turned and surveyed the apartment. "Not bad," she said.

"This used to be a warehouse, and the woman who bought the gallery wanted to retain some of those elements up here."

And she'd done pretty well at it, Robin thought. Wooden floors, lots of exposed brick, tall windows to her right that probably looked down onto the street, and a tin ceiling reminiscent of 1920s structures. If it wasn't original, it was faithful to the era. The furnishings, however, were modern Scandinavian style. A black leather couch with smooth steel legs, matching chair, and coffee table occupied one of the corners near the front windows, resting on a thick maroon rug. To the left was a kitchenette. A rectangular table of some dark reddish wood sat a few feet away, surrounded by four chairs. In the back corner opposite the living room looked to be a bedroom of sorts, though she couldn't be sure because plain Asian-style screens provided privacy.

"The bathroom is there," Jill said, pointing at a door near the screens. Her phone rang, a Lady Gaga tune. "And that would be the food. Be right back." She flashed Robin a smile and bounced out of the room. Robin heard her progress down the stairs, and she smiled. Jill lived in a place like this during college, and Robin had learned to recognize her footsteps on the stairs.

Strange, how she felt as if she was straddling past and present, but how familiar it felt, being here. She thought about the breakup, but it didn't conjure the pain it used to. Instead, it left a little echo of sadness, a memory whose edges no longer cut. Even the last night with Jill no longer tightened her chest or sat like a weight in her stomach. There was a comfort to it now, because it was a connection they'd once shared, and Robin no longer wanted to run from it or bury it.

Jill's steps sounded on the stairs again, and then she reappeared, carrying two full plastic bags.

Robin took one and set it on the counter next to the stove. Jill put her bag there, as well.

"Smells great." Robin removed the Styrofoam containers while Jill took plates out of the cabinets and set them on the counter.

"Load up." Jill opened the drawer next to Robin's left hip, exposing various silverware. "Here." She handed Robin a spoon, and her fingers brushed Robin's. A fleeting, light touch that Robin felt all the way up her arm. She hurriedly shoved the spoon into the rice and dug a scoop out.

"I got a curry for that." Jill opened one of the other containers and spooned the contents over the rice. "There's a veggie noodle dish in that one. Grab a couple more spoons." She motioned at a container closer to Robin, and Robin dutifully took another spoon out of the drawer and placed servings on both plates.

"What's this?" Robin opened the third container.

"Some kind of spicy chicken. I hope you still eat stuff like that. If old age hasn't stopped you," Jill teased.

"Hell, no. Not yet." Robin put a scoop next to the curry along with more rice. She did the same to Jill's plate. "Okay, that's enough to feed an invading army. Hope you still like leftovers."

"Love them. And I even got Madison into the habit."

"Good. It'll serve her well in college." Robin carried the two plates to the table, and Jill followed with silverware and a roll of paper towels.

"I've got water, Diet Sprite, and a pretty nice Pinot Grigio. If you feel like wine."

"I think I do, actually. Water and wine."

"How very biblical of you." Jill grinned and took two small waters and a bottle of wine out of the fridge. After she set them on the table, she grabbed the wine glasses and corkscrew. Robin opened the bottle and poured as Jill sat next to her, back to the kitchen.

"To art." She raised her glass in a toast. "And to you and your journey. May it become the one you want."

Robin clinked her glass against Jill's. "Thanks. And to you and yours." She sipped. Jill was right. It was a nice wine, with smooth fruity notes that finished with a dry citrus flavor.

"This place reminds me of that one apartment I had in Eugene. Remember that?" Jill dug into her curry.

"Yeah. I was actually thinking that when you went to get the food." The spicy chicken exploded on her tongue like a firecracker, and she reached for her water bottle.

"It occurs to me that this might be really strange."

Robin looked over at her. "What? Seems to me that spicy Thai food is the most normal thing there is."

Jill laughed and reached for her wine glass. "Okay, I get it. Let's stay in the moment."

Robin took another bite of the spicy chicken. This time, she didn't take a water chaser. "I do think that the current moment is pretty good. But I also understand where you're coming from. Yeah, this should be really strange, but it's actually not. I think I'm getting past some old stuff, and I'm glad to be here."

"I am, too. What do you think you're getting past?"

"Fear and anger, I think. There's a time and place for them. I have to figure out what works now, because it doesn't seem that what I did in the past is good for the present." Or the future, she silently finished. "Kind of deep, there." She took a bite of curry. "And this is really good. Can I help pay for it?"

"Next time's on you."

"All right."

Jill tried the chicken and immediately reached for her water. "Damn," she said after she'd had a couple of swallows.

"Right? Spicy Thai. Who knew?" Robin drank some wine and smiled. Jill had already set the stage for another meal. She liked the idea of rebuilding some kind of connection, even if they didn't see each other that much. Jill was in Seattle, after all, on the opposite coast.

"I think I agree with you," Jill said after she'd put her water down.

"About the Thai?" Robin teased.

Jill looked at the ceiling, a give-me-strength expression on her face, but she was smiling.

"Okay. Seriously, now." Robin set her fork down.

"Thank you. As I was saying, it should be strange, but it's not. I've wondered over the years what it would be like to talk to you in the wake of what happened, and then here I am…It's fine, and I still like you as a person."

"Yeah, well, I've done some pretty crappy things, and I've been thinking a lot about them because they're not pretty. They're actually kind of ugly."

"So try not to intentionally do ugly things from here on out." Jill poured more wine into both glasses.

"I feel better when I don't. I'm trying to figure out where I went off the rails. I don't like thinking there might be a lot of my dad in me." Robin finished the curry on her plate and moved on to the vegetables.

"He's a product of circumstances, and he didn't make the choice to change." Jill picked up her wine glass. "What's the deal with this off-the-rails thing?"

Robin shrugged. "I'm not sure when specifically it happened. I know when my mom died I was a train wreck, and then you leaving after that added to my armor and my attempts to protect myself—and I'm not saying that to cast blame," she said, in case Jill wanted to address that. "You had your reasons," Robin continued. "And who knows? Maybe had you stayed, I would've driven you away anyway because I couldn't deal with losing my mom. But sometime after that was when I went in this other direction, and for whatever reasons, it suited me in some ways but not in others. Hence the not-so-pretty stuff. I feel like I have a lot of amends to make, but I don't even know where to start."

Jill didn't respond for a while, and Robin continued to eat. This setting with Jill—far more intimate than a restaurant, though it wasn't even her house—made her comfortable talking to her like they used to.

Often, after one of their sounding board sessions when they first got together, they'd go looking for found objects for art projects and end up making out in whatever private places they could find. Jill had been reserved then, and not effusive in showing physical affection, but she must have felt safe with Robin, because she was always touching her after they'd started dating. A hand on her arm or the back of her neck. Lots of touches, as if she was assuring herself that Robin was real or maybe she'd just repressed that and Robin made her feel comfortable enough to do it. And hugs, Robin thought. Jill really liked hugs after they'd been together a couple of months. Robin must've taken those things for granted, because she missed them now.

"We all do things we're not proud of," Jill finally said. "And all we can do is forgive ourselves so we can do better."

"You make it sound easy."

"Do I? It's not."

Robin heard what might have been old wounds in her voice, and she knew what that was like, carrying those around. But Jill had managed to come to terms with hers. Had forgiving herself allowed her to do that? "Yeah. And that's where I'm kind of hung up."

Jill set her wine down and squeezed Robin's arm, and though it was a gesture meant to commiserate and comfort, it made Robin's skin tingle even through her shirt. "I think you'll be okay," Jill said. "You just have to remember that you can't do everything by yourself. And that requires that you take some of that armor off." She pulled her hand away, and Robin picked up her fork right away so that she wouldn't do anything stupid like try to grab Jill's hand.

"Glad you think so."

"So catch me up on life. Leave out the stuff you want." Jill smiled, and Robin got tangled up in that and in Jill's eyes, and she quickly took the last bite of spicy chicken, which helped burn any wayward ideas out of her head.

"This I can do," Robin said after she took a gulp of water. "But only if you do the same."

"Good trade."

And Robin relaxed a little more and filled in some of the intervening years. She did share a couple of things she'd done that she wasn't proud of, but not necessarily to drive Jill away. Rather, she wanted to be honest about the kind of person she'd let herself become. Somehow, it made her feel as if she was trying to do things differently, because she was owning parts of her past.

"And that about sums it up," Robin said after she'd talked for a few minutes. "I can't say I'm totally thrilled with how I've handled some things, looking back on them.

So I'm trying to figure out how not to be that way. At least not intentionally." She'd opted not to talk about the latest developments at work since those were still in motion and she didn't want to throw everything out on the table.

Jill poured their glasses full again. "I've told you, everybody screws up. It's what you do in the aftermath that can come to define you."

"I might be a little slow on the uptake."

"But you're working on it. And that's more than a lot of people can say." Jill took a sip of wine. "My turn. I'll just put this out there, though I know you're not really into dissecting our past. Regardless, I really screwed up when I left you."

Hearing it should have made her feel vindicated, but instead, Robin only felt sad. "I don't hold that against you anymore. I did, but that's changed."

"Clearly. Because you're sitting here eating Thai food with me."

Robin smiled. "Well, it's really good."

"Smart-ass. Moving along. I screwed up again when I let my family dictate not only that, but my initial career choice. Marrying a man was not the best decision, either."

"Hey, you got an awesome daughter out of it, and you obviously picked a good guy, because he's a good father." Robin almost reached over to squeeze Jill's hand again but fought the urge and kept her hand on the stem of her wine glass.

"True, but I put him and her, actually, through a lot of unnecessary pain. I hadn't accepted myself—who I am—and it took me a while to get to that point."

"And now?"

"I got to that point, though it hasn't been easy."

"Your family?" Robin asked, though she knew what the answer would be.

Jill took a swallow of wine. "They're a large part of it. There are some things about traditional Chinese culture that haven't translated across the diaspora. I was born in this country, and I speak English as a first language. My parents wanted me to be American, because they wanted me to succeed here. What they didn't count on was the whole lesbian thing. They blame America for it because, apparently, there are no Chinese gay people ever." She laughed wryly, but Robin heard the weight Jill still carried in the statement.

"I don't think I grasped that when we were together. You talked about it, but I don't think I really understood how hard that was for you, to navigate being gay with your family."

"I don't think I really grasped it, either. Things got a little better after Madison, since I'd done my womanly duty and produced a child. But when I went lesbian again—not that I had ever left—things got a bit strained."

"Has that changed?"

"A little. I'm not seeing anyone seriously, so my parents don't have to deal with the reality."

Robin finished her water and reached for her wine. "What about your sister?"

"She married a Chinese man, and they have two kids."

"And congrats to her, but is she supportive of you?"

Jill smiled at Robin's editorializing. "More so than my parents, but she tries to keep the peace if I get a little too rebellious." Jill shrugged. "They have been to a couple of my art showings, but for the most part, I think they see me as this odd foreign exchange student they ended up with."

Robin thought about all the things she'd put Frank through, and how he continued to defend her, even in the future she hoped wouldn't come to pass. And here Jill was, without that kind of support, and yet she'd made her way through. "How about Madison?"

"She's wonderful."

"I have no doubt. But does she know about you?"

"The whole lesbian thing?"

"Yeah. That." Robin set her wine glass down.

"Yes. And again, I'm very, very fortunate that Drew is the man he is, because he's been supportive of me even when we were divorcing. He knew deep down, as I did, but both of us opted to be in denial."

"He sounds cool."

"He is. I hope you get to meet him and Madison."

"Same here," Robin said, wondering if saying that created expectations that Jill shouldn't have. "So how are you now, overall?" she asked, to deflect from her previous statement.

"Pretty good." She smiled again. "I've worked on things, and had an epiphany or two along the way." Her voice trailed off, and she moved her hand, swirling the wine in her glass.

A lot of those going around. Robin sipped, noting Jill's choice of word to describe her revelation. Agent Tolson had said the same thing. So had Krampus. Maybe some day she'd broach the Bureau with Jill. She caught herself. That was a long-term kind of thought, and maybe not entirely appropriate.

"Point being, making mistakes is part of the human condition," Jill said. "It's what you do with them that matters."

Robin nodded slowly and stared at her wine glass for a while. "So why am I here?" she finally asked.

"Is this an existential or situational question?"

Robin laughed, because Jill had always been droll. "Both, but for this context, situational."

"I invited you."

"I get that part, but I guess I'm wondering why you did."

"I had a lot of fun the last time we had lunch. And I've enjoyed our conversations since then."

Robin held Jill's gaze. "I'm actually having a really good time."

"Good. Because I am, too. Seemed stupid not to have you over for Thai after you almost fell on me after however many years. I've learned to take advantage of an opportunity, because it may not come around again."

"Opportunity, sugar. Don't leave her on the porch," Magnolia had said, and it sounded as if she were right next to her. Robin glanced to her right and was relieved to see nothing there. She looked at Jill, who was frowning.

"You okay?" Robin asked.

"Thought I heard something."

"What?"

"I'm not sure. Probably somebody on the street." Jill's phone sounded with a little whistle. She pulled it out of her back pocket and swiped her thumb over its screen. "The helpers will be here a little early to work on the setup for the show." Jill set the phone down. "Sorry. I have to cut the afternoon a little short," she said, and she sounded genuinely disappointed.

"Don't be sorry. I had a great time." Robin stood and picked up both their plates.

"So did I. Want to take some leftovers home? I'm not going to eat the rest of this spicy chicken."

"Sure. Put whatever you don't want into one. Save some for yourself, though." Robin helped clean up as Jill bagged up the leftovers.

"Everything good to go?" Robin asked as she moved to the door.

"Yes, though I wish we had more time to talk."

"Same here. But you've got an art gallery to decorate and a daughter to talk to." She put her coat on, draped her scarf around her neck, and grabbed her hat.

"Which doesn't preclude the original statement," Jill said with a smile as she opened the door.

"Good." Robin smiled back and followed her down the steps. Jill put the plastic bottles in a blue recycle bin and then dug a set of keys out of her pocket as they crossed the main room of the gallery to the front entrance.

This side of the street was already cloaked in early evening shadows, and Robin remembered that she had to go back to work tomorrow and deal with whatever crap Frost decided to throw at her. Her stomach clenched a little. Jill set the bag of food carefully on the floor, and Robin moved to the side so Jill could unlock the main entrance.

"Thanks again for lunch," Robin said as she put her hat on and adjusted her scarf.

"You're welcome. I'm really glad you indulged me."

Robin started to button her coat, but Jill's hand on hers made her stop. She looked at Jill, confused, her hand sparking from Jill's touch, and fell right into Jill's gaze. For a few moments, Robin forgot what she'd been doing with her coat in the first place. And then Jill took her hand off Robin's and pulled her into an embrace, one of her arms around Robin's waist inside her coat, the other around Robin's neck. Robin froze, a potent combination of fear and desire cartwheeling through her chest, but she reacted to the feel of Jill's body against hers and returned the embrace.

This is not a good idea. But God, it felt amazing to have Jill in her arms. This close, the notes of Jill's cologne seared themselves into her brain, and even through the layers of clothing between them, the warmth of Jill's body seemed to pour into the hole in the middle of Robin's heart, both soothing and enticing.

"See you Tuesday." Jill released her and picked up the bag of food.

"Yes. Looking forward to it," Robin managed as she finished buttoning her coat and put her gloves on. She took the bag, glad for the extra protection of her glove between her fingers and Jill's, because right now, Robin was a maelstrom of emotions and just one more touch could open a floodgate that she would not be able to control. "Later," she said as Jill held the door open for her, an enigmatic smile playing at the corners of her mouth.

Robin took a few steps, willing herself not to turn around. She lost the battle and threw a glance over her shoulder that Jill captured with the expression in her eyes. She waved, and Robin responded in kind then turned back into the biting wind, hoping it might freeze the heat that stirred at her core. It didn't. Instead, it slowly spread through her limbs, burning openings in her armor. She envisioned herself walking toward the subway, bits of flaming metal lying in her wake, and when she actually did board the train, she sketched the image in the pocket notebook she'd taken to carrying around.

When she got home, evening had succumbed to nightfall. Robin put the food in the fridge, turned the lights out, and sank onto her couch to stare out across the city. How was it even possible to feel something for a woman who had dumped her all those years ago? Had she acquired a masochistic streak in the wake of her dealings (delusions?) with the Bureau?

What she was feeling was probably one-sided and had only flared up because she was in such a weird place emotionally after the past two weeks. Hopefully, Caroline and Jill would spark on Tuesday, and then Robin could rest easy, knowing that she'd ensured a future for Jill that wouldn't be like the one Krampus had showed her. She turned a light on and retrieved her laptop from her bedroom. Though she'd rather be drawing, she needed to start working in earnest on her own future, because from how things were going, it probably didn't include Frost Enterprises.

Chapter 12

ROBIN ARRIVED AT THE OFFICE ready for battle—whatever form it took. She'd spent some time dealing with work email the night before and doing her usual prep for the day's meetings. As far as she was concerned, her demeanor would be business as usual, no matter what the day brought. She took up her new work position on the couch, her feet on the coffee table, and sent her latest set of figures around to the relevant email list for discussion.

Laura entered and shut the door behind her. Robin looked up, and from Laura's expression, something was on her mind.

"What's up?" she asked as Laura approached.

"Mr. Frost wants to see you."

Robin's stomach knotted. "He called?"

She nodded.

"Why didn't he call me directly?"

"I don't know."

Robin set her laptop on the couch next to her. "Can't be good."

Laura shook her head. "Megan hasn't heard anything, but Brady Herrington was in Mr. Frost's office early this morning for over an hour."

Robin sighed. "Hell." Let the games begin. She grabbed her wingtips and put them back on. Since she couldn't wear motorcycle boots at the office, these were her corporate power shoes. Laura stood nearby, holding Robin's blazer.

"Thanks." Robin put her jacket on. "If you don't hear from me in an hour, send a search party."

"Or rescue mission."

"Hopefully it won't come to that." Her stomach continued to roil, though she knew it wasn't obvious from her tone or appearance.

"Good luck." Laura's expression was a mixture of worry and empathy. She followed Robin out of the office and shut the door behind them both. Robin heard it click as she strode down the hall to the elevator. She pressed the up button and waited, trying to calm her nerves. After all, she'd seen this coming. There was no place for a rebel in a corporation like this. Especially not a woman.

The elevator door opened, and she stepped on and pushed the button for Frost's floor. She was the only occupant and it gave her time to steel herself for whatever corporate was about to give her.

"What do you really want, sugar?"

Robin rolled her eyes. "On the elevator, too?" she muttered. She glanced around, but nobody else was with her. Christ. So she had voices in her head, now.

"Only ours, honey," Lady Magnolia said. "Tell the Lady what you really want."

"I don't know. That's the point of this exercise," Robin snapped.

"Sugar, denial ain't a river in Egypt."

"Perhaps we should allow Ms. Preston to find her own way."

Krampus, too? "Why is the Bureau still hanging around? It's past Christmas."

"Consider it charity," Magnolia responded.

"You didn't answer her question," Decker piped in. "What do you really want?"

"Get out of my head, please," Robin snapped. "It's a bad enough neighborhood already."

Lady Magnolia laughed.

"So what's your answer?" Decker pressed, her voice bouncing around Robin's skull.

"I told you, I don't know. I'm still figuring it out." This was the longest elevator ride in history. Why weren't they moving?

"You do know. You just won't admit it," Decker said.

"Fine," Robin shot back. "I want to take this whole corporation and tell Frost to shove it where the sun don't shine."

"We know that, honey. And we also know you're far too savvy to engage that approach. But what *else* do you want?" Magnolia practically purred in her ear.

Robin stifled an urge to press the button to Frost's floor again. She doubted she'd get there any faster. "Maybe I don't want to be corporate anymore. I don't think I ever actually fit here. And why are we doing therapy on an elevator?"

"It's a metaphor," Decker snarked right back. "What goes up must come down. Anything else you'd want after that whole sun don't shine thing?"

"I don't know." But she did. She'd take Jill out to dinner, where they could look out over the water and talk about art and life and whatever else Jill felt like talking about. And then maybe they wouldn't want to talk anymore—Oh, God. As if her life wasn't complicated already.

"That's it, sugar. Just say it."

"What?"

"The dinner part," Decker said.

"Ladies, perhaps Ms. Preston would rather not voice some of her thoughts."

"Thank you, Kr—uh...Mr. Rampus. Maybe I wouldn't." Was this elevator going to the Moon? "Besides, it's a little rude, looking at my thoughts."

"Honey, you're more transparent about some things than an invisible negligee. No use trying to hide it. My mama always said that the person you lie to most is yourself."

"All right. Fine. I might...want to take Jill to dinner. There. Happy now? And it's really complicated, and I don't want to talk about it."

"Feels good, doesn't it, to acknowledge that?" Decker said as the elevator doors slid open, and Robin waited for somebody to say something else, but her head held only the usual cacophony of her own thoughts. Dinner with Jill. Seriously?

She stepped off and walked down the corridor to Frost's office, envisioning herself as a gladiator about to step into an arena. That would make a cool drawing, she thought as she approached Megan's work area.

"Mr. Frost is expecting you, Ms. Preston," Megan said as Robin approached. "Go right in."

Robin gave her a nod and a smile and opened the door into Frost's domain, an office twice the size of hers, with even plusher carpet and a more spectacular view. Frost also kept a bar in the corner. She had no doubt lots of decisions were made and deals done over the liquor therein. Most likely very expensive top-shelf brands.

"Mr. Frost," Robin said as she closed the door behind her. "My assistant informed me that you wanted to see me."

He looked up from his desk, and it was strange to see him there, because Robin never thought of him as actually working at his desk. She'd never seen him do it, the few times she'd been to his office. Rather, he ordered and directed, while pacing near the windows or from the plush black leather couch near the bar.

"Have a seat, Preston," he said as he looked back at the papers on his desk. Robin recognized it as the power trip it was and opted not to let it bother her. She chose the middle chair of the three facing Frost's desk and got comfortable, as if she didn't have a care in the world.

"Preston, I've been thinking." Frost took his glasses off and leaned back. She didn't respond and instead made herself appear even more comfortable and at ease.

"Frost Enterprises, as you know, has a set mission and a certain corporate culture," he continued, and it sounded rehearsed. When she didn't respond, he shifted a little, and Robin hoped he felt uncomfortable. "I recently spoke with several board members, and we think someone of your outlook and talents would be a better fit elsewhere."

There it was. Robin refused to respond as he probably expected her to. She raised an eyebrow and maintained her relaxed position. "I see," she said. "And what precisely does that mean?" *Besides me shoving this tower right up your corporate butt?* But that wouldn't accomplish much in terms of financial leverage, and she definitely wouldn't have the moral high ground.

He shifted again, and Robin read surprise and discomfort in his expression. "We'd like to transfer you to one of our start-ups in China."

Robin took a few moments to process that. She'd expected he might do a transfer, but not halfway around the world.

"Guangzhou," he said. "We've been working on getting a better base there, and we need someone who can hit the ground running." His enthusiasm sounded forced. "We'd increase your pay, and ensure housing and transportation, of course."

"Doing what, exactly?"

"Consulting," he said, and she gave him props for his political vagueness. Corporate-speak for "warehoused figurehead."

Robin had been to that facility. It was where Frost had sent a couple of his other "problem children." Most resigned within a year. "And if I prefer to stay here and continue in my current capacity?" Robin kept her voice and demeanor calm.

Frost leaned back again, but if he was trying to appear relaxed, it didn't work. Instead, he looked like a kid who'd been busted telling a huge lie to his parents. "We've decided to close your position and do some internal reorganization."

So her choices were China or layoff.

"We think Frost—and you—would be best served in China," he hastily added. "Especially given your talents and—" He stopped, as if searching for the best word. "Outlook."

They were pushing her out. Leaving was thus on her, since they could point to this "fabulous" opportunity they were offering her. "You said consulting. Does that mean I would be in charge of Guangzhou? Last I heard, there were problems with the current administration."

That took him aback. He glanced away, then back at her. "We could probably arrange a supervisory position of some sort."

"So I'd be supervising the current leadership? And I'd be the direct report?"

Again, Frost glanced away. Maybe he hadn't considered the possibility that she might take him up on this. Not that she would. But she didn't want to show her hand.

"I'll look into that."

"When will you know?" Robin liked pushing him a little. It suited her new perspective and current mood.

"The end of the week." His expression matched the sourness in his tone, audible even under the gravel that marred it.

"That gives me time to give some more thought to your offer." Robin smiled, but it wasn't genuine. She didn't care.

"I'll let you know what I hear." This conversation hadn't gone the way he'd wanted. Robin could hear it in his voice and see it in the way he kept shifting his weight in his chair. Relaxed people didn't do that.

She stood, sensing dismissal behind his words. "Thank you. I'll expect to hear from you at the end of the week, if not sooner." She threw the last dig in as she left his office. Megan looked up at her, and Robin shrugged and smiled in that conspiratorial way employees had when dealing with the boss.

Fortunately, the elevator opened almost immediately when she pressed the button and once again, she was alone when the doors closed. "Hello?" she said. No response. She exhaled, relieved, and then elation made her want to jump up and down, but she wasn't sure why. The CEO of Frost Enterprises had pretty much ensured her career with the company was at an end, but all she could think was "what's next?" She toyed with the ring on her pinkie as the elevator released her.

Laura looked up from her desk as Robin approached.

"Give me a few minutes." Robin smiled and entered her office before Laura could respond. Her business cell lay on the couch next to her laptop, and she picked it up and scrolled through her contacts until she came to the one she wanted and pressed it.

"Pruitt and Associates. How may I help you?" came the answer. Crisp, professional, bland. Robin envisioned the woman on the other end in a dark skirt suit, hair arranged perfectly. She had the kind of neutral voice that could have been on any radio station in the country.

"Hi, there. This is Robin Preston at Frost Enterprises. I'm wondering if Mr. Pruitt is available for a brief conversation."

Pause. "I'm sorry, Ms. Preston, but he's in a meeting. I'll be glad to leave him a message."

"I'd appreciate that, Ms.—" she stopped so the other woman could fill in her name.

"Brewster. Your message?"

"Please tell Mr. Pruitt that I may have solved his personal assistant problem. He can call me at this number for more details." She provided her business cell and Ms. Brewster recited it back to her. "Yes, that's it. Thank you."

Ms. Brewster provided a crisp, professional, and very bland signoff. Robin hung up and remained standing, tapping her phone against her chin. Her personal cell sat on the coffee table, and she exchanged her business cell for it. A text message from Jill made her heart speed up a little, though it shouldn't have. None of the feelings that had been coming up for Jill should be happening. Robin opened the message. Jill had sent a photo of the gallery wall, no longer blank. Four of her mixed media pieces hung on it. *Teaser*, she'd written. *You'll have to wait 'til tomorrow to see more.*

Robin grinned. *You are a total tease*, she texted back. *Looking forward to the show. Thanks again for lunch.* She hit send, and it felt dangerous. It was on the edge of flirtatious, and that could bring trouble. No, it *would* bring trouble. Robin texted Caroline to make sure she was still coming to the opening. Because now more than ever, Robin needed a boundary between her and Jill. Especially since she'd admitted aloud that she wanted to take Jill to dinner. Which meant that Robin would gladly do other intimate things with Jill.

"You should ask her out," Decker said.

"It does not endear you to me when you poke through my personal thoughts," Robin said as she looked up. Decker was leaning against her desk, wearing jeans, penny loafers, and a button-down blue Oxford shirt.

"And here I thought we were finally making progress in our relationship." Decker pointed at Robin's cell. "You've already had a couple of lunches with Chen. Why not go the next meal up?"

"Are you trying to make me cause a future for her that really sucks?"

"Get down off the cross, honey. Someone needs the wood."

Robin started and turned her head. Magnolia was seated on the arm of the sofa, dressed in a dark blue form-fitting gown and what looked like a sapphire necklace. She wore a matching ring on her right hand, and it sparkled against the white of her glove. Her hair was done up like it had been the first time Robin had met her.

"Sugar, if you're attracted to someone, you try to spend time with them. And the Lady is nothing if not versed in the laws of attraction." She gave Robin a dazzling smile.

"But the future I saw—"

"Is one of infinite possibilities," Magnolia said. "And we can have a hand in each, according to the decisions we make. It's all about what's in here, sweetie." Magnolia placed her hand in a graceful motion over her heart. "Examine your intentions." She faded.

"Wait," Robin said, but Magnolia was gone. So was Decker. When, exactly, had this happened, that she'd allowed herself an attraction to her past? Or rather, a recognition of it? She'd been head over heels in love with Jill when they were together. The kind of love that sometimes drives the young to passionate declarations of forever and makes them hold on maybe a little too desperately because they haven't discovered the wisdom that age brings. She remembered how that felt with Jill back then. She wasn't sure what head over heels was like at this age, but she did know what she was feeling for Jill was not just attraction. It was connection and comfort and, if she was being honest with herself, exciting and deep and delicious.

Robin was way past her youth, shaped by a cynicism born of grief and loss. Since Jill, there'd only been one other woman who came close to getting past her barriers but she'd left a few years back. Robin realized now that she'd probably helped drive her away. Nobody but Jill had ever gotten past her armor, which Robin understood now that she had already been forging in college. Jill had sensed that. She'd seen in Robin not the gothy, punky persona she presented but the fragile artist who craved a sense of security and enough trust to be young rather than the bearer of responsibilities way beyond her years. Little wonder that Jill felt so familiar to her now.

Her phone signaled another text message—Caroline, with an affirmative. It should have made her feel better. It didn't. Why was the Bureau encouraging a hook-up with Jill? Was it some kind of test? She turned the sound of her phone off, set it on the coffee table, and opened her office door. Laura looked up from her monitor.

"Got a minute?" Robin asked.

Without a word, Laura followed her into her office. Robin shut the door behind them and gave her the rundown of her meeting with Frost. "I've probably got this week," she finished. "Maybe a couple days more, but that's doubtful. I'm pretty sure I pissed him off even more today." She moved to her conference table and sat down.

Laura took a chair next to her, and smiled, though Robin saw sadness in her eyes.

"Don't worry. I'm working on an angle for you. I'm not going to leave you alone in the shark tank."

"A month ago I wouldn't have believed that you'd try to help me," Laura said. "Actually, you wouldn't even be talking to me about this."

"You're right." Robin leaned back and stretched her legs out. "So, about the shark tank."

"Don't worry about me. I have resources, too."

Robin grinned. "So with both of us working on it, it'll happen."

"What about you?"

"I have a few resources my own self."

"But where will you go?"

"I don't really know. I'm not quite sure what I want to do next." It was scary, not having a plan. But also liberating. She had a little bit of time to decide, and she'd been working her networks already, so something was bound to shake out, even if it was a contract position or something she could do for a year or two. She could use that time to think a bit more about where she might want to go.

"A month ago, I wouldn't have told you this—"

"Because I was a major jerk," Robin finished for her. She sat up straight.

Laura laughed. "Well, yes. But since you seem to be on the road to recovery, I'll let you know that you have a really excellent head for business. You're a natural leader and when you act like yourself—like you are now—people really respond to you. That's the problem with a lot of corporate leadership. Arrogance. It doesn't instill loyalty or respect. People don't want to work for people like that."

"So how come you've stayed this long?"

"It hasn't even been eighteen months."

"I have an idea as to how big a jerk I can be."

"I do, too. But I saw something underneath it, and I know how hard it is for women to make it as far as you did in this world. I admire that about you, and I could tell you knew what you were doing. After eighteen months, I'm right. You do know. And it scares Frost. That's what happens in places like this. Somebody who's secure would let you do what you do best and offer you opportunities to branch the company out. But he's not. And you have to be careful in environments like this. Insecurity can be contagious."

Robin studied the rings she'd taken to wearing. "Wise words. And would you like something to drink? I've got some water and iced tea in the fridge." She gestured at the mini-fridge next to her couch.

"I've got something at my desk." Laura stood. "But thanks. Besides, you have a meeting in twenty minutes."

Robin groaned, and Laura laughed as she left. After she'd shut the door, Robin got up and went to her couch. She sat down and checked her personal cell. Another text message from Jill, and Robin tried to ignore the giddiness that ran up her spine, but she couldn't entirely.

> *Thank YOU for spending time with me yesterday.*
> *And you have no idea how much of a tease I've*
> *become.*

She'd included a winking emoji, and Robin stared at the message, then reread it a few more times. Heat spread through her chest, then her thighs. Was Jill flirting with her? It sure felt like it. And oh, God it felt good. Better than good. Shit.

Hmm. I think I can guess, she texted back. Oh, Jesus. She was flirting back. And enjoying it. More than enjoying it.

This was probably bad. And maybe inappropriate. She read Jill's previous text again. Wasn't it? It was just some harmless flirting with an ex. Who Robin had been totally in love with even after Jill dumped her. Oh, God.

Her phone lit up with another text from Jill. *We'll see. Back to more art. Looking forward to tomorrow.*

Same here. And I have yet another meeting. Later. Robin hit send and sank onto her couch. Could she still close this box? Pandora hadn't been able to. She leaned back and sighed. Because it was probably not a good idea to get hung up on an ex.

Robin closed her eyes and saw Jill that night after Lady Magnolia had dropped her onto the sidewalk right next to her. So different than she'd been in college, but also so much more comfortable with herself. Maybe Robin had never lost her feelings for Jill.

She set her phone on the arm of the couch and reached for her laptop. Weird. The screensaver hadn't turned on, instead it displayed a web page Robin didn't remember loading. As she studied it, she knew for sure she hadn't brought the site up, because she would have remembered if she had. The page advertised a job opening as the director of an arts foundation in Seattle. What the hell? Robin stared at it. Was she losing her memory? Or her mind? Because that should probably have happened already, and she should be waking up soon in a drab room with an iron-frame bed and a medical tag on her wrist. And that hadn't happened. Which meant that the past two weeks were for real, and there were things in the world that she didn't understand.

"Or it *is* the *Matrix*," she muttered as she read the job description. It was a really good fit for her. The foundation wanted someone with experience in management, business, and an eye for attracting new donors and developing funding partnerships. The application deadline was coming up in the next few days. Not a problem. She'd already updated her résumé, so all she needed was a cover letter, and she was pretty good at those.

A chime sounded on her business phone, alerting her to an appointment. The meeting. Robin grabbed her tablet, phone, and scratch pad and stepped out of her office and paused at Laura's desk.

"Did anybody go into my office while I was with Frost this morning?"

Laura looked up at her, puzzled. "No. I was here the whole time. Why?"

"No reason." She adjusted the items she carried and walked toward the other side of the building, nodding and smiling at various people as she passed them. This area outside her office was a typical open space like the lobby of a hotel, tastefully furnished and with a coffee station along the far wall. Robin didn't like the coffee, so she usually bought her own downstairs. As she passed it, she slowed down. A familiar figure was stirring her coffee with one of the provided plastic stir sticks. Robin stopped, staring.

"Seattle's more your speed, don't you think?" Decker gave her a lopsided smile and raised the Styrofoam coffee cup to her lips. Robin approached, making sure nobody was paying attention to her.

"Jill's in Seattle," Robin said, keeping her voice low. She got herself a cup of coffee, because if nobody else could see Decker, Robin didn't want people to wonder what she was doing, standing over here chatting to the air.

"That's totally a perk."

"What—" she started to say when Hodges interrupted her.

"Hey, thanks for the figures you sent out this morning. Appreciate it."

She jerked her attention to him. "Sure. No problem." She turned back to Decker, but she was gone, again.

"You going to the meeting?" he asked as he fixed himself a cup of coffee.

"Wouldn't miss it," she said dryly. Robin stood for a few moments, studying all the people she saw moving around or standing and talking. No Decker. Not that Robin was surprised.

Please don't let this mean I'm nuts. On the other hand, if this was what going nuts was like, it wasn't so bad. Maybe she was like that character in that Russell Crowe movie, *A Beautiful Mind*. The one where he kept seeing and interacting with people who weren't there.

"You okay?"

Robin glanced at Hodges and said, "Yeah. Thought I saw someone I needed to talk to." Should she go to a doctor and get evaluated? There had to be a test for this sort of thing. But if she were going crazy, why was all the stuff currently happening to her kind of good? Even her attraction to Jill wasn't a bad thing. It felt good, though Robin still wasn't sure what to do with that. Was she even ready to get involved with someone who had the potential for real emotional engagement? Plus, she had all these other things going on, and she had to think about what to do in terms of employment, and that included the art foundation.

Which was in Seattle.

Close to Jill.

Robin entered the conference room with Hodges and took a seat at the end of the table. Brady wasn't normally in this meeting, which was some relief, but as she settled into her chair and arranged her materials in front of her, she realized that she wouldn't have cared if he was. Now she had to use her epiphanies for good, and that was exactly what she intended to do. But right now, she had to get through this meeting. She pulled her scratchpad close and started drawing.

Decker entered Agent Tolson's office. Usually the case manager was at her desk, going through files or checking the progress of various field agents. Right now, however, she stood staring out the window at the city.

"Ma'am," Decker said, though she knew Tolson was well aware of her presence.

"And how is Ms. Preston?" Tolson asked without turning from the window. She always dressed just shy of 1940s Hollywood glamorous. Her suits were cut in such a way to keep her on the professional side, but Decker could totally picture her as a character in a Cary Grant movie. Decker herself preferred a more casual style, but she appreciated that Tolson could pull the look off.

"Busy. Pretty sure she'll be sending a résumé out soon. Probably tonight."

Tolson turned from the window and regarded Decker the way she always did—a mixture of amusement and patience in her eyes. "Excellent. This remains under special ops, you understand."

"Yes, ma'am." No formal reports, no recordings, though Tolson sometimes requested a live feed.

"It's why I put you, Magnolia, and Mr. Rampus on this assignment."

"I figured." Decker smiled. Tolson sometimes picked cases for personal reasons. Clearly, this was one of them. The Bureau was strict with its epiphany schedules—Christmas only—but sometimes the case managers would give a little more juice to the epiphanies after the fact, if they felt the subject warranted it. Decker could count on one hand the number of times Tolson had special op'ed epiphanies after Christmas, but when she did, it was usually to ensure a particular outcome.

"Sometimes discordant notes need to be tuned," Tolson said, as if she'd read Decker's mind. "You understand, of course, that it is imperative that we keep Ms. Chen and Ms. Preston on their merging paths."

"Yes, ma'am. But I think after Christmas Future, Preston's not that amped about starting anything up with Chen."

"We're working on convincing her otherwise."

Decker nodded, hoping that Preston got it together. Decker kind of liked her, even though she'd been sort of snotty. Underneath that, Preston was probably fun to hang out with. Decker figured that whatever she sensed in Preston, Tolson did, too, or she wouldn't have launched a special op. "Anything else?"

"Not at the moment. Thank you." Tolson smiled, and it lit her features up. Totally a forties movie star look.

Decker nodded and moved to the door.

"Oh, I did think that was a nice touch with the coffee today," Tolson added.

Decker stopped at the door. "Preston seems to be someone who needs a few reminders now and again. And I think she might consider sightings a support system, in a strange way."

"I agree." Tolson returned to staring out the window, and not for the first time, Decker wondered who she'd been before she joined the Bureau. "Thank you again," Tolson said.

Decker closed the door quietly behind her.

Chapter 13

"What new and exciting things do I have to worry about today?" Robin paused at Laura's desk and handed her a large cup of coffee from the café across the street, one of her fave coffee stops.

Laura raised her eyebrows in surprise, but she smiled, too. "No calls from Mr. Frost."

"Thank God."

"No meetings."

"The Lord is indeed smiling upon us."

Laura laughed.

"Oh, here." Robin pulled a sticky note out of her pocket with a phone number on it. She placed it next to Laura's keyboard.

"And whose phone number is this?"

"Daniel S. Pruitt, senior board member of Frost Enterprises."

Laura looked at it again, then up at Robin, clearly confused.

"He's in need of a really good personal assistant, and he would, and I quote, 'very much like to formally meet you and chat with you a bit.' I told him he could schedule you any time today or after tomorrow—holiday, after all—to do just that. So when you call, Ms. Brewster will probably answer. She's normally the administrative overseer for Pruitt's main office, but she's handling possible hires for him, too. Tell her who you are, and she'll get that set up."

Laura's smile widened. "Thank you. But what did you tell him about why I might be interested in such a position? Won't he wonder why you're giving up such a wonderful assistant?"

Robin smiled. "Because he knows that Frost wants to close my position. There's no way Frost made that decision without consulting the board. Pruitt probably thinks I'll take the China transfer, and that I can't take you with me. But that's not something he'll discuss with me while it's a decision still in the making. So don't thank me yet. Wait until he offers you a job. And don't let him lowball you."

Laura laughed. "I can handle it," she said in a way that told Robin that, yes, she definitely could.

"Great. Just let me know when he schedules you for the chat so I don't freak out because you're not here." Robin moved toward her office door but turned back to Laura before she went in. "Oh, and if you don't have anything on your plate this afternoon besides babysitting me, go ahead and leave. It's New Year's Eve, after all."

"Can I say that I really like this version of you?"

"Yes. And I expect that you won't forget me when you move on to greater things."

"Not a chance." Laura's desk phone range and Robin left her to it, enjoying how it felt to not be a dick. She was learning that it didn't make her vulnerable. Rather, it made her feel stronger, somehow, and more grounded.

She settled herself onto her couch, shoes off, feet up, laptop propped on her knees, and went through emails. The arts foundation in Seattle had sent her a benign reply thanking her for submitting her materials for consideration for the job of director. Robin had sent them in last night, after she wrote a kickass cover letter. She'd been inspired, dancing around her apartment to New Order between paragraphs, fueled by a sense of adventure she hadn't felt in years.

Decker had probably left that web page on her computer. She hoped so, because thinking that she didn't remember doing it was a little scary. Instead, she entertained the idea that the Bureau was going guardian angel with her. It did still creep her out a bit—she still couldn't completely scrub the image of Krampus out of her head—but going crazy wasn't supposed to be like this, she was pretty sure, so she'd just keep traveling this epiphany road, see where it led.

Robin finished answering emails then started looking for a place to live in Seattle, but caught herself when she opened the first website. She was getting ahead of herself. And why the hell did she think Seattle was a good idea? Jill was there, after all. And in the bad future, Robin had ended up in that city. But why had Magnolia said what she had today? And why had Decker told her to ask Jill out and then told her that Jill being in Seattle was a perk of the job posting?

Was the Bureau messing with her? Maybe this whole thing was a test, to see what she'd do. She frowned. That didn't make sense. The Bureau was supposed to help you find your better self. Why would it deliberately put stuff in your way like this that you weren't supposed to do? Robin sipped her coffee, thinking.

God, she wanted to go home. Seattle would always be that to her. And it was a big city, so she probably wouldn't run into Jill. Much. All these revelations were making her sentimental. She toyed with one of her earrings and thought about how it felt as if she'd been entombed in a massive ice floe for several years and it was finally thawing all around her. Her thoughts wandered to Jill again and the evening's event. Fortunately, Jill would be really busy tonight, and that would definitely help Robin maintain boundaries.

Finishing a couple of work projects would help keep her mind off things she probably shouldn't be thinking. With an effort, Robin picked up her business cell. She still worked for Frost, after all, and she had calls to make. Sighing, she settled herself more comfortably on the couch.

Nine o'clock rolled around, and Robin texted Caroline before she bundled up for the trip to the gallery, a little nervous because Caroline hadn't checked in. Caroline could be a little flaky—but tonight, it irritated Robin. She needed a clear boundary between her and Jill, and Caroline was meant to serve as that, though she didn't know it. Robin didn't want to bias the outcome of their meeting by telling either woman why she'd really invited Caroline.

She grabbed her keys and left her apartment. The opening was slated to start at nine, but Robin didn't want to arrive too early because that would mean fewer people, and less of a buffer between her and Jill. Since lunch on Sunday, Robin had been dealing with a slow, delicious burn when it came to her thoughts of Jill. Normally she enjoyed an attraction, and normally she'd act on it. But she was trying to change her approach to lots of things, and that meant Robin had made herself vulnerable to sticky things such as feelings and emotional attachments. And this heat she carried for Jill was clearly a gateway drug to the future she'd seen with Krampus.

So why the hell was she going to this event? And why the hell did it feel so good, thinking about seeing Jill? No matter how much she tried to fight it, the connection between them remained, and there was something poetic about being with her on New Year's Eve.

She remained standing on the subway, though there were seats available. Most people were in a festive mood and probably on their way to parties somewhere. One guy in the corner had his headphones blaring so loud that Robin could have danced to the song. Times Square would be emptying after midnight, and Robin dreaded the ride home. Maybe she'd get a cab after the event. Or maybe she'd leave early, which was probably the best course of action.

The train lurched, and she held on to the metal bar, staring down at her black leather motorcycle boots, so much a part of her years ago. Why Robin had kept them, she wasn't sure, but she was glad she did. They still fit, even with thick socks. Old, forgiving friends. She wore a pair of faded jeans and a casual button-down black shirt. She'd put a dark purple sateen vest on over her shirt and Robin felt more like herself than she had in—well, in a while.

The closer she got to her stop, the more revelers packed the train, until she was pressed against the doors. A couple of half-drunk young guys wearing goofy red glitter top hats talked about a party nearby and bumped into her. Repeatedly. She exhaled with relief when the doors opened at her stop, and she tripped her way onto the platform, free of the train's pungent combination of winter sweat and alcohol. It had been a while since she'd been out on New Year's Eve. Last year she'd spent it at a small gathering of friends, and the year before that she stayed home. The year before that—was she working? Robin walked up the steps to the cold night air. Yes, she'd been working. Christ.

Once at street level, she moved out of the way of pedestrian traffic and dug into her back pocket for her phone. Caroline had texted about twenty minutes ago, saying she'd be late. At least she was on her way, but Robin was ambivalent about her attendance, torn between the future she'd seen and her own feelings for Jill, coupled with what Magnolia and Decker had said earlier. Robin started walking the five blocks to the gallery, actually enjoying the expectant, celebratory mood of passersby.

Her phone buzzed in her pocket, and she checked it. Caroline again, saying she'd be later than she originally thought. Robin took her glove off and texted back, asking her when. She held her phone in her ungloved hand and shoved both into her pocket. The wind between the buildings blew raw across the exposed skin of her cheeks and nose, and she hunched deeper into her scarf and coat collar.

A few minutes later she arrived at the gallery. A small group of people stood outside, smoking and talking. Robin's phone buzzed in her hand, and she stopped upwind before she entered the gallery to check it. Caroline again. She wouldn't make it after all and she was sorry.

Robin frowned. The Bureau at work? Or really just a coincidence? One of the women who was smoking looked over at her, and Robin forced a smile. She texted a quick acknowledgement back, trying not to seem pissed.

Caroline responded seconds later. Her ex had some kind of emergency and needed Caroline to watch her kid. Robin replied with hopes that things would be okay, and she understood. Hell, she might actually have been relieved, because she'd feel obligated to hang out with Caroline all night.

The gallery was already busy, which meant Jill would be busy, too. Robin should just relax and see how things went. For all she knew, somebody was here who Jill was already interested in. Or somebody else would take an interest in her. So just go in and enjoy yourself, Robin remonstrated herself. She liked art crowds, and she'd had a good time at the last event. And she could always leave early, which was probably the best idea, since she wasn't really sure what she was doing in terms of Jill.

A sleek white limo drove slowly past on the street, and Robin froze. No. Not another ride with Lady Magnolia. Not tonight. The car kept going, and she relaxed. The Bureau should probably implement some kind of program to help people get past their damn visits. White limos would forever make her think of Lady Magnolia. Another white limo cruised slowly past, but Robin couldn't see through the tinted windows no matter how many streetlights were burning. She relaxed. There were lots of limos out tonight. New Year's Eve, after all. She took her other glove off and shoved it into her coat pocket with the first and glanced through the windows into the gallery's interior.

At least forty people milled around, some looking at Jill's pieces, others chatting. A guy in a white tuxedo shirt and bowtie was walking around with a tray of wine. Robin didn't see Jill right away, which was probably good. God, she was really nervous about seeing her tonight, and it was like the first time she'd ever asked Jill out, this jittery anticipation, wondering if Jill liked her *that* way—Christ, she wasn't twenty-one anymore, and Jill was an ex with a future riding on decisions that happened here and now.

Robin entered the gallery with a couple of the people who had been smoking. She took her hat off and added it to her coat pocket, then ran her hand through her hair before she took her coat off. The din of voices and laughter filled the room, but underneath she heard some kind of electronic chill music, and she wondered if that was Jill's choice.

The wall to her left featured the four large mixed media pieces Jill had texted to her, but she'd added a few smaller ones between them. The lighting in here definitely made her art stand out. Jill apparently also did art in picture boxes—found objects and photographs in wooden boxes with glass fronts.

Robin moved to that wall first and studied the first of these, about two feet square. Jill had painted the background of this piece, a nearly translucent Chinese pagoda, and over that she'd arranged clippings from Chinese- and English-language newspapers from Seattle along with black-and-white photos of a small Asian girl, dressed in American clothing. Robin leaned in a little closer and realized the photos were of Jill as a child. At the bottom of the piece was a pair of chopsticks with a fork lying haphazardly across one of them, as if pinning it to the bottom of the picture box.

"It speaks to the artist's dual ethnic identities," said a stuffy male voice behind her.

Robin looked at him, a squat, balding guy wearing round glasses and a light brown suit. "So I gathered," she said, more amused at his pronouncement than annoyed. She took a glass of white wine off the tray of a passing server and sipped. Better than the stuff at the last opening. "And I'm pretty sure she has a hell of a lot more identities than just two," Robin added with a smile.

The man sniffed and moved away. Robin watched him as he tried to impress another woman checking out one of Jill's large mass media pieces, and clearly, he got shot down again. She smiled and caught sight of Jill a few yards away talking to a tall woman dressed in black wool trousers and a matching blazer, her long dark hair pulled into a bun, two long ivory hairpins holding it in place. Attractive.

But then the woman moved, revealing more of Jill. Oh, God. Sparks skittered down Robin's spine and heat rolled through her chest and thighs. Jill wore a form-fitting red evening dress that left her shoulders and the very top of her cleavage exposed, along with part of a tattoo across the top of her right shoulder. A simple silver chain hung around her neck, but she'd kept the studs and gems in the multiple piercings in her right ear, and she'd spiked her hair up like the night they'd first run into each other. The incongruity of the classic, almost vampish lines of Jill's dress and the art girl hair, piercings, and tattoo made Robin's heartbeat speed up.

Jill was saying something animated, and then she suddenly looked over toward Robin, as if she sensed someone was watching her. She held Robin's gaze for a beat, and a strange, deep longing pulsed at Robin's core and in her chest, and then Jill smiled. She said something to the woman, made a gesture as though she was asking her to wait a moment, and then Jill moved toward Robin, who was transfixed by this vision, this exuberant, grounded woman whose smile set all manner of Robin's parts ablaze.

"Hi," Jill said. "I'm so glad to see you."

"Likewise. And you look absolutely stunning," Robin said, relieved that she sounded calm. Hopefully charming.

Jill touched the top button of Robin's vest. "Why, thank you. I like this look on you much more than corporate. Very nice."

"Oh?" Robin's gaze remained locked on Jill's, and it seemed that the two of them were the only people in the room, the only two people in the entire city.

"Definitely. In Chinese symbolism, purple represents spiritual awareness, and physical and mental healing." Jill let go of the button.

"Huh. Appropriate. And black?"

"Several meanings, one of which is delving into the depths of something. Other meanings are adaptability, spontaneity, and power. Emotional protection, too."

"But I'm trying to get rid of my armor."

"You don't need it for emotional protection. Can I take your coat? I'll put it somewhere safe." She smiled again, and Robin fought the urge to kiss her as sound and light returned to the moment. Christmas Future, she reminded herself, but it was much harder to convince herself that taking a vow of chastity with regard to Jill was the best way to go.

"Are you sure? This is your grand soiree, and I don't mind carrying it around. Or I'll just take it to the coat check." She figured there was one in the back, since nobody else in here was wearing or carrying winter wear.

Jill rolled her eyes and took Robin's coat and scarf as she leaned in and gave her a quick hug. As brief as the contact was, she left Robin on the verge of trembling. Robin clenched her teeth as Jill's cologne triggered another round of heat. She transferred her wine to her left hand.

"Come on," Jill said. "I want to introduce you around. We'll start right over here," she said as she led Robin toward the tall woman she'd been speaking with earlier. "Danielle," Jill said, "I'd like you to meet an old friend of mine, Robin Preston. Robin, this is Danielle Paredes. Be right back." She walked away, carrying Robin's coat, and Robin got a look at the skin of Jill's upper back and more of the tattoo, partially blocked by the top of Jill's dress. A stylized Chinese dragon across her shoulder blade, exploding with primary colors. Robin couldn't see its head, hidden by Jill's dress, and the idea of seeing the rest of it added to her very clear and very strong attraction. Somehow, she managed to smoothly redirect her attention to Danielle.

"Hi. Pleased to meet you." Robin offered her free hand, and Danielle shook it. Not too hard, not too soft. Neutral.

"Preston," Danielle said in a warm, well-modulated voice. "Your name sounds familiar. How do you know Jill?"

"We were both doing art at the University of Oregon back in the day."

"Are you still involved?"

"I was, but switched to business and ended up doing a master's in that. I've recently been engaging with it again."

Danielle sipped from her own wine glass. "Are you trained in a particular medium?"

"Photography, pastels, oils, charcoal, watercolors, mixed media. Jill and I have a history of found object hunting."

Danielle laughed, and Robin decided she sort of liked her, because the laugh was genuine. "That sounds like Jill.

She loves going on those. Maybe that's why your name is familiar. She's talked about someone she went to college with who got her started in that activity. Was that you?"

Robin remembered the first time they'd gone on a hunt, in an abandoned farmhouse near the Oregon coast. She'd finally persuaded Jill to come along. Robin smiled. "Yeah, it was."

"So you haven't seen her in a while?"

"No. We lost touch after college but recently ran into each other and reconnected." Robin took another drink of wine, realizing that might sound a little too intimate, but she liked how it sounded.

Danielle didn't appear to take it that way, though. "That's nice to hear. She's a fabulous artist and an all-around wonderful human being. Our foundation has provided grants for her work, and we're always so pleased to do it."

"I'm glad you have. What foundation?"

"North by Northwest, in Seattle."

Robin stared. "Wait. Are you D.L. Paredes, then? On the North by Northwest Board?"

Danielle smiled, surprise in her eyes. "That would be me. Are you familiar with us?"

"Not as much as I would like to be." Robin gave her one of her most winning smiles. "I applied for the directorship."

Both of Danielle's eyebrows raised, and her smile broadened. "*That's* it. The reason your name is so familiar. I just read your materials this morning. Jacob—Burns, the current vice-president—forwarded them as soon as he got them."

"Well, I don't want to make this awkward for you. I'm sure there are plenty of applicants you're considering. We can discuss something else." Robin handed her now empty glass of wine to a young woman carrying a tray.

Danielle cocked her head, a thoughtful expression in her eyes, as if she was assessing Robin with a different perspective. "Jacob is very selective about résumés he forwards to me." She paused. Then, "Tell me more about your own art."

"I have a particular taste for pastels and charcoal. Pen and ink, too. But I don't have anything that's public. I enjoy doing art, but I also enjoy being around it and thinking about ways to support it. One of the projects I did while working on my master's was to develop a funding plan for an art cooperative. It worked pretty well. I have a knack for things like that."

"I can tell." Danielle took another sip of wine.

Robin wasn't sure what she meant by that, and before she could say anything more, Jill returned.

"Sorry for the delay. I was accosted," Jill said with extra dramatic flair.

"Hopefully in a good way." Robin raised an eyebrow and sipped her wine, trying to look innocent. Danielle smiled.

"If only. Can I borrow Robin for a bit?"

Danielle nodded, still smiling. "Certainly. A pleasure to meet you," she said to Robin. "If things don't get too busy in here, I'd love to chat more."

"Great. Take care."

Danielle moved away, and a server approached. "Wine?"

Both Jill and Robin took glasses.

"Danielle is on the board of one of my funders," Jill said as she started toward another group of people.

"So she said. Maybe I should pick your brain about how you go about getting grants and funds and all of that."

"Improving your business acumen?"

"Branching out." Robin smiled and took another quick swallow of wine because Jill's shoulders were proving a major distraction. She'd better go easy on the wine, she thought as Jill introduced her to a few more people. Robin had seen a table filled with food toward the back, and once she was done with this group of people, she'd head over there.

Jill left Robin to chat with a woman named Tasha or something like that, with maroon streaks in her blond hair. She said she'd just finished art school and was working with a writer friend on a graphic novel. They were joined by two young men holding hands, who introduced themselves as Matt and Derrick.

"Robin," she introduced herself.

"Girl," Matt said to Tasha. He leaned close to her, conspiratorial. "I have it on good authority that she's single," he stage-whispered.

Tasha looked hopeful, and Robin pretended to be interested. "Who?" she asked.

"Jill. Chen," he added as further explanation.

"Are you sure?" Tasha looked from him to Derrick, then back at Matt.

"Eighty percent."

"Good odds," Derrick chimed in.

Robin sipped her own wine, listening as Matt tried to convince Tasha to go talk to Jill a little more. Maybe she should encourage this. Tasha was cute. Artsy. Probably fun. She'd definitely provide Jill with a distraction. Robin steeled herself, because the thought of Jill with someone else really wasn't sitting well with her. "Sure," Robin managed, "you should go talk to her—"

"Sugar, how about you get me a glass of wine?" Lady Magnolia said to Matt as she smoothly inserted herself between Tasha and Robin.

He stared and, with a goofy smile, went to find the required beverage.

"Hello, sweetie," Magnolia said to Robin. "Fancy meeting you here."

Robin stared, too, and cleared her throat. At least others could see her. Then again, this whole gathering could just be a giant delusion. She hoped not. Tasha and Derrick appeared to be waiting for introductions because Magnolia cut a celebrity-style figure, in her black evening dress and matching gloves. Her hair flowed down her back in perfect queen waves.

Before Robin could respond, Matt returned with a glass of wine and Magnolia took it. "Thank you, sugar," she said, her low drawl steeped in Southern charm. "Do y'all mind?" She gestured at Robin as if she was selecting her in a store. "It's been longer than it took my mama's sourdough to rise since I've seen her and we've got to get caught up." Magnolia sipped as the three smiled, looking starstruck, and moved away.

"Hi, I guess," Robin said when they were gone. "Another charity visit?" Maybe the Bureau really did think she was a lost cause. Robin's stomach clenched.

"This one's extra credit, sweetie. The Lady loves a good romance." She smiled against the rim of her glass, which now held a perfect lip print. "Change the now, you change the later."

"What does that mean, exactly?"

Magnolia raised one perfect eyebrow, and Robin was immediately chastised.

"Sorry. I think I know what you mean, but I'm still not convinced it's a good idea."

"Honey, the future is never set in stone. It's an outgrowth of the choices you make and the motivations behind those choices. My mama always said that you can't go wrong with genuine."

"But Jill—"

Magnolia raised a hand to keep Robin from continuing. "Girl, have you not been paying attention? She knows what she wants. So do you. And sugar, you are more obvious than a pig in a double-breasted suit at a barbecue. If you don't want the future you saw, then work on who you are in the present and remember, it's all about intent and motivations *now*." Magnolia winked. "You run along, sugar. Relax. Enjoy the party." And she sashayed into the crowd, leaving Robin to stare after her.

She frowned, and took a sip of wine, trying to calm her thoughts. How could something that could prove to be so wrong make her feel so right? And what would happen if they hooked up? Could Robin maintain her good intentions and not slide back into bad habits? A man walked past with a plate piled high with goodies. Food first, Robin decided. More thinking later. She went to the tables set up in the back and ended up chatting with another gallery owner for a while.

By eleven-thirty, Robin had managed to eat even more of the seriously delicious hors d'oeuvres and chat up several more people. She'd never had a problem at social gatherings, and after Jill had spent a few minutes introducing her around, Robin had told her to go mingle with her adoring fans. It helped Robin, too, because the closer Jill was to her physically, the more intense Jill's effect was on her. And if Robin had to keep staring at her in that dress, she'd start coming across like some perv who undressed women with her eyes.

Taking a break from the socializing, Robin stood studying Jill's smaller watercolors—delicate landscapes and seascapes. These were earlier pieces, according to the tags, and both had already sold. In fact, quite a lot of her work was marked as sold, which pleased Robin immensely. The music—just loud enough to register—had changed to a faster-paced, danceable beat. She tapped her foot in time.

"Those are the vineyards of a winery in Oregon, not far from Portland," Danielle said, bobbing her chin at one of the landscapes. Robin hadn't noticed her approach.

"Yes. I've been there. It's really beautiful. Jill nailed it."

"That's right, you're a Seattle native. How do you like it all the way over here?"

"It has its good points. But I really miss the Northwest. That'll always be home." Robin turned from the painting to look at Danielle. "Did you fly out specifically for this event?"

"Yes. I'm based in Chicago these days, but I always try to attend a couple of Jill's showings that we help fund. I'm originally from Portland."

"Do you miss it?"

"Quite a bit. I'm looking to get more involved there and perhaps move back or to Seattle in the near future. I think it would be easier for me to be more involved at the grassroots level that way."

Robin nodded. "Admirable. How long is your term on the board at North by Northwest?"

"A while, yet."

"Good." Robin meant it. Danielle seemed savvy, and she clearly wanted to advocate for artists.

"So tell me, Ms. Preston, why you would pull up stakes here, travel across the country, and settle for a position that lacks the prestige and salary that you're no doubt making now."

Well. Doesn't mince words. "That's an apples and oranges comparison. And it's Robin." She sipped and motioned at one of Jill's seascapes. "I spent most of my childhood immersed in art, because it made me feel safe and creative, two things that I didn't get to feel much as a kid." She turned her gaze back to Danielle. "Hard times. But I always had art. I thought I always would have it, but my mom died when I was in college, and my dad wasn't in the picture, so I chose business school, hoping to keep things together for me and my brother." She shrugged. "I turned out to be pretty good at business, and maybe because I have an art background, it gives me a different perspective on the kind of tool business can be."

Danielle nodded and gave her an encouraging smile, so Robin continued.

"I can navigate corporate America very well, Ms. Paredes. But I've not ever been a hundred percent comfortable in it. Regardless, I know how it works, and I know how to make it work for others. I saw the opening at North by Northwest and jumped on it because that's what I'd much rather be doing, not only to put my skills to work for it, but also because it'll feed my soul in ways that money and prestige simply can't."

"Thank you for that. And it's Danielle."

"Oh, damn," said a thirties-ish man nearby in tight black pants and an even tighter blue shirt cut to expose his well-sculpted arms. "I wanted to buy that one." He was looking at one of Jill's found object pieces, a city scene.

An equally buff man with him shook his head sadly. "Let's check on the other one." He caught Robin's eye and gave her a little nod. Robin nodded back.

"Jill's work is quite popular at these events," Danielle said.

"And I love that. Does she ever sell out?"

"There have been a couple of times that she has. Jill is on her way to even greater things."

"That's why foundations such as yours are so important." Both she and Danielle turned back to Jill's work, a shared silence of admiration for it. "I really appreciate you taking the time to talk with me," Robin said. "I hope I didn't bias your selection process. Too much, anyway." She smiled, and Danielle laughed.

"I actually enjoy meeting potential candidates for positions with the foundation. I'm only one aspect of this process. There are others, of course, who will want to meet the top choices."

"Danielle," said a tall man who might have been African. "Oh, pardon me." He saw Robin and inclined his head in apology.

"No, it's fine. Carry on. Thank you again, Danielle."

"The same to you." She engaged the man, and Robin wandered away to look at a few more of Jill's pieces. Had she said too much to Danielle? Made her think she was strange? Or disingenuous? A server moved toward her.

"Can I switch you to champagne?" he asked. "It's almost midnight."

Robin looked at him and grinned. "Already?"

"Yes, ma'am." He smiled back. Cute, in an emo kind of way.

"Then, absolutely." She placed her half-full wine glass on his tray and took one of champagne that was almost two-thirds full. He was one of several servers trading people's wine for champagne. Robin took her phone out of her pocket. Five minutes to go before the new year. The music faded, to be replaced by what sounded like a live feed from Times Square. She didn't sip her champagne yet, wanting to save it for the stroke of midnight. Robin got caught up in the palpable excitement in the room, and she was glad, actually, that Caroline had bowed out. It dawned on her, then, that Lady Magnolia might have had something to do with that. Robin looked around for her, but didn't see her. So the Bureau was...what? Match-making?

She caught sight of Jill, who was working her way through the people toward her, carefully carrying a glass of champagne, and Robin shoved the Bureau to the back of her mind.

"Hey," Jill said when she was next to Robin. "Three minutes." She smiled. "Enjoying yourself?"

"Very much."

Jill started to reply when someone on the other side of her said something, and Jill gave Robin a tiny shrug and turned to address him. Robin allowed herself to watch Jill's profile. And her neck and the shape of her shoulder. Her gaze dropped lower, to the tantalizing curve of Jill's breast down to her hip and lower still to the top of the slit in her dress, about halfway up her thigh. Robin's heart pounded harder, and she remembered the first time they'd made love all those years ago, Robin stripping Jill out of her jeans and rain-damp shirt as thunder rumbled beyond the windows of Jill's warehouse studio apartment, both of them impatient with need and want.

"One minute," somebody shouted. Several others cheered.

Jill put her left hand on Robin's right shoulder as she continued to talk to the man on her right, and Robin was sure the fabric of her shirt was melting, fusing to her skin under Jill's palm. Jill looked at her and gave her another smile, then turned back to the man to her right, who was clearly a fan. Robin didn't care how long Jill talked to him, as long as her hand stayed on her shoulder. Small pleasures, things like that, and she'd be grateful for them as long as she lived. Opportunity echoed through her brain, standing there with Jill so close, her hand making a physical connection between them.

"Twenty seconds!" somebody else yelled, amidst cheers. The sound emanating from the speakers increased, and Robin heard the announcers at Times Square, and the din of the crowd that had gathered there.

And then somebody shouted "Ten!" and the rest of the people in the gallery started counting down, too, glasses of champagne poised to toast. Jill still gripped Robin's shoulder, and she joined the crowd in the count.

"Five! Four! Three! Two! One!"

The gallery broke into whooping and cheering as "Auld Lang Syne" blared from the speakers. Several people started kissing, and Jill's hand was suddenly on the back of Robin's neck. Before Robin could figure out what was happening, Jill pulled her head down and Jill's lips were suddenly on Robin's, and all Robin knew at that moment was the warmth and softness of Jill's mouth moving against hers, tasting of champagne, and a roaring in her ears and fireworks in her chest and thighs.

Jill pulled away, but her hand stayed on the back of Robin's neck, and her eyes seemed to sparkle beneath the gallery lights. She tapped her glass against Robin's. "Happy New Year," she said.

"Yeah. Happy New Year to you." Robin drained her champagne in one long swallow, trying to cool the molten heat still circulating through her blood.

Jill drank hers in similar fashion. "Are you going to hang around?"

Robin hesitated. She should go. But the feel of Jill's fingers still on Robin's neck and the aftermath of the kiss pretty much overrode that idea. "Yeah."

"Good. If you're tired, though, I'll understand."

"Nope. All good." The music changed to something more danceable, and a few people nearby laughed and started moving and swaying.

"More champagne?" Jill pulled her hand away from Robin's neck and pointed at her glass. "I'll get some for us both."

"I'm good. Maybe a little more wine. Here, don't worry about it. I'll handle it. Go mingle." She took Jill's empty glass and moved away, heart still slamming her ribs, her thoughts completely muddled. She placed the empty glasses on a tray stand and got herself a white wine from a server and weaved through the crowd to find one with champagne.

There was emo boy now, talking to a tall, curvaceous woman in a black dress.

"Good work, sugar," Lady Magnolia said with a smile and a wink as she handed Robin a glass of champagne.

"I don't—"

Magnolia placed a gloved finger over her lips. "The Lady is nothing if not a romantic at heart, sweetie." She straightened, and took a delicate sip of champagne. "Not bad."

"I'm not sure—"

"Oh, yes you are." Magnolia took another sip and set the glass back on the server's tray. He moved away. "Opportunity and intent," Magnolia said authoritatively. "Make sure yours are honorable." She winked. "Take care, sugar." She turned away, a regal, elegant movement.

"Wait."

Magnolia did.

"Thanks for—everything, I guess." She smiled. "And you look fabulous."

"Girl, don't I know it." Magnolia blew her a kiss and moved into the crowd. Robin lost sight of her, but a flash of red in her peripheral vision captured her attention. She turned to see Jill nearby, talking to a small group of people. She walked the champagne over. Jill took the glass.

"Thanks," she said with a smile that made Robin ache. "Hold on. I have to say some goodbyes."

Robin nodded and watched her walk away, needing to push that dress down so she could see the rest of Jill's tattoo. And a lot more. She took a swallow of wine, noting that the gallery was actually clearing out, and as that happened, the music seemed to get louder. The current song was a slow, sexy groove. It matched everything she was feeling right now, as she watched Jill near the door, smiling and clasping hands. A few people Jill hugged, including Danielle, who caught Robin's eye as she was leaving. She waved at Robin before she stepped outside, and Robin returned the gesture, marveling at coincidences.

Then again, Lady Magnolia was in the house. Maybe nothing was a coincidence. She sipped her wine and said good bye to a few people she'd chatted with earlier. Robin had to wait around, anyway, since Jill had taken her coat. Lady Magnolia was nowhere to be seen, and Robin wondered again if she'd been hallucinating. She watched an older straight couple talking earnestly to Jill, and she took another sip of wine. She really hoped she wasn't hallucinating, because this was a lot of fun.

She did a quick trip around the gallery to assess how many pieces had sold. Only three were left. This had clearly been a good night, and Robin smiled, pleased. She took her phone out and checked messages. Frank had texted New Year's greetings, and she responded. Several other friends and acquaintances sent texts or photos of various scenes from celebrations. She replied to a few, then held up her phone, took a selfie in front of one of Jill's larger pieces, and sent that to Frank as well as a few others with the message, *hanging with the artists on New Year's!*

"I want in on this," Jill said at Robin's elbow.

"Good idea. Photo for Madison." Her voice remained steady though Jill's proximity made her ache.

Jill leaned in, and she and Robin made goofy faces. Robin took the photo then checked it. "Totally ridiculous," she pronounced as she showed it to Jill.

"Definitely. Send that to me."

Robin did, then looked up from her phone. The gallery was mostly empty with the exception of a few servers and a couple of people Robin assumed were gallery staff. Groups of people stood outside, talking. A few smoked. They'd move on to other parties, Robin was sure. The clock on her phone read 12:43.

"This was a lot of fun," Robin said. "A ton of work for you and the crew, but well worth it."

"It was, wasn't it?"

"You sold everything but three."

"Really?" Jill grinned. "Go, me."

Robin grinned back. "Second that. Go, you."

Jill took Robin's empty glass from her. "Let me check in, and then I'll get your coat."

"Okay." Robin watched her walk away, and it was almost painful, the effect Jill was having on her. Good thing she'd be out of here soon. Because if she stayed any longer she wasn't sure she'd be able to keep her hands to herself, especially after that kiss. But thinking about leaving hurt in ways much less pleasant than thoughts of staying. The music had been turned down, and the selection changed to a relaxing electronic chill and Robin again perused Jill's art, marveling that each viewing brought new things to light.

"Anything in particular that caught your eye?" Jill asked, bringing Robin out of her examination of one of her large mixed medias.

Oh, the many meanings that question held. Robin cleared her throat a little before she answered. "I really like the art box pieces. The one on the other wall with the photos of you as a little girl was really moving. I wish I had seen those photos when we first met."

"I actually didn't discover them until I graduated. But you're seeing them now. I have a bunch of others, too. Family shots from China included."

"I'd love to see them sometime."

"I'd love to show them to you." Jill's gaze bored into Robin's, warm and welcoming. "Care to join me for a nightcap? Which is generally hot tea in my world."

"That would be great," Robin said before she talked herself out of it.

"I was hoping you'd agree. Come on." Jill headed toward the back, where the gallery owner was talking to three servers. "Going upstairs, Amber," Jill said. "Go ahead and lock up. I'll let Robin out." Jill shook the hands of all three servers and thanked them.

"Wonderful event," Robin said, and Amber smiled.

"Thank you for coming. Good night," she said.

"And thank you," Robin added to the servers. They nodded at her and returned to their conversation with Amber. Jill caught Robin's eye and motioned with her head to follow her.

At the base of the steps, Jill slid her shoes off, black velvet heels. "God, how do women wear these all the time?"

"I did kind of miss your Converse. And combat boots." Robin kept her tone light, because she didn't trust herself around Jill, and the intensity of her attraction scared her because of its potential in so many arenas.

Jill laughed and went up the stairs, holding the bottom of her dress up with her free hand to make movement easier. Robin's throat went dry at the sight of her exposed thigh, and she grabbed the handrail, as if the cool metal would help ground her.

Once inside, Jill turned on a couple more lights and shut the door behind them. "Give me a sec. I'm going to change."

Robin nodded and decided to take her boots off, since she generally took her shoes off when she got home. Seemed rude to stomp through this nice apartment with her boots on. She set them by the door and went into the living room. She heard the bathroom door open then shut, and she stared out the window onto the street below, watching groups of revelers still out enjoying themselves. Noises from the kitchen area drew her attention there, to Jill running water into a kettle. She'd changed into a pair of baggy gray sweats, thick gray socks, a white V-neck T-shirt, and the blue flannel shirt she'd been wearing on Sunday. She was just as beautiful as when she'd been in her dress.

"I'd go full Chinese tea service on you," Jill said, "but all that stuff is at home and it's late. So we're doing electric kettle and teabags."

Robin grinned. "I'm going to hold you to that tea service."

"Then you'll have to come to Seattle." Jill finished filling the kettle and plugged it in. She retrieved two cups from the cabinet and a box of tea.

"I just might," Robin said.

"I'll hold you to *that*." Jill raised an eyebrow at her, and Robin smiled as she took two teabags from the box and put one in each cup. The faint smell of jasmine from the teabags accompanied her motions. She closed up the box, and Jill set a small squeeze bottle of honey on the counter. The water was already boiling so she poured it into each cup, then handed Robin a spoon.

Strange, how intimate and familiar the simple act of preparing tea like this felt, as if they'd been doing it for years. Robin stirred honey into her cup and handed the spoon back to Jill. Their fingers brushed in the transfer, and Robin looked to see if sparks were hovering above her fingernails, but she kept cool throughout. Jill finished with her cup. "Come and sit down," she said, and she carried her cup into the living room.

"Be right there." Robin made a quick trip to the bathroom, returned to the kitchen for her tea, then joined Jill in the living room on the couch. Jill had turned music on, and though the sound was low, it sounded like an indie band. Something mellow. Robin sighed as she settled herself. "This was a great night. Thanks for the invite."

"I'm glad you still like art." Jill stretched her legs out and put her feet on the coffee table.

"Same here. And you know, you didn't tell me what the color red means."

Jill smiled as she blew on her tea. "Dynamic, celebration, vitality, creativity, happiness. To name a few."

"Perfect choice for the evening." Robin sipped. "When do you go back to Seattle?"

"The third. Do you have tomorrow off?"

"Yes." And no way was she going in. Frost could fuck off.

"Good. Want to have lunch?"

Robin laughed, giddiness ricocheting through her chest. "Is this going to be a thing with us?"

"I hope so. And maybe we'll work our way up to dinner. Different kinds of food, you know. Get some variety going." She gave Robin a sly smile.

In spite of the tea, Robin's mouth went dry. "I've decided you're right. I really don't know how much of a tease you've become."

"Depends on the company. Some I prefer much more than others." She raised her cup to her lips, and her eyes seemed to sparkle.

"Here's hoping I make the cut."

"You did."

Dangerous, flirting like this. But she couldn't bring herself to stop. Robin started to say something else when Jill's phone rang with the main song from the movie *Frozen* and Robin almost exhaled with relief.

"Madison," Jill said. "She wanted to say Happy New Year before I went to bed."

"That's cool. Go on."

Jill smiled at her and picked up her phone from the coffee table. She answered and moved into the kitchen area.

Robin listened to her talk, fascinated by Jill's mom voice and interaction with her daughter. She thought about the Jill she'd known in college and wondered about getting hung up on memories. Was she attracted to the past? Maybe a little. But she really liked this Jill—the one who was becoming an established artist and who had a cool ex-husband and a daughter and at least one tattoo. Robin had only just begun getting to know this Jill, and she wanted more.

Jill laughed from the area near the bed, behind the screens, and Robin remembered the first time she'd heard her laugh, about a week after they'd met, on their way to another class with a couple of other students. Robin had barely known her then, but when Jill laughed, Robin wanted to hear more of it, and she wanted to know what was underneath it, and what kinds of things made Jill who she was.

She had that feeling now, and it collided with her confusion about what any of this meant and how much stock she should put in a future, regardless of what shape it took. Robin picked up her nearly empty cup and Jill's, which was just less than half full, and took both into the kitchen. She set them on the counter just as Jill emerged from behind the screens, no longer on the phone.

"I sent Madison the selfie we took tonight. She's trying not to act like it, but she's interested in meeting you."

"Well, you did invite me for a tea service," Robin said as she cleaned her cup and wiped it dry with a dish towel before she put it back in the cabinet.

"And that is a perfect formal gathering for a meeting. I'll have to ponder that. Tired?"

"A little. Not as much as you must be, though. Done?" She motioned at the cup that had been Jill's.

Jill looked at the cup, then at Robin, as if she was considering something. She moved closer and gently pulled the dish towel out of Robin's hand. She set it aside. "Stop for a minute."

Robin stared into her eyes. Something in Jill's tone and expression caused that deep longing she'd felt earlier to resurface.

Jill moved closer still and ran her fingertips over the back of Robin's hand, braced on the counter. Robin froze, most coherent thoughts paralyzed. Jill continued to trace patterns across Robin's knuckles, and then she gently moved Robin's hand so she could briefly interlock their fingers. A current shot up Robin's arm and raced right to her thighs. She wasn't sure she was still breathing.

"When are you going to stop denying that there's something happening between us?" Jill's fingertips traced more patterns on Robin's palm, and these small, slow touches would have brought Robin to her knees, if she hadn't been leaning against the counter for support.

Robin cleared her throat. "I'm not denying it."

"Then what's going on?" Jill moved her fingertips to Robin's wrist and stroked under her shirt cuff. Robin's heart was pounding so hard she wondered if she'd faint.

"I'm scared," she managed, her words thick with emotion and truth.

"Of what?" Jill continued the exquisite, maddening motions with her fingertips, but she held Robin's gaze with her own, searching, going past whatever defenses Robin might have had.

"Hurting you."

Jill's fingertips stopped moving, but they remained on Robin's hand. "So don't."

Was it really that simple? Would that keep the future she'd seen from coming to pass? Jill's hand was warm on hers, and staring into Jill's eyes, Robin realized that yes, it just might be that simple, that her motivation for being here with Jill in this moment was because she wanted to feed the connection between them.

Robin raised her free hand to Jill's face and cupped her cheek. She stroked her skin with her thumb, then slowly leaned in and kissed Jill's forehead. Jill sighed and covered Robin's hand with her own. Robin pulled away, but Jill stepped closer. She slid her arms around Robin's waist and put her head on Robin's shoulder. Robin closed her eyes and held on, excruciatingly aware of Jill's body, even through the bulky clothing. With one hand, she ran her fingers lightly through Jill's hair, enjoying the way the buzzcut on the sides and back felt against her fingertips.

One of Jill's hands tracked slowly up Robin's back until her fingers moved beneath her hair on the back of her neck and lightly grazed her skin. The sensation sent chills down her spine. Jill moved her head, and Robin opened her eyes and held Jill's gaze as she gently stroked the side of Jill's face. Jill kept her motions slow, too, and ran her hands along Robin's shoulders then back to her face, where she carefully moved Robin's hair out of her eyes and rested the fingertips of one hand against Robin's lips.

Robin kissed them and gently took that hand in her own. She entwined their fingers and held both their hands against her chest, still stroking Jill's face with her other. Jill pulled her hand out of Robin's grasp and ran both her hands up Robin's arms, then down the front of her vest to the top button. Jill's eyes held a question. Robin nodded once, and Jill undid the top button, then moved slowly to the next and then the next until Robin's vest was open. Jill swept it off her shoulders, and Robin let it fall to the floor.

Jill's hands rested on Robin's hips, and she brushed her lips lightly against her cheek, and then her chin, perilously close to Robin's mouth but just out of reach. Robin's knees went weak with the promise and the feel of Jill's breath against her skin. And then Jill undid the top two buttons of Robin's shirt, and her fingertips on Robin's skin sent heat through her veins.

Jill carefully pushed Robin's shirt collar out of the way and placed her lips against Robin's neck—a delicate, light kiss that became many more on the skin between Robin's ear and throat. Robin shuddered and gasped and moved her head to give Jill better access.

So slow. Achingly slow. Fingertips trailing lightly over exposed skin and ghosting lightly over lips. Robin had never spent so much time touching someone like this, standing so near, watching Jill's reactions in her eyes and seeing her own mirrored within. Robin ached and throbbed, the intensity between them unlike anything she'd ever experienced. The hole she'd been carrying deep in her heart filled with hope and relief, and she didn't want it to end, the connection between them flaring to life once again.

Robin brushed Jill's lips with her own, a brief, gentle touch, and then Jill's hands were in Robin's hair, and Jill kissed her slowly and deeply, and Robin's hands were on Jill's face, holding her in place until she pulled away, her grip dropping to Robin's shoulders and then to the remaining buttons on Robin's shirt. Jill kept her gaze locked on Robin's as she undid these and pulled the shirt out of her jeans. Robin let her, and pushed Jill's flannel shirt smoothly off her shoulders.

Jill worked Robin's shirt off her, taking her time. It joined the other articles of clothing on the floor. Robin shivered, but not from cold. Jill's fingertips left chillbumps in their wake as she ran them across the expanse of Robin's chest and stomach, only to start over again on her arms and back.

Carefully, Robin pulled Jill's tee off, and she couldn't breathe for a moment, struck by how beautiful she was, partially nude with the tattooed tail of a dragon dropping over her shoulder and brushing the top of her breast. And then Robin mapped Jill's torso with her hands, taking care, letting the heat continue to build between them as she unfastened Jill's bra and let Jill undo hers.

So achingly intimate, the touches between them and the unhurried, burning kisses. Jill undid Robin's belt and the button of her jeans, and their kisses increased in intensity, until they ended up on the bed, though Robin wasn't sure how, so lost she'd gotten in what Jill stirred within her.

There was no fumbling here, no desperation for quick release as they finished undressing each other and journeyed across each other's skin with lips and hands. These moments between them were framed with care and patience, and a deep, almost primal tie that they strengthened with each touch, each kiss, each movement. Jill's sighs and soft moans drove Robin to even greater care as she entered Jill with first one finger, then two, letting Jill guide their rhythm until she clung to Robin, staring into her eyes as she let go with a long, aching groan and a shuddering wave.

Robin held her, unaware that she herself was crying until Jill brushed her tears away along with her own, and kissed her, the look in her eyes bringing a fresh round to Robin's eyes. And then she surrendered to Jill's continued explorations, her hands leaving even Robin's skin aching for more.

By the time Jill slid her fingers in, Robin was so close that Jill probably could've made her come with a kiss, but instead she drew it out somehow, made Robin crest in several waves until finally she exploded, clinging to Jill and gasping, every particle of her body both sated but somehow still aflame.

And then she cried against Jill's shoulder, not sure why, but letting herself release that way, too. Jill stroked her hair and held her close, until Robin fell asleep, aware of the

heat from Jill's body, the sound of her breathing, and early
morning light spilling through the front windows.

"Lord have mercy," Lady Magnolia said as she sank into
the chair on the other side of Agent Tolson's desk and fanned
herself. "Those two are meant for each other. Two little
lesbian sugarpeas in a pod."

"Did Ms. Preston go home last night?"

Magnolia arched a perfect eyebrow. Tolson was thorough,
and Magnolia knew that, but a little bit of faith in the Lady's
abilities, please? "Word on the street says no. But to be sure,
I checked the alarm records at the gallery. It was set once at
one-sixteen A.M. and was not disabled or reset the rest of
the night. And the Lady knows neither was drinking heavily.
Lady's intuition suggests our cute little lesbian didn't need a
drunken crash pad. She did, however, need a Chen infusion."

Agent Tolson smiled. "Excellent work."

"It is, isn't it?" Magnolia pretended to preen because she
knew she could get away with it.

"There are a few loose ends." Tolson tapped Preston's
hardcopy file with one manicured fingertip. Magnolia liked
that about Tolson—her attention to personal grooming
details. Her nail polish perfectly matched her suit color, a
deep rose red. And her hair was never out of place, no matter
how she wore it. Tolson would have made an excellent queen.
"Mr. Rampus will ensure the final stage of the operation,"
Tolson added. "But if you and Agent Decker could continue
to monitor and aid as needed—run interference as Agent
Decker would say—I would of course be immensely
appreciative."

"My mama always said that it ain't finished 'til it's finished."

"Thank you, Lady. I am extremely grateful for your assistance on this case."

Magnolia stood and straightened her gown. "Anytime. The Lady is always up for a challenge." She gave Tolson a saucy little wink and swirled out of the room, closing the door with a firm click.

Chapter 14

ROBIN WOKE UP SLOWLY, EVERY part of her relaxed, the faint scent of sex and sandalwood—or maybe teak—teasing her nostrils. Jill was cuddled up close, her thigh over Robin's and her arm across Robin's chest. Jill's head was on her shoulder, and Robin realized her right arm was asleep, but she didn't care because Jill was the reason. There was nothing important enough for her to move, nothing important enough to disrupt the feeling of Jill against her.

Memories of what had happened between them suffused her limbs with warmth. If this was part of a delusion, it was delicious. Perfect. The best delusion ever. Jill stirred, and Robin felt her lips on her neck. Whatever nerves were there, Jill's lips set them off and the message went directly to her crotch. Robin sighed with pleasure.

"Hi," Jill murmured against Robin's skin.

"Hi, back."

"How are you?" Jill's breath was warm on Robin's skin, and Robin wanted nothing more than to wake up every day to that sensation, though she probably had no business wanting such a thing so soon.

"Is there a word with a stronger meaning than stupendous? Maybe in Chinese?"

Jill chuckled and kissed Robin's jawline.

"How about you?" Robin moved her head slightly and kissed Jill's forehead.

"Same boat as you."

"Good. You can help me steer it."

Jill snuggled closer, and her shift in position allowed Robin to move her arm and stroke Jill's hair, valiantly ignoring the protestations of her nerves as they fired awake.

"I think we probably missed lunch," Robin said after a while.

"Guess we'll have to go with dinner. But I don't really want to leave this bed yet, especially with you in it."

"I say we eat in, then. There's a really good pizza place a couple blocks away. Seriously. You will never have pizza that good in Seattle."

Jill laughed. "Fine. I'm in." She shifted again and was suddenly on top of Robin, staring down into her eyes and there was nothing else in the world in that moment beyond Jill. But from somewhere within, Robin's newfound emotional responsibility kicked in.

"I suppose we should talk about this," she said, not taking her eyes off Jill's.

"About..."

"These new circumstances."

A slow smile tugged at the corners of Jill's mouth. "We should. But I think over pizza is a more appropriate time, don't you?"

Robin smiled back. "Works for me."

And this time their lovemaking heated quickly, and it tore the bedsheets off the mattress, and erupted several times between them, until they both collapsed, tangled in blankets and each other, breathing heavily. Robin held Jill close and remembered that the last time she'd spent this long in bed with a woman had been with Jill, a month after they'd slept together the first time.

This was different, though, for both of them, she sensed. Newer, somehow, and deeper. So much deeper, both of them bringing to the bed their wounds, scars, and extra years, their vulnerabilities and strengths, revealing them only to each other. Robin's chest tightened. She'd never felt like this with anyone, not even Jill the first time they'd connected. Something had changed, triggering even more between them, and as much as it scared and confused her, it grounded her, too. She wanted more. But she wasn't sure how to make that work, especially as she tried to get her own life back on track.

"Shower and pizza," Jill said after another long delicious while. "Join me."

Robin obliged, though the shower stall only served as another venue for continued exploration. Robin traced the lines of Jill's dragon tattoo with her lips down her shoulder and back, and Jill traced more than that until the water cooled, and they hurried to finish, laughing and kissing.

Robin went to pick up the pizza—thank God for pizza joints open on New Year's Day—while Jill stayed behind to make some phone calls. The first day of the new year, and the late afternoon sun reflected off building windows, creating patterns and shadows on neighboring structures. Robin took a few photos with her phone on the way, and thought about the North by Northwest Foundation and the possibility of moving to Seattle.

It occurred to her that even if she didn't get that job, she'd go to Seattle anyway. That's where she had to be, and not necessarily because of Jill or a job, but just because it was part of her journey and maybe, in a way, part of getting back on track. Robin knew that with a weird certainty, and she also knew that she and Jill would have to decide what this was between them and what they wanted to do with it. Christmas Future still made Robin nervous, but what had happened between her and Jill felt so mind-blowingly and utterly right that she decided that wasn't the problem.

The problem, she knew, was her. And Jill's solution was really that simple. Don't hurt her. Did Robin have the wherewithal to overcome the bad coping strategies she'd used over the years? The ones that drove people away, elevated her to queen bitch, and ate a hole in her soul?

She had to. It *was* that simple. And that hard. Robin carried the pizza back to Jill's, and she knew she had to tell her some things. Maybe not her experience with the Bureau, but some other things. Jill could make any decisions about what she wanted to do once they'd talked, and whatever her decision, Robin would respect it.

"Okay, you're right. I have yet to find pizza this good in Seattle." Jill finished her first piece. She'd never eaten the crust ends, and Robin smiled as Jill tossed one into the box.

"Told you." They were sitting on the couch, the pizza box on the coffee table along with their bottles of water. Robin finished her piece, crust end and all, and picked up another.

Jill reached over and brushed a strand of Robin's hair away from her face, an intimate and tender gesture, and Robin stopped chewing, caught in it.

"So talk," Jill said. "You first."

Robin finished chewing and swallowed. She took a drink of water and set the rest of her pizza on a napkin. "Okay." She hesitated. She wasn't sure where to start. Jill didn't say anything, just waited. "All right," Robin continued. "Remember Cynthia, who you met briefly when we were at the tree after our first lunch?"

"Yes. You said she was something you weren't proud of."

"Yeah." Robin grimaced. "I'm not." And she told Jill about how she'd seduced Cynthia, thinking it would be fun but also an in at Frost, and about how she'd broken it off only to get into Cynthia's crosshairs. And then she told her about what Frost had said to her on Monday, about closing her position and sending her to China. She stopped, watching Jill's face, looking for judgment or recrimination. It never came.

"Damn," Jill said instead. "That's a lot on your plate. I see now why you've been saying you're going through a transitional period. How do you feel about the Cynthia situation?"

"Fucking stupid. I told you, I've done a lot of shitty things, and that's up there at the top of the list. And not just because it probably helped cost me my job." And maybe a lot of other jobs in corporate America. Robin didn't voice that part. "I don't know, exactly, why I did it, looking back on it. I can justify it by saying I wanted to try to get ahead with Frost through Cynthia's husband. Or I was bored, and she was hot. I can make all kinds of excuses, but none of them justify it. That was the bad side of me, and I hate that I have one of those."

"Well, it's done. And now you have to work with what you've got."

"I also hate that you know that story."

Jill sat back, expression inscrutable. "Why?"

"Because it puts me in a really bad light."

"So tell me a couple of good things to balance it out."

"All right. And fortunately for both of us, I can. I did undo a couple of my layoffs."

"What do you mean?"

"I laid a couple of people off before Christmas, saw the error of my ways, and brought them back into their positions."

Jill smiled. "I'd say that's a much better light."

"And I did a presentation that was supposed to be a ticket to my next promotion, but I didn't believe in the company anymore. Or maybe I was just seeing things differently about my life. I'm not sure yet. Anyway, my assistant put together a really great presentation that highlighted better business practices, and I did that one. Totally not the company line, and I'm sure it helped cement my boss's decision to get rid of me. But the board liked it, and I gave credit to her."

"There. That's a good balance." Jill squeezed Robin's hand. "We all screw up, and we all do things that we can never be proud of. What you can be proud of is you're owning it and learning from it. And doing things differently as a result."

Robin shrugged and picked up her piece of pizza. "I hope so."

"The woman that Drew caught me with wasn't the first I'd slept with after we married."

Robin stopped chewing and stared at her.

"The first was also married to a man, who happened to be a friend of Drew's. I'm not sure how it happened. It seems one afternoon we were just hanging out in her kitchen, and then we were in bed together." Jill shook her head. "Bad scene, and you can imagine how weird it was to be around her. Neither of us ever mentioned it after it happened."

Robin finished chewing and swallowed. She didn't say anything.

"I was so unhappy," Jill continued. "Not with Madison, of course. And not with Drew. I liked him then, and I like him still. But I was so unhappy being in a situation where I couldn't be myself. I couldn't express who I truly was with him, and I felt I had been pressured into the marriage by my family. I also had a tremendous amount of guilt because I could never be the woman Drew needed or wanted, and I only compounded it by cheating on him. So I can empathize with hating that you know something about me that I'm not proud of." Jill reached for another piece of pizza. "Like I said, it's done. And you have to work with what you've got. So in light of all this revelation between us, do you think you want to stay at Frost?"

Robin shook her head. "It's weird, but even when Brady pulled that crap in the conference room, I was already thinking about leaving."

"Oh? Why?"

"Long story." And it involved secret agents who may or may not exist, time travel, and possible hallucinations. But that she wouldn't talk about. Not yet. Maybe not ever.

Jill gave her a look, as if she knew Robin wasn't going to tell her everything. "And China's out of the question?"

"Yeah. In this instance. No offense to China." She gave Jill a sheepish smile. "I've been to that branch. It's sort of the Siberia of Frost Enterprises."

Jill finished her pizza and tossed the crust end into the box before she took Robin's hand. "There are many parts of China that might be like Siberia, actually. My own family says things like that. So you don't want to pursue this particular transfer."

Robin shook her head. "No. Maybe a year ago I would have, but realistically, even then it wouldn't get me any kind of advancement. I had some blinders on regarding Frost and the overall work culture there."

"Okay, quick. What's the first thing you think of when you think of Frost Enterprises?"

"Hell."

Jill fought a laugh, but Robin could see it pulling at her mouth. "Can you be a little more specific?"

Robin thought for a moment. "Did you ever see the movie *The Matrix*?"

The laugh escaped. "You're saying you took the red pill."

Robin looked at her with appreciation. "Exactly. That movie is a good description for how I've been feeling lately. I was a cog in a wheel, only there was no chance for advancement no matter how hard I worked, and I could easily have stayed doing that. But then everything shifted, and I saw the error of my ways, I guess. That's why I was already thinking about leaving before Cynthia—well, anyway."

"The same thing happened to me at the bank where I'd been working," Jill said. "Basically, I was a drone for about four years. I had epiphanies myself, for lack of a better word, and I realized that if I wanted to make my life better, and become the person I wanted to be, I had to do it. I had to just fucking do it. That was part of my red pill moment. I actually thought about that movie, too, when I was going through my self-evaluation. That's when things started to change, and not all of it was easy."

"No, clearly, changing is not easy." Robin leaned back, acutely aware of Jill's hand in hers, Jill's thumb brushing over her knuckles. Curiously arousing but comforting, too. "What's next?"

"Not sure. I'll be okay for a while. I'm pretty good at investing, turns out. I'll be visiting Frank next month. I can stay longer, now. Not sure his wife will appreciate it." She sighed. "I have a lot of repairs to do in that area, too."

"I know how that feels." Jill raised Robin's hand to her lips and kissed it, letting her lips linger. "But people will respond to genuine effort and motivation. Just give it time."

Robin looked at her. Lady Magnolia had said something similar last night. "Can I ask what happened that put you in the position to pick the red pill?"

Jill didn't answer right away, as if she was considering her words. "Basically, a series of events forced me to think about some things I'd done, was doing, and would be doing. Sometimes, we don't like what we see in the mirror or how the things we do affect others. Repercussions can last for years."

"I can relate to that. Something similar happened to me. And I'm kind of sorry that you have to deal with me on the cusp of whatever the hell it is I'm trying to do."

"I'm not." Jill squeezed Robin's hand.

Robin's chest and throat tightened, as if she was going to cry. She swallowed. "Since we're in true confessions mode, I'm thinking about Seattle," she said, tentative.

"For what reasons?"

"I want to go home. I'm looking for a new beginning in a place that created me. The me I miss the most. And there's this thing that's telling me to go, that it's what I'm supposed to do."

"The directorship at North by Northwest is open." Jill ran her fingers up Robin's arm, exposed because she'd rolled the sleeves of last night's shirt up, and delightful little chills accompanied her touch. "I might have hoped Danielle would have mentioned it." She put extra innocence in her tone.

Robin grinned. "She did. But only because I'd already applied."

"Well. Small world. Good luck." Jill smiled and leaned in and kissed her.

After a few moments, Robin pulled away, as loath as she was to do it. Her sense of responsibility had kicked in again. "Let me say something."

Jill sat back, waiting.

"I want to make sure that you understand that as great as it is that you're based there, I don't expect you to drop everything—or anything, for that matter—and invite me into your life. I know that you've got things going on, and that you don't want to bring just anybody into Madison's life. And it may take me a while to get there, by which time you might have something else entirely going on. Point being, go on doing what you're doing and don't feel obligated."

Jill raised an eyebrow. "I appreciate that, but maybe you're jumping a whole bunch of guns. So how about this—we stay in touch and see where things go and what the situation may be? Because I actually want to do that."

Robin nodded and smiled. "Or that." Jill always could distill things to the most logical point.

"You don't need to make things any more complicated than they already are." She stroked Robin's face, and Robin leaned into her touch. "There's something happening here. I'm not sure yet what it is, though it's clearly something, and I'm enjoying it, but both of us have some sorting and thinking to do."

"I agree." And Robin did. It should have made her anxious and either clingy or standoffish, but it didn't. After last night and today, she was entirely ready to let go and trust whatever this process was. And maybe she should have worried that Jill would bail again, but she didn't feel that, either. Besides, they were older now, and better equipped, for the most part, to deal with things. Robin hoped that was the case, though she seemed to be the one who had some catching up to do in that department.

Jill kissed her again. "So live with me in this moment. Because I really don't want it to end."

Robin did, and when she finally left, it was nearly nine that night. When she got off the train at the stop near her apartment, she checked her phone. Jill had texted her. *Have dinner with me tomorrow.*

Tell me when and where. She entered her building.

By the time she got on the elevator, Jill had texted her again. *It could go longer than just dinner.*

Robin grinned, sparks shooting down her thighs. *I'll keep that in mind.* Once inside her apartment she pulled her boots off. What a New Year's Eve. And Day. What was the old saying? That whatever you're doing on the first of the year will determine how you spend the rest of the year? God, she hoped so. Her phone dinged with another message from Jill, with a time and a restaurant. Whatever Robin had going at work, if it conflicted, she'd cancel it. Tomorrow was Jill's last night in town, at least for a while, and she liked that—

delusion or not—much more than anything Frost could dole out.

Got it. See you then. Can't wait, she texted back. And then she sighed, because she did have to engage with reality for a while and check her emails. She changed into sweats and settled herself on the couch with her laptop, blinds open, and thoughts of Jill in the back of her mind.

Chapter 15

"Good morning," Robin said to Laura. "What's on the agenda today?"

"Morning." Laura checked her monitor. "The usual. Nothing new."

"No word from Frost?"

"Not on my phone." Her eyes narrowed. "Something's different about you."

"What?"

Laura regarded her. "I'm not sure. But it's good. Did you have a good New Year's?"

"Spectacular." Robin grinned and went into her office, leaving Laura to wonder about that. She set the duffle bag she'd brought onto her couch along with her work satchel. The duffle bag contained a set of after-work clothes and another set of work clothes for tomorrow, since she was hoping she'd be spending Jill's last night in town with her. And Robin didn't want to wear corporate to dinner. She didn't like how it felt on her. Come to think of it, she never really had.

Robin checked her desk phone because the message light was blinking. Ah. Frost. He wanted to see her as soon as she got in. "Here we go," she muttered as she erased it.

"Going to Frost's," Robin said to Laura when she stepped out of her office a few moments later.

Based on her expression, Laura sympathized. "On the plus side, I just heard from Mr. Pruitt's office."

Robin waited. "And?"

"I'm meeting with him at three today."

"Excellent. I'll be all right on my own for a couple of hours." She tried to sound plaintive, but ended up smiling. "Have you heard anything from Megan?"

"Not where Frost is concerned, though Brady Herrington was in there twenty minutes ago."

"The boys' club." Robin shrugged. "Back in a bit." She went to the elevator, and imagined herself once again suiting up for battle, only this time looking like the Black Widow character in the *Avengers* movies. That was a badass image and helped settle her nerves.

"Hey, Megan," Robin said as she approached. "Mr. Frost left me a message this morning."

"Go right in." Megan gave her a pleasant smile, but Robin saw what might have been pity in her expression.

Robin opened Frost's door and was pleased to see that Brady wasn't in the room. Just Frost, seated at his desk, suit jacket off. "Mr. Frost," she said as she closed the door behind her.

"Have a seat, Preston," he half grunted.

She settled herself in the middle chair again, presenting as cool and relaxed.

"I've looked into what we discussed on Monday, and I'm afraid overall supervisory status is out of the question."

"So what would my position be?"

His lips twitched, as if he was fighting a scowl. "Primary consultant."

"Salary?"

"Three percent more than your current."

"Do you have a job description?"

His jaw muscles clenched. Clearly, he hadn't expected these questions. "I'll email one to you."

"When do you need a decision?"

"As soon as possible."

She smiled. "And I'll make one, once I have the description. When are you closing my current position?"

"As soon as we can."

Hell, she'd quit today, but she wanted to go through the appearance of procedure. "Then I'll get right on it." She stood, bypassing his dismissal, and he frowned, because he probably hadn't expected that, either.

"Anything else?" she asked.

He shook his head, and she left, pretty sure that the position description would be in her office email when she got back. Megan was on the phone, so Robin waved at her and took the elevator back downstairs. She motioned Laura into her office to give her the latest then prepared for the usual business of the day. Sure enough, Frost had sent the job description. Robin read it and almost laughed aloud. Basically, it was a professional babysitter with no real influence. Frost would have her decision tomorrow.

Robin's personal cell rang, and she checked the number, an area code that looked vaguely familiar. "Preston," she answered.

"Good morning. It's Danielle Paredes."

"Oh, hi. Did you get back to Chicago all right?"

"I'm still in New York. And in an interesting turn of events, Jacob Burns will be here on Monday, as well as the two other members of the selection committee. They're interested in chatting with you, since they'll be here."

Robin grinned. "Excellent. Can we set up a time, place, and day for that?"

"Certainly. I'll check with the others and get back to you with some options."

"That's perfect. Thank you so much."

"You're welcome. We'll be in touch. Cheers."

"Thanks. Bye." Robin hung up and did a fist pump. Lots of things in motion, and she felt freer and lighter than she had in years. Plus, she was having dinner with Jill. That would get her through the rest of today. More so than all the meetings she had to deal with. She'd make sure everybody had the right figures, that she said all the right things to clients, and that her colleagues were briefed. And she'd do it well. But she didn't care anymore about the bottom line or possible accounts for Frost. Instead, she'd been reaching out to various people in her networks across corporate America seeing who might be interested in donating some money to an art foundation in Seattle.

Quite a few, as it turned out. Useful, for the upcoming meeting with the North by Northwest committee. One thing, however, chewed at her. When she put in her notice, Frost could give her all kinds of bad recommendations. He could even bring up the accusations Brady had thrown at her. If the foundation called for a reference, he could do some damage.

Or maybe he wouldn't. Maybe he'd think some podunk arts foundation wasn't worth a blackball. Tomorrow might reveal how far Frost would go, when she resigned. That would determine whether she'd address calling Frost for a reference with the foundation. Robin put that thought aside and focused on the things she had to do right now, and the client calls she had to make.

By one-thirty, she was ready to grab a quick bite before her next meeting. As she was logging out, Laura stuck her head in.

"I'll be leaving in a few minutes."

"Okay. Hope it goes well."

Laura started to leave, seemed to think better of it, and instead came in and shut the door behind her. She moved toward the couch where Robin was working. "I just talked to Megan."

"And?" Robin moved her duffle bag aside so Laura could sit down.

"Something odd happened. Frost came out of his office about twenty minutes after you left and wanted to know why Megan had let 'that man' into his office."

"What man?"

"That's what Megan said. Nobody went into Frost's office after you left. Nobody can get into Frost's office without Megan seeing them, if she's at her desk."

"So I'll ask the obvious question, now."

Laura didn't let her. "Yes, she was at her desk, and even if she was on the phone, she's still positioned to see the door. She didn't take a break until Frost came out of his office."

"Did he say anything else about this man?"

"No. But it seems odd. Right after you leave, some mysterious man goes into Frost's office that Megan doesn't see, and then Frost tells her to go to lunch on the company."

"Why?"

"She doesn't know. That's what he told her to do."

Robin frowned. A similar thing had happened to her, when Agent Tolson first stopped by. Laura didn't see her, and there was a weird time warp effect. Did the Bureau send someone to visit Frost? That made no sense. It wasn't Christmas. They only opened cases at Christmas. Or did they? She'd seen Decker and Lady Magnolia since Christmas. "Well, as long as he's buying lunch for people, we're probably all okay. For now."

"Just be careful," Laura said, and she sounded genuinely concerned. "Megan said he seemed upset."

"I will. Thanks. And shouldn't you be getting ready to go uptown?"

Laura stood and smoothed her skirt. She'd worn a very professional dark brown suit. "I guess I should. You never know what the trains are going to do between here and there."

Robin smiled. "Good luck. Let me know how it goes."

"I will. And thank you."

After she'd left, Robin decided she had just enough time to grab a sandwich. She did, thinking about Frost's mysterious visitor, and she wondered if it was a dapper man with a German accent and a nicely fitted suit. Well, if it was Krampus, Frost no doubt had a lot of crap to go through. She almost felt sorry for him. Almost.

On her way back through the main lobby of her building, her personal cell rang with another call from Danielle. "Preston," Robin answered, moving out of the way of people coming in from the street.

"Hi. Danielle again. Do you have any time Tuesday morning at ten? Say, a late breakfast meeting? The committee will be involved in other things the rest of the day Tuesday and Wednesday, and they have to fly back to Seattle on Thursday."

"Yes. Where?"

"There's a restaurant near the building they're meeting in." She gave the name of the restaurant.

"I know it. Ten o'clock, Tuesday. I'll see everybody there. I can be reached at this number if anything comes up."

"Great. We'll see you then. Cheers."

"Thanks. Bye." Robin smiled and nodded to herself as she entered the appointment into her phone's calendar. She went back to her office. Just enough time to eat half her sandwich before the meeting. This one would include Brady, but Robin didn't care. After all, she was seeing Jill tonight, and she had a meeting in a few days with North by Northwest. Things like Brady didn't bother her anymore. She stepped off the elevator and went to her office.

"I like how this dinner ended." Jill pulled Robin against her, both of them sweaty and breathing heavily, once again tangled in the sheets on the bed above the gallery.

"Who said it's ended?" Robin kissed her.

"Good point," Jill murmured against Robin's lips as she started moving beneath her again.

Much later, Jill was wrapped around Robin, and Robin stroked her hair, wondering how things had gotten to this point, and what kind of luck that took. Maybe luck had a little help. How did one send a thank you card to the Bureau?

"I'm really enjoying this," Jill said.

"Well, sex can be a lot of fun, if you do it with the right people."

Jill laughed and nuzzled Robin's neck. "I believe I am."

"Same here. It's amazing. And mind-blowing."

Jill propped herself on her elbow and looked down at Robin. "Amazing and mind-blowing?"

"And stupendous. Plus the Chinese word for whatever's better than that."

Jill lightly nipped Robin's neck, and Robin groaned involuntarily.

"I really like that," Robin managed.

"I know. So tell me more about your revelations this past month."

"I've told you most of them."

"Most?" Jill nipped Robin's lower lip.

"Some day, I'll tell you what really happened with my red pill decision. A lot of it I'm not sure about, because it's extra weird." And she wasn't sure how much of it was real, though she didn't want to think about that.

"Try me."

"I did. I have. I hope to again."

Jill chuckled. "Same here." She brushed Robin's hair out of her eyes and stroked her face. "Okay, how about this? When you decide to tell me your red pill story, I'll tell you mine."

"Did yours make you wonder if you were going totally nuts? Like you might possibly be delusional?"

A shadow of a memory flickered in Jill's eyes. "I did think that was a possibility. But sometimes, things just happen, and the best you can do is go with it and hopefully learn something, even if it might defy imagination. I went with it. Still learning."

"Me, too. Took a major kick in the teeth, but I think I might be getting there. More work to do, though."

"There always is." Jill brushed her lips across Robin's. "I couldn't believe when you just kind of appeared next to me that day."

"Same here," Robin said wryly. "Do you ever think that there are—I don't know—forces beyond your control that sometimes do things to get people on the right track?"

"Like the red pill contingent?"

Robin laughed. "Okay, yeah. Like that."

"I do sometimes think that. Because otherwise, what are the odds that you would be in that spot at that time on that day?"

"Not very high." None, if Magnolia hadn't intervened.

"Exactly."

Robin pulled her close. "Why the hell did you invite me to your opening?"

"I don't know. Seemed like the right thing to do. And honestly, being that close to you again, I just fell into old habits. The ones I like." Jill pressed her lips against Robin's shoulder. "There were flashes of the you I remembered in there. But you seemed a little raw, like you'd just been through something."

"I had."

"And you will tell me all about it some day." Jill's lips moved against Robin's neck.

"Yes. Some day." She stroked Jill's back, marveling at the warmth of her skin and how something as simple as touching her could inspire such emotion. "I was thinking that night that you were how I remembered, too, but with all of these new and interesting layers, combining in different ways with who you were when we were in college."

"I like that image a lot." Jill's fingers tracked between Robin's breasts, sending a cascade of sparks down Robin's spine.

"So how exactly did we end up here?"

Jill's laugh, husky and warm, soaked right through Robin's skin. "Do I really need to answer that?"

Robin grinned. "No, come to think of it. I'll just go with it."

"Good." Jill's fingers trailed over Robin's abdomen. "You're a really nice mixture of your old self plus the pieces of you I don't know yet. I get that you have things to think about and things to do, but I like what you've got going on, Robin Preston."

Robin laughed. "Good. Because I like what you have going on, Jill Chen." And she did. So much.

"We need to do this again." Jill's hand moved lower, much to Robin's delight.

"You mean the extended dinner?"

"Yes. That."

"It's a date. Text me the time and place."

Jill smiled against Robin's mouth. "I will." And she ended further conversation.

Krampus found the affairs of mortals mostly tiresome, but he did enjoy the sheer variety of cultures and the types of drama each engaged in. Humans were, however, remarkably similar at their deepest levels, driven by very basic things such as fear, lust, anger, and hunger, much like other species. Except humans imbued these things with often strange meanings, as if seeking to understand their very essence. Which, he thought, only made things exceedingly complicated.

He entered Tolson's office. She was on the phone, a heavy black thing that he recalled from offices in the UK in the late forties. Tolson held up a finger, signaling that she'd be done in a moment. She didn't bother motioning at the chairs, since he never sat down when he visited her. He'd been working with her a long time, but she'd figured some things out about him early on, and he liked it when a human was intuitive.

Tolson hung up. Her suit today was a lovely olive, her nails neutral. "Mr. Rampus. I trust things are continuing to move smoothly."

He clasped his hands behind him. "Yes. Ms. Preston continues to engage the choice you had hoped, and with little urging. I must admit I'm a bit surprised by that." He saw by her smile that she was not.

"Sometimes humans are easy to understand, Mr. Rampus. You have to look for the logic within the irrational."

He pursed his lips, puzzled.

"Ms. Preston's early years were formed in a context of love and support, even within circumstances that were less than ideal. Ms. Chen comes from a very strong support network, but it was and remains constrained in some respects. She was drawn to Ms. Preston because of the latter's ability to adapt to changing situations and her spirit of exploration, no doubt acquired from her mother. Ms. Preston, for her part, was drawn to Ms. Chen because of the sense of stability and security she offered, instilled by her own background. Ms. Preston, as you know, didn't have much stability, as hard as her mother worked to provide it." Tolson leaned back in her chair.

"Fascinating." It was. Humans provided him much food for thought.

"The Bureau, Mr. Rampus, exists to effect change in as unobtrusive a manner as possible. We may seem limited in

271

scale, but for every one person we reach, there may be change across myriad generations. It's one of the many intriguing things about this work, and it's why we're relatively selective with our cases. After all, one can only do so much. As you are well aware."

He nodded once but did not respond, since Tolson rarely expounded on the duties of the Bureau, and she often had interesting things to say.

She tapped one of the folders on her desk. "Chen and Preston complement each other very well. Together, they can accomplish great things. Which may not be at first visible, but change doesn't need to be of large magnitude to have lasting effects. It can build momentum over time."

"Ah. This makes sense as to why we have expanded the parameters of Ms. Preston's case."

She regarded him for a moment, and Krampus marveled that he found her so difficult to read. "Sometimes the Bureau must take a few extra steps to point a case in a direction that hopefully allows a freer expression of change." She tapped the file with her finger again. "And sometimes, certain parties within those parameters must be made less effective, shall we say."

He inclined his head, signaling his understanding.

"I appreciate your discretion in this matter."

"We shall see, I suppose, whether my methods with said party were effective."

"I did like the approach. Not your usual style, but I think it was appropriate for the situation."

"I can be versatile as necessary."

Tolson smiled. "Thank you for your time, Mr. Rampus."

"Of course." He turned and was out the door in less time than it took to blink.

Chapter 16

THE AFTERNOON CITYSCAPE OUT HER office windows held Robin's attention much longer than usual. She'd never really looked at how sunlight bifurcated some of the taller buildings, or how it sparkled off the surface of the river at this hour. Somewhere in that pale blue sky, Jill's plane was on its way to Seattle, taking both Jill and a part of Robin with it.

She set her coffee on the floor and took several photos with her phone. It really was an incredible view. Someone knocked on her door.

"Come in," Robin called. She turned from the window as Laura entered and shut the door behind her and joined Robin.

"Mr. Pruitt would like to know when I can start."

Robin grinned. "Great news. Did you hold out for the salary you wanted?"

"I didn't have to. It's an excellent offer."

"So go on and give your notice."

Laura stared out the window. "I just did. How did it go today?"

"He wasn't surprised that I resigned, but he was subdued, which was strange for him." He'd also avoided her direct gaze.

Typical of an old boys' club. Bullies, but when confronted directly, they didn't know what to do.

She turned to look at Robin. "When's your last day?"

"I told him I'd stay on consultative status until the end of the month to get Hodges up to speed on my client base and accounts, but that I'd be off-site for the most part. I don't think he'll mind that I'm not in the building all that much." Robin smiled. "And I won't, either. Want to make a bet that he's not closing my position after all?"

"And that he'll rename it, stick Hodges in there, and then hire somebody else at less pay for Hodges's old position?"

"I see you've played this game before."

Laura smiled. "I haven't been here that long, but some things you figure out pretty quickly."

"I'm really sorry that this place isn't what you thought. Or what I thought. And I'm also sorry that I made most of your time here crappy."

"Accepted. But you made up for it at the end."

"Good to know." Robin raised her cup in a toast. "If you ever need anything, contact me."

"The same to you."

Robin checked the clock on her phone. "It's almost four on a Friday. Feel like having a drink?"

"I'd love to. Let me finish up a few things."

"I'll do the same. Twenty minutes?"

"That should be enough." Laura left, and Robin stared out the window again, thinking about Jill, the meeting on Tuesday with North by Northwest, and Seattle. She should have felt out of control, resigning from a position like this without definite backup. Instead she felt anticipation and excitement, like she was about to embark on an adventure she'd been looking forward to for a long, long time.

She thought then about the absurdly generous benefits package Frost offered. Robin had been prepared to highball it so she could bargain him down to what she expected, but he'd already prepared an offer greater than what she'd wanted. Even the corporate secrets clauses that every severance deal included weren't as restrictive as some, and pretty much had nothing to do with the work she'd be doing if North by Northwest hired her. Or a comparable organization. Though at this point, she'd settle for working in some funky café if it got her back to Seattle.

Robin finished her coffee and went back to her desk. That wasn't like Frost, to have such a generous offer ready to go. All the years she'd been here, Frost never let money go without a fight. But he was clearly relieved when she signed, and he offered recommendations for any future employers. Something told her he would, and that she had nothing to worry about in that regard. Almost like she had guardian angels or something.

Or maybe a posse of secret agents. "Thanks, you guys," she said softly. On a whim, she took a clean sheet of letterhead from her desk drawer and wrote a quick note: "Thank you, Agent Tolson, Decker, Lady Magnolia, and Mr. Rampus. I can't say it was all fun, but I can say I definitely needed it." She signed and folded it and slipped it into a blank envelope and wrote *Agent Tolson* on the front. She left it faceup on her desk then packed her laptop and tablet up, grabbed her coat, and went to wait for Laura.

⬥

Robin parked the rental in a public parking structure, deciding she'd rather do that than battle traffic for a spot on the streets, especially this close to Pioneer Square. Seattle traffic felt different than that on the East Coast. Especially in midtown Manhattan. No comparison. Still, it was much easier to just do public parking, especially since she didn't know how much longer Jill was going to be at the gallery.

Her phone rang, and she picked it up immediately because it was Frank, and she hadn't talked to him in a week.

"Hey," she answered.

"Rob? Are you okay? What's going on?"

"I'm fine—"

"What the hell? I get this weird text about big changes, and you'll talk to me later—"

"I knew Deb's folks were visiting this week, and I didn't want to lay it on you until they left." She opened the car door.

"Lay what on me? Please tell me you're okay."

"I did. But I'll tell you again. I'm fine, Frankie. Fine. Better than fine. Things are pretty great, actually."

He was quiet for a second. "Then what's up?"

"Okay, promise me you'll just listen? And then you can ask whatever questions you want." She knew he probably wouldn't be able to stay quiet. He never could, since they had been kids, but it was a habit with them, the promise-me-you'll-listen! tactic. And when he broke it, they'd always end up giggling about it.

"Tell me."

"First, don't worry about me. Everything's good."

"Jesus, Rob. Did you kill somebody? Are you on the lam in Mexico?"

Robin laughed. "Oh, my God. That's what you think of me?"

"Okay, okay. Sorry. What?" His impatience was obvious.

"First, I left Frost."

"You what?"

"I quit my job. I'm not with Frost anymore."

"Oh, my God. That's what I thought you said. When?"

Robin stretched one leg out of the car. "Last Friday. This is my one-week anniversary." She waited for him to freak out.

"That is the best news ever," he said, completely surprising her.

"Wait. You're okay with it?"

"Okay? I'm goddamn ecstatic! Rob, you were losing your soul there. I kind of understood why you went into business, but after your first few years there, I wondered why you didn't leave. And then..." He didn't finish, but Robin knew he wanted to say when things got bad between them. "Wow. This is such great news. I kept hoping that you'd leave, because if you did, you'd be yourself again. Maybe I'm going to get my wish."

Robin bit her lip, fighting tears though she wasn't sure why she felt like crying. Residue, Jill had called it the other night. Getting rid of toxic leftovers. Shedding an old skin. "I hope so."

"I'm pretty sure I will," he continued. "So are you all right? Do you have money? A place to stay?"

Robin smiled. Frank and Deb were teachers. Combined, their salaries were a third what she'd been making at Frost. And here he was trying to look out for her. "I'm good. Really great severance package, and I got another job."

Silence. Then, "What? Already?" There was a note of dread in his voice as if he thought she'd company-jumped to another place like Frost.

"Director of an art foundation. They're nonprofit, and they grant money to artists and art causes."

"Art? You're back in art?"

"In a way, yeah. I mean, I'll be responsible for fundraising and looking for new projects and helping find new avenues of coolness, I guess you could say."

"You're serious."

She got out of the car, shut the door, and leaned against it. "Totally. And I'm really excited about it."

"When the hell did that happen?"

"Kind of a weird story."

"Tell me."

"Well, I applied for the job a couple weeks ago—maybe not that long ago. And then I was at an art opening New Year's Eve, and the director of the foundation board was there because they happened to have funded the artist whose opening it was. And then a couple days after that, the director of the board called me and said the people from the hiring committee were going to be in New York on Tuesday. So I went to chat with them, and they offered me the job that evening. It was all pretty amazing." And when she said yes and got off the phone, she did the nuttiest, craziest party dance ever, knocking all kinds of things over in her apartment.

He laughed, then, but it was his really happy laugh, the one he did when he was super glad about some news. "I'm just—I don't know. Really excited for you. And you sound so much better. So where is this foundation?"

Robin was grinning now, so wide it almost hurt. "Ready for this? Seattle."

"Shut up."

"No, it is. I'm in Seattle right now."

"What? You're there now?" He was practically shouting over the phone, and Robin had to hold it away from her ear.

"Yes. Just got in about an hour ago. I'll be here for a week or so, because I want to find a place to live."

"Holy shit. You're house hunting in Seattle. Do you think—" He stopped.

"Yeah. I'll drive by the old house and take a picture."

They both lapsed into a shared silence before Frank spoke again. "Man, this is the best news. I am so happy for you. Are you still going to visit us?" His voice carried a note of worry.

"Hell, yes. I don't start at the new job until mid-March. I figure I can find a rental on this trip, and then when I get out here, look around for something else. I'll be able to stay a few extra days with you. I can help with the baby's room." She pushed off the car and with the phone braced between her ear and her shoulder, she buttoned her pea coat.

"That would be so great. Because I haven't gotten much done, what with Deb's parents visiting, and them going all loony over her because, you know, baby. I'm kind of chopped meat, basically." He laughed. "Plus, with school starting up, it's been kind of nuts."

"Good thing I'm between jobs, then," she teased. "So speaking of the baby. Have you and Deb come up with possible names?"

"Actually, yes. Travis if it's a boy, Mallory if it's a girl. What do you think?"

Again, Robin's grin almost hurt. "Love them both."

"But it depends on the baby, too. When it's born, it might not want either name."

"Guess you'll find out." But Robin was pretty sure Travis would be fine with his name. She locked the car and put the key fob in her jeans pocket.

"Yeah." And then he went quiet again, probably in a daddy haze. A few moments later, he said, "Damn, this is so amazing. Great news from you—I know it's scary, to quit a major job like that. But I'm just so glad because you sound like my old Robin, and I was so worried I had lost you." He stopped and cleared his throat, and Robin knew it was because he was trying not to cry.

She wiped her eyes.

Frank continued, "I love you, Rob. You have to know that."

"I do. And I love you, too."

He cleared his throat again. "So is that all the big news?"

"That wasn't enough?"

"That was pretty big. But I know how you are. You usually hold some stuff back."

"There is some other stuff, but I'm not ready to talk about it yet. I'll probably be able to tell you more when I see you next month."

"Oh, come on. Really?" He used a tone from their childhood, when he'd cajole, coax, and sometimes outright bribe her until she finally spilled whatever she was keeping from him. This time, though, it wouldn't work.

"Really. February."

"Is it good?"

"So far." Thoughts of Jill filled her mind. It was very, very good.

"And you're not going to tell me until next freaking month?"

"Nope."

"Challenge accepted. Operation Robin's Secret will commence as soon as we hang up."

She laughed. "Not this time. But if anything changes between now and then, I'll let you know."

"Don't be so sure." He did a cartoon villain laugh, and Robin laughed, too.

"Okay, I have to go," she said. "I need to get some stuff squared away, since I just got in. I'll let you know how things go here, and I'll get that photo of the house."

"Sounds good. I know it's weird to congratulate somebody on quitting their job, but in this case, congratulations."

"Thanks."

"I know there's more to that story, too."

"A very long one. For February."

"But I'll talk to you before then?" He sounded tentative, as if this might be too good to be true.

"You'd better. I'll send you photos of my house-hunting adventures. Now go take care of Deb. She might want some kind of weird food or something."

"No doubt. Later."

"Bye." She hung up and slipped her phone into the back pocket of her jeans. She'd worn her motorcycle boots, and as she left the parking garage and walked the three blocks to the gallery, a sense of homecoming washed over her. She felt as if she could fly, as if she was twenty years younger, ready to take on the world.

A coffee house drew her in a half block before the gallery, but once she had her drink, she went back outside. Cloudy and cold, but not unbearable. Typical January weather here, as familiar as the view of Puget Sound and the Needle. She sipped, enjoying everything about this day. Since Robin was a few minutes early, she loitered near the gallery and drank a bit more coffee. A nearby bench outside the restaurant next door gave her a nice place to do that, and she sipped, idly watching a woman walk by with her dog, a big goofy black lab. A guy across the street who looked like a grizzled sea captain who'd spent way too much time with his grog was talking to a man holding what looked like a tourist map. His wife was tugging on his sleeve, pulling him away from the sea captain. Pioneer Square attracted characters, cranks, and down-and-out as well as sightseers.

A young girl exited the gallery, carrying a military-style backpack. It was decorated with hand-painted cartoon figures, interspersed with big, colorful stylized peace signs and flowers. She wore a lightweight blue coat—the kind of coat ubiquitous in this part of the country, made for rain but probably with some space-age fleece as a lining—that fell to mid-thigh. Her jeans were rolled up in a style from the eighties, over skateboard-style sneakers. Robin approved.

The girl approached, and as she did, Robin realized who it was. She kept her revelation to herself.

"Hi. Do you mind if I sit here?" Madison asked, sounding much older than she looked, the expression in her eyes reminiscent of Jill when Jill was in her serious moods.

"Sure." Robin slid over. "Waiting for someone?"

Madison sized her up, gauging what degree of stranger-hood Robin represented. "Yes. And he'll be here any minute." She sat down and put her backpack between them on the bench.

"Cool." Robin sipped her coffee, wondering if she should reveal who she was. Better not. Jill hadn't seemed ready for Robin to meet her daughter.

Madison took her phone out and engaged in some texting. Robin continued to watch pedestrians.

"Are you waiting for someone, too?" Madison asked after a couple of minutes.

"Yes."

Madison went back to her phone, then looked up at Robin again, brow furrowed. "Are you Robin?"

"Yes. Hi, Madison. Good to meet you." She stuck her hand out, and Madison took it. Her handshake was firm. Jill was teaching her well.

"Why didn't you say something?" Another question, sounding much older than Madison looked.

"Didn't feel it was my place."

Madison smiled. "Because my mom probably wants to conduct some kind of special introduction between us."

Robin smiled back. "Well, yeah. Not sure this is the trip she wanted to do that, though."

"Probably not." Madison's eyes seemed to sparkle mischievously. "But this is okay with me."

"I'm glad. Because it's okay with me, too."

A maroon late-model Honda SUV pulled up to the curb.

"That's my dad," Madison said as she stood.

"Okay. Guess we'll get the special introduction from your mom later."

Madison grinned. "Yep. Bye."

Robin watched as she got into the front passenger seat, and as the car pulled away from the curb, Madison waved. Robin waved back and marveled at how natural it felt to interact with Jill's daughter, as if they'd known each other a while. She thought about that. If things got more serious with Jill, Robin could end up a stepparent, which meant a lot of responsibility. Was she ready for something like that?

She finished her coffee, rolling that thought around. Yes. She was. If she was going to be with Jill, then she had to make room for Jill's family. And it wasn't a matter of "had to." It was a matter of "wanted to," something she felt deep. Robin got up, tossed her empty cup into a nearby trash can, and went to the front entrance of the gallery. This one was devoted primarily to Jill's work, a lot of which was visible on the walls through the front windows. It reminded Robin of New Year's Eve, and a flush raced down her legs. She pulled the door open and stepped inside, immediately comfortable as faint art smells teased her nostrils.

Robin unbuttoned her coat and loosened her scarf. Somehow, seeing Jill's art here in Seattle made it even better.

"Hi," said a woman Robin estimated to be in her mid-twenties. She wore loose black linen pants and a rust-colored blouse, also linen. She wore her hair in an afro, and her glasses were so trendy that Robin immediately felt old.

"Hi. I'm actually here to see Jill—"

"Hey." Jill emerged from the back, quickened her pace, and was in Robin's arms before Robin could say anything else. "How was your flight?"

"Fine. Long."

"You're probably tired." Jill stepped back, much to Robin's disappointment.

"Hasn't hit me yet."

Jill smiled and took Robin's hand, and that was almost as good as the hug, because she intertwined their fingers. "This is Amira. She's practically my third arm around here. Amira, this is Robin."

"Hi."

"Good to meet you," Amira said. "Would you like any coffee or anything?"

"Just had some, thanks."

Jill shot her a smile. "Robin's going to be around for a few days, so I'm sure she'll be back. Right now, though, I'm calling it a day and taking Robin to an early dinner before she passes out from traveling. If you need anything, call or text."

"You know I will. Good to meet you," Amira added to Robin.

"Likewise. Chat with you later."

"Bye," Jill said as she pulled Robin to a door in the back of the gallery that opened into what was clearly storage and a work area for Jill, though Jill did most of her creating in a studio at home, she'd told Robin a few conversations back.

"Ah, art stuff," Robin said as the door closed behind her. But she didn't say anything else because Jill pulled her into a kiss that made Robin's insides flip.

"I know it's only been a week, but it feels like a lot longer," Jill finally said after a while.

"Yeah, it does. But here I am, and I'm really glad to see you. And maybe get a tea ceremony."

Jill gave Robin a look that made her ache. "You'll get more than that. Hold that thought while I get my coat."

Robin did, and she allowed herself to appreciate Jill's ass in her jeans. She knew what was underneath the loose black shirt, and oh, how she wanted to see it all again. Jill was wearing her combat boots and had her hair spiked up today, and when she put her leather jacket on, all she needed was a battered guitar case to make her look like a renegade indie rocker.

"Ready?" Jill asked.

"Yes. What's the plan?"

Jill guided her out a metal back door that locked automatically behind them. They stood in an alley. "Where are you parked?"

"The garage about three blocks that way." Robin pointed.

"Okay. Do you feel like going out to eat?"

"Whatever you think is the best plan of action. I'm just really glad to be here, and I'm still on East Coast time, so I might not be the best person to make the plans."

Jill smiled and kissed her again. "So how about this?" She took her phone out of her pocket. "I'm texting you my address, in case we get separated. We'll go to my place, and we can either eat there or go somewhere close."

"I like that plan."

"Good. I'm parked right over here. I'll drive you to the garage and partially block traffic on the street while I wait for you."

"Sounds excellent."

Jill took her hand again. "God, you look good," she said as they walked.

"I was thinking the same about you." Better than good, Robin thought. Fucking amazing.

"So, as I told you last night, Madison is at Drew's for the next week, so you're welcome to stay with me."

"Um. Yeah. About that."

Jill stopped, puzzled. "What?"

"I accidentally met Madison."

Jill raised an eyebrow. "Accidentally?"

"I was sitting on the bench outside the restaurant next door, giving you a few extra minutes, and she came out of the gallery and sat there to wait for Drew." Robin shrugged, sheepish. "She asked if I was Robin. I didn't want to lie."

"Oh, really?" Jill sounded more amused than anything else.

"And we both said we were okay meeting outside the special introduction you might have planned for us."

"Special introduction? Did she say that?"

Robin bit her lip. "Damn. I'm totally throwing a twelve-year-old under the bus, aren't I?"

Jill laughed. "She'll let me know what she thinks. Although, yes, I would have preferred a special introduction."

"And not on this trip, I know. Sorry."

"You have really interesting timing. It seems you were supposed to meet her today." Jill started walking again.

"Probably for the best. She seems like she's a really good judge of character. She'll let you know if I'm good for you." Robin remembered Christmas Future. Madison would definitely let Jill know what she thought of Robin.

"She is." Jill opened the passenger side of her car, a black sport utility wagon whose back seat was covered with art supplies. "And you're right. She will."

Robin got in and buckled up while Jill went around to the driver's side. She got in but didn't start the car right away. "I think I prefer eating in tonight," Jill said. The look in her eyes made Robin's mouth go dry.

"And will this be an extended dinner?"

"Damn right." Jill leaned over and kissed Robin into a delicious, heated fog, her lips and tongue making Robin throb, making her ache in ways she didn't know she could. "The things you make me feel," Jill murmured against Robin's cheek. "I'm so glad you're here."

Robin smiled and kissed her again, but pulled away before she got to the point where she couldn't. "Okay. I'll stop now before we get ticketed for indecent window fogging."

Jill grinned and drove her to the garage and dropped her off. When Robin pulled onto the street a few minutes later, there was Jill, partially blocking traffic. Robin flashed her lights, and Jill stuck her hand out the window in a wave before she accelerated. And Robin knew, as she positioned her car behind Jill's, that just like that first day she'd met her in that art class, she would follow her anywhere.

Agent Tolson opened one of the two files on her desk and added a plain white envelope to it. She closed the file and tapped it, undecided. She took the envelope out and turned it over, to the side that had her name handwritten on it. For the third or fourth time, Tolson took the sheet of paper out and read the thank you note again. Finally, she carefully folded it and put it back into the envelope. She picked up the copy of the note from the corner of her desk and placed it in the top right drawer of her desk, which was one of a few concessions to privacy from the Bureau she allowed herself.

She closed the file and checked the name, ensuring that it matched the official closed case ledger before she consigned it to the vault. *Preston, Robin Anne, DOB June 15, 1978// Seattle, WA.* Correct file, correct protocol. She entered the information onto her tablet with her stylus then placed the paper file aside so she could enter the second file into the closed case ledger. Match the name, enter the data, close the case. Tolson set Chen's file on top of Preston's once she'd finished and poured herself a cup of celebratory tea from the ornate teapot that sat on her desk. She carried the cup, along with the saucer, to the window.

Some cases took a bit longer than others, but that was the nature of change. The Board of Advisors would be pleased at her next debriefing and Tolson's undiminished record of success would continue unabated. That was because she chose her cases carefully, and conducted myriad inquiries before undertaking the more difficult ones like Chen-Preston, which required long-term coordination and resource juggling to ensure proper timing.

Not to mention providing extra incentive. Of course Preston was redeemable. She had been all along. Tolson wouldn't have taken the case if she weren't. But Tolson knew a few things about human nature. Preston would respond to a challenge, and being told she might not be salvageable would galvanize her to extra effort. Chen had been the same way, when the Bureau initiated contact with her while she was still working at the bank. Tolson sipped from the cup, the china delicate against her lips. A lot can happen in a few years.

She would see that her field agents—she'd chosen them herself—on the Chen-Preston case received extra benefits and commendations. And copies of the thank-you note, which helped them realize the importance of the work they did here.

Tolson smiled as she raised the cup to her lips, and drank a silent toast to the Bureau, her team, and the quixotic nature of change. May it be ever possible.

About Andi Marquette

Andi Marquette is a native of New Mexico and Colorado and an award-winning mystery, science fiction, and romance writer. She also has the dubious good fortune to be an editor who spent 15 years working in publishing, a career track that sucked her in while she was completing a doctorate in history. She is co-editor of *All You Can Eat: A Buffet of Lesbian Romance and Erotica* and the forthcoming *Order Up: A Menu of Lesbian Romance and Erotica*. Her most recent novels include the romances *The Secret of Sleepy Hollow* and *From the Hat Down* as well as the mystery *Day of the Dead* and the Goldie science fiction finalist, *The Edge of Rebellion*.

When she's not writing novels, novellas, and stories or co-editing anthologies, she serves as both an editor for Luna Station Quarterly, an ezine that features speculative fiction written by women and as co-admin of the popular blogsite Women and Words. When she's not doing that, well, hopefully she's managing to get a bit of sleep.

CONNECT WITH THIS AUTHOR:
Website: http://andimarquette.com/

Other Books from Ylva Publishing

www.ylva-publishing.com

Caged Bird Rising
A Grim Tale of Women, Wolves, and other Beasts

Nino Delia

ISBN: 978-3-95533-319-5
Length: 237 pages (62,000 words)

In a world dominated by men, it should be Robyn's greatest fortune that the handsome Hunter Wolfmounter sees her as the perfect fertile wife. But an encounter with a mysterious wolf changes her worldview. She flees into the woods, where she meets Gwen, who helps her to change— into one of the independent beasts she has always been warned about. But the men are hot on her trail.

The Secret of Sleepy Hollow

Andi Marquette

ISBN: 978-3-95533-515-1
Length: 166 pages (45,000 words)

Graduate student Abby Crane schedules a research trip over Halloween weekend for Sleepy Hollow, in search of material for her doctoral thesis and answers about her long-lost ancestor, Ichabod Crane. Local folklore says he disappeared at the hands of the ghostly headless horseman— or did he? With the help of the attractive Katie McClaren, Abby finds much more than she ever thought possible.

The Tea Machine

Gill McKnight

ISBN: 978-3-95533-432-1
Length: 346 pages (97,000 words)

Spinster by choice, Millicent Aberly has managed to catapult herself from her lovely Victorian mews house into a strange future full of giant space squid, Roman empires, and a most annoying centurion to whom she owes her life.

Decanus Sangfroid was just doing her job rescuing the weird little scientist chick from a squid attack. Now she finds herself in London, 1862, and it's not a good fit.

All the Little Moments

G Benson

ISBN: 978-3-95533-341-6
Length: 350 pages (132,000 words)

Anna is focused on her career as an anaesthetist. When a tragic accident leaves her responsible for her young niece and nephew, her life changes abruptly. Completely overwhelmed, Anna barely has time to brush her teeth in the morning let alone date a woman. But then she collides with a long-legged stranger…

Coming from Ylva Publishing

www.ylva-publishing.com

Driving me Mad

L.T. Smith

After becoming lost on her way to a works convention, Rebecca Gibson stops to ask for help at an isolated house. Progressively, her life becomes more entangled with the mysterious happenings of the house and its inhabitants.

With the help of Clare Davies, can Rebecca solve a mystery that has been haunting a family for over sixty years? Can she put the ghosts and the demons of the past to rest?

Rewriting the Ending

hp tune

A chance meeting in an airport lounge and a shared flight itinerary leaves Juliet and Mia connected. But how do you stay connected when you've only known each other for twenty four hours, are destined for different continents and each have a past to reconcile?

The Bureau of Holiday Affairs
© 2015 by Andi Marquette

ISBN: 978-3-95533-549-6

Also available as e-book.

Published by Ylva Publishing, legal entity of Ylva Verlag, e.Kfr.

Ylva Verlag, e.Kfr.
Owner: Astrid Ohletz
Am Kirschgarten 2
65830 Kriftel
Germany

www.ylva-publishing.com

First edition: November 2015

Credits
Edited by Jove Belle
Cover Design & Printlayout by Streetlight Graphics

83931045R00182

Made in the USA
Middletown, DE
16 August 2018